Harmony by Sienna Mynx

Brown sugar lassie,
Caramel treat,
Honey-gold baby
Sweet enough to eat
— Langston Hughes

ISBN-13: 978-0615645209 (Custom)
ISBN-10: 0615645208

~ Foreward ~

Harmony is a fictional tale based on a time in history where the arts, talents, and identities of people of color were shifting toward a renaissance of change. I chose the early 1920's in Harlem New York as the setting for my book, because I discovered a small window of opportunity to turn fact and spin fiction. Why? As always my stories aim at creating an unlikely love affair that resonates with dramatic flare and sexual heat. However, I'm a lover of this time period. I'm a lover of Duke Ellington and Bessie Smith. I'm a lover of Langston Hughes and even Marcus Garvey. Though my story barely references these great talents, the feelings of empowerment, and creative expression was indeed an excellent muse to begin my tale from. I wanted to explore a story with characters that fictionally would be the catalyst for the changing times in Harlem during prohibition.

A wonderful book I used as reference for Harmony is *The Harlem Renaissance (Hub of African American Culture 1920-1930) by Steven Watson.* I suggest lovers of African American history give this book a read through. I found maps of Harlem, timelines of important events, even pictures of the Negro elite to submerge myself in the story of Harmony Jones.

I'd like to share a couple of facts versus fiction for you before you read. Harmony picks up in 1923. Prohibition was indeed a reality for the country. Sicilian mobsters, Irish and Jewish mobsters ran the underworld of bootlegging. Vincenzio Romano is fictional, but the gang wars and associations he has in this book were borrowed from events during that time.

The Cotton Club musical direction wasn't under Duke Ellington in 1923. A man by the name of Fletch Henderson led the orchestra. Furthermore, Dutch Schultz had not moved in to claim Harlem's dark underworld and is not referenced in this tale. After the sale of Club Deluxe by Jack Johnson to Owney Madden (while Madden was serving time in prison) Club Deluxe underwent a transformation that catered to white only clientele and perpetuated the stereotypes of black artist by even labeling jazz as 'jungle music'. Before Dutch Schultz moved in on Harlem a black woman from Martinique named Queenie Stephanie St. Clair was twenty-six and had aligned herself with one of New York's most notorious street gangs known as The Forty Thieves.

Think about it for a minute, because I certainly did. We're talking about a gang, of white men who were both murderers and thieves, that has been in existence since the 1850s fell under the control of a French speaking black woman in 1920? If that doesn't inspire the imagination what could?

Harmony touches on these events, and exaggerates the facts around the Forty Thieves and how Madame Stephanie St. Clair made ten thousand dollars to open the first numbers bank in Harlem.

Also, I want to note that the story does make references to Lucky Luciano and The Five Points Gang, along with the Sicilian mobsters of that time. Everything borrowed was done so for the fictional purpose of strengthening this tale and any similarities are solely coincidence. It's my hope you will read this and enjoy my version of fact versus fiction. Hopefully at the end of my tale you will fall in love with Harmony and Vinnie as I did.

Sienna Mynx

CHAPTER ONE
The Blues

1923 Harlem, New York

Milo's horn blew sultry and seductive through the swing beat. This was their music, their time, and no instrument other than the smoky wail of his saxophone could say it better. Harmony closed her eyes and let the rhythm flow through her. The melody calmed, and emboldened her in sinful ways she refused to put a name to.

"One, two, three, four," she mumbled without parting her lips, swaying a bit behind the cover of the stage curtain—slipping into her zone. Milo's horn demanded patience, selective timing—now she was ready.

Harmony emerged from stage left. Her stride became grace in motion. Each step set the sequined strands that dangled from her curvy hips to dazzle under the hot chorus spotlights. Milo blew sweet melodies from his sax that trailed her as she crossed in front of the all-Negro orchestra to the microphone. The lights of the club dimmed in every corner and pale faces lifted from their dinners or turned from their jovial conversations transfixed.

Ladies and gentlemen The Cotton Club presents to you, Miss Harmony Jones.

Harmony's lips, plump as fresh plucked strawberries, drew near the magnified chrome bulb. She offered her audience a taste by joining the brass section through their warm up, her *bee-bop-skat-shubbie-dee-bop* riding along effortlessly. Fletcher Henderson, the bandleader, gave her the cue. Harmony extended her arms, parted her lips and her voice sailed to unattainable heights. So did her hopes. Tonight she'd send both soaring. For Harmony, fate left her little choice when it came to her chosen profession and the personal demands in her life. And thanks to The Cotton, life had improved considerably. She now lived well in the northern part of Hamilton Heights, a neighborhood referred to as Sugar Hill. Nonetheless, it never escaped her that this stage, with Milo on his horn and Stickman thrumming a bass, was where her stardom exceeded a colored girl's dream. That's why tonight she intended to use what she's got to get all that she needs, namely an alliance with notorious mob boss, Vincenzio Romano.

Harmony's delivery got the band rocking before Fletch ended the jam session with Milo blowing through her intro. Her song eased in on a sexy escape of breath, sweet and low. She watched the audience through a thin veil of her lowered lashes. Inch by inch her hand eased down the microphone's stem, her nails glistening like rubies. She was often told her beauty, whether real or perceived, under the glamour of the stage lights, was nothing compared to her voice. Even the racist gangster who'd bought Club Deluxe and renamed it The Cotton Club said the same. The man known as Owney 'The Killer' Madden, gave her top billing to sing what he, and those now staring at her in anticipation, called 'jungle music'. Harmony knew different. The music of her people, jazz and all its tangled roots, came straight from the soul. Absolute, commanding, and enchanting, her voice often inspired white men to send her gifts of chocolates, perfume and dozens of her favorite roses after a single performance.

Harmony's gaze focused past the burn of the lights. Through the pearly wave of smoke and shifting shadows, ladies all dolled up with long-stem cigarettes between gloved fingers, glared. Often this was the case. Harmony had grown used to it. The men however, were a different story. In dark crisp tuxedos, tailored, with perfectly groomed mustaches and hair neatly oiled back from their faces, she held them captive through her song.

Willie's out there. Willie needs me to see this through. He's all I've got. And Vinnie Romano is gonna help me dammit.

With surreptitious glances, she searched the crowd for her guy. It happened. A current of excitement rippled through the atmosphere sparking hurried movement from the doorman to the waiters, each of them looking pointedly at the other. Killer Madden dashed past the stage, breaking for the club's entrance. Someone of importance had entered.

He's here. It's him. Has to be.

Harmony believed tonight of all nights he'd show. Not because he was expected, but because she needed him. See Romano and she shared something. It was unspoken but each time she sang and he sat in his favorite booth and watch, she felt it. She wasn't one to normally hang her hopes on a white man, in fact she wanted nothing to do with the lustful glares often shot her way by these mobsters. But this man was no ordinary fellow. Willie's life depended on his affinity for her songs. Harmony's gaze followed Romano as she eased into the whimsical allure of the lyrics with her voice. Dropping a little sway to her hips she ran both hands, palms flat and fingers spread, down her curves, stirring up a couple of wolf whistles from the crowd. Romano hadn't noticed. Not yet.

Tonight would be like all others. Always the same booth, the coal-black velvet drapes parted just enough to reveal his omniscient-like presence. Romano would sit, watch, and she'd sing. Under the glare of the stage lights she'd see little. The shadows covered his face, yet she felt his eyes—a woman always does. Often from the distance his hand appeared as he gestured to someone at the table.

At The Cotton, Harmony soon became familiar with the faces of the notorious as they came and went, each vying for a moment of this most powerful gangster's time. Mickey Collins and Madden were close. Collins imported the bootlegged liquor filling the club patron's glasses. She even believed he had something to do with how Owen Madden managed to purchase and muscle Jack Johnson out of the Deluxe. But if Collins, a reported ex-member of the Five Points Gang, was to be feared and respected for his connections to the mob, Romano's ruthless reputation made him the god they all bowed in respect to.

Her friend, a cigarette girl by the name of Paulette, told her just days ago *he* had asked for her schedule one night when she was absent. It was the first time she knew her suspicions were true. Romano had eyes for her. She was sure of it. Tonight, Harmony hoped that attention would pay off.

For Willie's sake.

Vincenzio 'Vinnie' Romano eased back into the soft leather of his booth seat. This club had become a habit. *She* was becoming *his* habit. Otherwise he'd stick to his own territory.

Romano wasn't unfamiliar with the nightlife along Lenox Avenue. He grew up cracking skulls and breaking the law with his best friend Lucky around the gambling dens and brothels in Five Points. Lucky went on to become a part of the Five Points Gang. Vinnie had no intention of trying to belong. In fact he created the Black Hand, a gang that helped him earn his respect, elbows to fist all the way. His reputation was rumored to have reached his powerful father in Sicily. No one questioned his authority, at least not to his face. His Sicilian blood and being the son of Don Giuseppe Romano had sealed his destiny.

Signaling for another whiskey, Romano ignored the prattle of his kid brother and focused on the vision of beauty before him. Lately he couldn't get Antonio to shut the fuck up about the money flowing in and out of Harlem. It was Antonio who originally brought him to the club after he had refused several invitations from Madden. The Cotton was a whites only establishment, no race mixing in or near its doors. Still Romano thought the club beneath him. That was until he saw her. He wouldn't have paid her any mind if it weren't for her voice, it took him by surprise when he first heard her. He wasn't a man often surprised. After witnessing the songbird's talents he ordered one of his men to go out and buy the best jazz records in the city.

Romano licked the bitter taste of his half smoked cigar from his lips and she drew him in. They called her Harmony. He chuckled when he first heard her stage name and discovered it was indeed her Christian name. The doll had class. He had to give her that.

Harmony's hips swayed, her hands eased up and down her curvaceous sides as her voice went from smoky to wickedly sexy and low. Romano leaned forward, Harmony was in rare form tonight—and something was different. Sweetheart was singing to him. He was sure of it. Songbird was looking him directly in the eye. He liked that.

What a dame.

Medium in height with skin sepia brown as if brushed with ginger, Harmony Jones had full succulent red lips that made him lick his own. Her cheekbones were high on her heart shaped face. A distinct feature that made her almond shaped eyes slant and disappear under dark lashes when she flashed a coy smile through her performance. And her trademark was always present in her dark wavy hair. A white rose, pinned behind her right ear. She sang of desire. How she burned for more. And she dressed the part. Demure from the front but unashamedly provocative when she turned to the orchestra and revealed the low cut back. Tonight her clingy garment was the deepest shade of purple and seemed to sparkle with violet lights as if the most precious stones were woven into the thin fabric. A sweetheart-shaped bodice separated and lifted her ample breasts upward. *What a rack!* Romano was a breast man; she was full in the hips and chest, as he liked his women.

Harmony's shifting loose sequined hem flattered her legs. When Harmony moved, and her hips often did in time with the melody, it provoked every man in the place to wonder about the softness between those thighs. Romano held back. Taboo barriers between coloreds and whites didn't mean shit to him. If he wanted anything or any woman, the rules never applied. No. Romano held back for his own reasons. Boredom would set in when a conquest became too easy, especially after a dame's submission made her think his prominence meant something profitable for her. He'd rather worship this beauty, untouched, from afar. Still he wasn't a man to be teased, and his songbird was tempting the beast in him tonight.

"So as I was saying," Antonio's nasal drone mowed down his wandering thoughts.

Romano dropped his gaze over to his second in command. "What? What were you saying?"

Antonio Romano was short, and thin, with a scar that ran from his left brow down to the middle of his cheek thanks to a nasty childhood knife fight. Antonio wasn't a thinker. He was a doer, and without the strong hand of his older brother he would have wound up on the same path as any stick-up man with a trigger-happy temper.

"Out with it." Romano said.

Antonio cleared his throat. "Collins's on the level. He's square. This I know for sure. Take a look around Vinnie. This joint is tops. Cops don't bother Madden, and the booze is constantly flowing. Give me the okay and we can own this scene. All of it Vinnie, the numbers banks, I'm talking top to bottom... it's prime for picking, Harlem and all."

"You feeding me a line?" asked Romano.

"No. I'm just weighing in is all. I got the right to speak my mind. This isn't Sicily. Papa has no say in the men we become or the way you do things. Still we're blood, and we're in this together. Hey, forget about it. What do we need with Harlem? Bronx's doing alright." Antonio took a quick sip of his drink, his gaze bounced from his brother's ashtray to his watchful stare. Romano could smell a setup. His brother stunk of it.

"You're restless little brother. I see it. Doesn't mean I have to act on it. You got rights? You have the rights and privileges I say. *Capice?*" Romano asked.

Antonio's jaw tensed. Romano eyed him, waiting. His brother didn't respond. He threw back the last of his whiskey then slammed the glass on the table. "Hey toots!" he barked at the cigarette girl. "Get a wiggle on over here. Will ya?"

The leggy toffee brown skinned brunette walked over in fishnet stockings and a corset with her tits packed tight in the front like cantaloupes. Around her neck hung a cigarette case. Romano's eyes cut past them both to Mickey Collins off at the bar. Mickey lifted his glass to him. *So now Collins had Antonio making his case?* Romano smirked. There was something to it.

The foxy brunette flicked her lighter, sparking a flame that burned down the tip of Antonio's ciggy. She cut her hazel brown oval eyes over to the mob boss. "Mr. Romano, what can I do you for—cigar, cigarette?" She dipped so he could get a full view of her wares accentuated by her breasts.

Antonio leaned out of the booth. His eyes did a slow climb up her legs and under the ruffled hem of her chorus-girl skirt. He exhaled a wave of smoke from his nostrils and smiled in approval. Paulette ignored Antonio. She flicked her golden lighter open and leaned in to ignite Romano's cigar. Standing upright, the brunette struggled to hide her disappointment.

"You new?" asked Antonio.

8

She blinked her reply, turned her boobs to his line of view. "No sir. They call me Paulette, I'm tall, tan and terrific!" she said. It was a canned response that the girls must all say in greeting.

"Yea well beat it, Paulie. Can't ya see we discussing business here?"

Paulette made a quick exit. Antonio chuckled. "Check out the gams on that dame," he said with a sly grin. "Always been a leg man. Not into dark meat though."

"Tell me, exactly when did you become the *man* to sing and dance for Mickey Collins?" Romano asked.

"Aww Vinnie, I was just flapping my gums. Pay it no mind," Antonio gave a double shoulder shrug. Romano remained unconvinced, but he let it go.

Fletch waved his hand in front of the orchestra and ended the set. Harmony took her cue and gave a curt nod of thanks to the applause. She didn't look over at Romano. She didn't have to. The pull of his stare rained heat through her bones.

I should walk over there and lay it all out for Romano. Tell him about Willie and ask for his help. Isn't that the way of the Sicilians? The powerful men are lord and master over the weak and needy. I heard Milo call this one the boss of all bosses. That's how Lewis would address him too, Boss Romano. He'd say you give a man like Romano your burden, and for a price the boss will relieve you of it? Funny he didn't look old enough to be so powerful. He definitely had a liking for my singing. Harmony laughed bitterly to herself. *That may be but this is Harlem, girl, and you're a jazz singer that can't even enter through the front door of the club everyone comes to hear you sing at. Since when did the desires or needs of a colored woman mean a damn thing to a dangerous Sicilian like him? And if Madden gets wind of my plans I'll be on my hands and knees scrubbing floors again.*

Blowing a final kiss to the audience in gratitude for the applause, she bowed to Henderson then quickly switched off the stage, but stopped short of the arriving tap-dancing girls to catch her breath. From her concealed position she stole another look to the Sicilian, he continued to watch with the same blank expression he wore when he arrived. Without the glare of the stage lights she could see him clearly. Romano had dark olive skin for a white man, with hair smoothed from his face in a golden brown wave, tapered low at the nape and with extended long sideburns. His serious features were chiseled into a strong jaw line and squared, dimpled chin. Deep-set eyes under a straight silken brow were intense, profound. Romano had no facial hair. He didn't smile but she did notice a brief reaction. The corner of his mouth tipped upward to something Mr. Madden said, when he arrived at his table to offer a welcoming. She wondered what color his eyes truly were?

"Did you hear me Mony?"

Harmony stole a glance back over her shoulder at Milo, and then returned it to the mob boss across the room. Milo followed her stare.

"Oh no, Miss Mony, no," Milo said, taking her hand. He walked her further away behind the curtain. Beyond earshot, he took hold of both of her arms tightly.

"What's eating you?" Harmony struggled, trying to break free.

"Mony, what'chu think you're doing? Do you know who that there man is?"

"Let go, Milo."

"Do you?"

"It's Vinnie Romano. Yes! I know who he is."

"No. Wrong. Vincenzio Romano and next to Collins, he's *the* guy. Dangerous. Very dangerous Mony, do you understand? He's not someone you want to tease. And if Madden sees you giving him the eye, lord Mony, have you lost your senses? I've been trying hard to keep them white boys off you, and you giving *that* man eyes? I seen ya, during the act. You was singing to him. Christ, I think he knows you were singing to him."

"Willie's missing, Milo. He ain't been home. I don't know where he went or how long he's been gone for. Just that he is."

"That ain't a Romano problem. That's a Willie problem," Milo hissed, lowering his voice under the soft patter of more girls in sailor shirts and miniskirts running by in their tap shoes.

"But Willie's my problem, and Romano may be the only way to fix this. Mickey Collins sure as hell won't."

"Why Romano?" Milo asked.

"Paulette say that Antonio Romano was seen with Collins men and Willie out back during an unload. Mr. Madden was angry. Yelling. He struck Willie and then Willie run off. Paulette say Antonio Romano went after him. That's the last anybody seen of my brother. Now folks saying that Collins think Willie stole from him. None of it make no sense. I'm hoping I can get to the bottom of this mess."

"Paulette? That girl would sell wolf tickets to her own mama's funeral. I heard the rumors and they mostly lies. What the hell would Antonio Romano care if Madden gets rough with Willie?"

"Dammit, he missing, you hear anything I said?"

Milo stepped back. He looked at her as if her head had rolled off her shoulders. What she said deserved the response, but she was the only help her brother had if these gangsters were after him. Harmony trusted Milo. She trusted him with her life, and Milo was right. He had kept the advances at bay from men that thought they were entitled to cross the line. But his perceived power was as far as Madden and his band of thugs would let it be. If he stepped out there and into this mess, Milo would be swatted back like a fly.

"He's missing. I gots to find him. He could be in all kinds of trouble."

"What's your plan? Boss Romano won't help you if Willie's on the lam, or worse if he got mixed up with that crazy brother of his. I hear all kinds of tales about Antonio Romano. And if Willie stole Collins' money, he's a dead Negro."

"Maybe, maybe not. If what you say is right... but what if'n it ain't? What if I can change that?"

Milo threw his hands up. "You one confused girl if'n you think you can." He mumbled then walked off. Harmony stopped herself from going after him. Turning, she leaned out and looked across the club. Romano was still there. Dangerous or not, she had to try. Besides, they had a connection. It wasn't her imagination. And not since Lewis had she ever felt so drawn to a man. That would be her secret though. Nothing she did or said from this moment would make her secret desires a reality. For now Willie would be her reason. Harmony was all her little brother had.

After the beauty left the stage Romano checked his timepiece again. Mickey Collins had requested a meeting. His gaze lifted to see the gangster at the bar. Collins raised his glass to him in a mock toast. Romano dismissed him. Antonio was in his element in Harlem. Tonight however he noticed his brother kept checking the faces of the men and women serving. He seemed a bit surly as well. Which meant Antonio was holding back.

"Any word on when we can move my shipment? The boys are ready to do it tonight?"

"Huh? No. We need a few more days."

Romano's gaze narrowed. "Days?"

Antonio pulled on his collar as if it were choking him. His face flushed as he downed the shot of whiskey on the table.

"What the hell do you mean days?" Romano said his voice steely and low.

"Thing is Vinnie, the cops are all over the shipyard because of some mess with the Germans. I think it best we cool it for now. Just to be sure there's no hassle."

"I want it moved tonight. Chief O'Brien will make sure it's no problem."

Antonio sighed.

"Something else on your mind?"

"Wondering if you should talk to Collins. I hear he'll be dry soon. Might be wanting to do some business."

"Can it." Romano ordered. "I know you've met with these men. I also hear you've offered protection for the Forty Thieves from their trouble with the same cops you claim are holding up my booze. I'm giving you a pass, a chance to come clean, something I need to know?"

A deep shade of pink stained his brother's cheeks. Romano may not care to do business in Harlem but it didn't mean he didn't know the players. Right now there were hustles run by a black woman named Madame St. Clair or as most called her, Queenie. She had big designs to open her own numbers bank and force the Sicilians out, but no funding. Add to her lofty goals was her influence and control over a white gang of men. The bitch had balls.

However crafty Queenie's Forty Thieves were they continued to have a persistent problem with the authorities and Antonio was generously helping by using his name. His brother's pet projects were of no concern to him on this turf, with these Negroes. Except when it came to his booze. He'd put Antonio in charge of a twenty thousand dollar stash that was to be sent down to Atlantic City. A week of it being locked up in a warehouse had him on edge. He wanted that business done.

"I can explain."

"You will explain. And you'll tell Collins there's no room at the table for any meeting. If that changes, it's when I say. Not a day before. Understood?"

Antonio narrowed his eyes but held his sharp tongue. He forked his pasta and slurped up his dinner with an obedient grunt. Romano had almost decided to leave when suddenly, she appeared. His Songbird was brought to his table by the maître d'.

"Excuse me, Mr. Romano," said Charlie with a polite nod.

Antonio stopped chewing. Sauce dripped from his chin. He frowned, getting a better look at the jazz singer who shyly stood behind Charlie. He glanced over at his brother a bit curious.

"What is it?" asked Antonio, wiping at his chin.

"Miss Harmony. She wants to speak with you, sir." Charlie looked pointedly at Romano, ignoring Antonio altogether.

Romano set his glass on the table. He leaned forward and saw her clearly through heavily lidded eyes. Harmony met his gaze dead on and a hint of a smile touched the corner of his mouth. "By all means," he said.

He watched her straighten her back and step forward to the edge of the curtained booth. She seemed confident he would grant her wish. This intrigued him. "Mr. Romano, sir, my name is Harmony Jones."

"Take a walk, Antonio."

Antonio's pout clouded his judgment. "I wasn't done Vinnie."

Romano cut down his brother's objection with a silencing yet commanding look. Wiping sauce from his face Antonio slammed the napkin on the table. He eased out of the booth. Charlie bowed deeply and backed away, signaling the waiter to bring Antonio a complimentary whiskey to ease his mood.

Romano nodded once and she accepted his offer to sit.

"Harmony. Interesting name doll."

"My Grams named me. She said I was born feet first, screaming. She knew with my lungs I was destined to sing. Guess she was right."

"Ah, well she must be proud of the songbird you turned into."

"She's dead."

Romano nodded. He tapped his finger on the table and stared at her. She looked away, but it was evident she didn't approach him to fish for a compliment. She wanted something, as most dames did. That was fine with him. Her being able to get it was a different matter.

"Mr. Romano?"

"Call me Vinnie."

Harmony looked him in the eye. He liked that. "Vinnie. I asked to speak to you because of my brother." She pulled her hands down into her lap and cleared her throat in an attempt to steady her shaky voice. She was nervous, he liked that too. "His name is Willie, Willie Jones. On the streets they call him Little Will. He works here at The Cotton, drink waiter to the tables. He also um, runs errands for Mr. Collins. Mickey Collins."

"I don't know your brother," he grumbled. *Maybe it woulda been better if she'd kept her mouth shut.* His interest in her tale was ebbing away by the minute.

"Yes, I know," she said quickly. "I mean to say, I know who you are. My brother's missing. I haven't seen him in nearly a week. Word is Mr. Collins is blaming him for something. Not sure what. There must be some misunderstanding. Willie would never do anything wrong. Never. I was wondering if you could possibly help me a turn." She hurried through the rest, to out pace his impatience. "Help me find him."

"Why not go to Mickey? He works for him."

Harmony stiffened at the question. "Not to be disrespectful, but surely you of all people know that Mickey Collins would snap my neck for asking about his business. And there is another reason."

Romano's brow arched curiously.

"I hear tale that your brother might have seen him last. He might know why Willie run off. Maybe he can help clear up the matter. I, uh, I couldn't approach him either. For obvious reasons."

Romano settled on the answer. This one here was smart. Harmony continued to maintain his stare, he knew men who weren't as bold. "I thought I'd have better chances with you, since I've noticed you watching me."

"Watching you?"

"Enjoying my show."

The tension in his jaw made it feel tight, and his gaze leveled on her pretty face under drawn brows. To say he was surprised was an understatement. The Negress was trying to turn him. How could she possibly know his lustful desires when she sang across the dining hall to a crowd of unappreciative bastards and never gave him a second glance? She couldn't know. Could she?

What chance did she think she could have for him to care about some hooch runner in Mickey's crew? And what's this with Antonio and Harlem? The more he heard about his brother's interest in the people here the more his suspicions rose. Especially considering his and Antonio's history with people of color. He dropped his cigar to the ashtray and blew a long stream of smoke through his nose. "Interesting. I'll need more information on your brother."

Harmony nodded quickly.

Antonio reappeared; a few of Romano's best men were in tow. His brother had a cold congested look of disapproval settled over his face, which seemed to disconcert Harmony because she lowered her gaze to her hands until Romano's words brought her focus back to him.

"Let's discuss this later, in private."

"Private?" Harmony glanced from his stare to their audience. It appeared she quickly understood what *private* meant. Crestfallen, she averted her gaze, if she had been a shade or two paler he was sure he'd see humiliation rising pink on her cheeks.

The band was warming up. Harmony glanced over and Romano noticed the saxophonist's beckoning stare. "I'll meet you at the front of the club, if that's okay."

Romano nodded. She was dismissed.

Harmony's gaze lifted to Antonio who made no effort to move. She glanced once more to the ruthless Sicilian that could possibly save her brother's life. He flicked his fingers for his brother to back off. Antonio did, with a snort of distaste.

"Thank you." said Harmony meekly, and she eased out of the booth. She straightened her dress with a tug at the sides. Her breasts heaved, drawing the stares of the others. Quickly, she stepped around Antonio. She could feel eyes on her backside as she sashayed to her safety zone, to the wings of the stage. She didn't dare look back. If she did she'd lose her nerve.

The orchestra played the vamp as Harmony returned to the microphone. Fletch shot her a worried look. Milo slipped her a warning nod that Mr. Madden was indeed watching her now. She closed her eyes to block the disappointment she'd read on the rest of her bandmates' faces, and began to sing. When she opened her eyes, Romano's table was again crowded with Sicilians. But only one pair of eyes was fixed on her. *His.*

****

"If you think Boss Romano is going to save Willie over some Negro in a skirt, you're crazy!"

"Oh pipe-down Milo, I know the man isn't the least bit concerned about Willie," Harmony said in a gentle but firm tone. She changed behind the dressing screen where only her silhouette could be seen.

"Mony, Lil Will isn't worth the trouble. If he's double-crossing these men, he's a dead boy either way!"

"Don't you dare say that, Milo! Say it again and I want you out."

"It's true. Willie has to be either suicidal or dumb to think he could get away with stealing. He hiding for that reason. Either way you won't be able to save him. You have to know this. Boss Romano wants one thing and if you leave with him, you won't have any choice but to give it to him."

Harmony came from around the screen wearing only her slip and a tight lip scowl. She opened her mouth to counter his prediction but dismissed the effort. Instead she picked up her peach and white floral dress drawing it down over her head. "Do me?" She turned to give him her back.

Milo rose and zipped her up, his hand lingered for a moment on her hip then dropped away. "Mony, listen to me. What would Lewis think?"

Harmony closed her eyes at the mention of her sweet dearly departed Lewis. The pain over his death was beyond her tears. She waited a beat for the anger and longing to shift to a bearable degree in her heart.

"Lewis is dead. He went out there and got himself killed working for men like Romano. I won't lose my brother too. He's all I have." She turned to face her friend. "What Lewis would think don't matter. What you think don't matter a damn either sugar. All that matters is the promise I made to Grams. Willie's seventeen and right or wrong he's *my* kid brother. I got to try to save him, even from himself. Vinnie Romano sits out there every night I sing and burns a hole in me from across the room. If there is a small chance that gangster will help deal with another, especially the likes of his rattlesnake brother Antonio and that racist pig Mickey Collins, then I'm gonna take it. That's the end of this discussion, Milo."

Harmony stalked over to the vanity. She dropped down in front of the mirror. Picking up pins, she captured her loose unruly curls and pinned them back, flat to her head. If she thought about what *could* happen, she wouldn't be able to pull it off. Willie's fate would be sealed then. *If it isn't already.*

From the mirror's reflection Harmony saw Milo drop in the chair behind her. She knew his fear. A colored girl in Harlem had few options and fewer choices. If your skin was medium brown to fair you might get a chance. At The Cotton they called mulattos 'tans' and gave them top billing. She barely passed that test. So for her, singing jazz for rich white folks by night liberated her from doing laundry for the same white folks by day. She was lucky. Milo had gotten her a brownstone in Sugar Hill, where all the other musicians, painters, authors, poets and Negro elite lived. It belonged to a friend of his. The person, whom she never met, allowed a reasonable sublease once she became a headline attraction at The Cotton Club. This is why Willie's fool hearted ways hurt her so. Here she was breaking her back to give him more, and he was running those streets.

Milo had been Lewis's best friend and an associate of Fletcher Henderson. Behind her back he hustled an audition for her at the newly opened Cotton Club when her washboard could no longer put food on the table without Lewis's earnings. His reasoning made little sense then, but now it did. Singing was all she had left. It was all she was.

"Singing jazz ain't the sin Mony, though, what them boys do out the back door with the bootlegging and gambling is. I'll give you that. What I'm asking really ain't no worse than singing in your church."

"That's baloney. I see them girls coming from 125th street. I'm tellin' you I ain't no jazz singer. Singing hymns is far from it." She spit on her heated iron and pressed back down on the linen for Mrs. Ward, running the steam over to flatten the wrinkles.

"Hear me out. Fletch is forming his band. You know Jack Johnson done sold Club Deluxe to those gangsters. The place is called The Cotton Club now and it's big time, bigger than the Apollo. Gonna make us all famous."

"What that mean to me?" Harmony grunted. She set down the iron to shake out the sheet she washed clean of stains for the Wards until her fingers cramped and the skin on her hands wrinkled.

"It mean a new start. You grieving for Lewis and I understand it, but he gone. I swore to take care of you. Best I can. That's what this deal means. And if you do it, I can get you out of here, to a better place."

"You talking crazy!" Harmony laughed.

"I'm talking opportunity."

Harmony folded the sheet to a sensible square and set it atop of the rest of the laundry. Sweat beaded over her brow and the bridge of her nose. It was hot as Hades with both windows open. Leaving the one room flat she shared with Willie and Lewis was a dream when he was alive. She had no hope that after losing him it would be any part of her reality. Milo was feeding her a line. She wiped at her face with the back of her hand. "I can't tap or dance, I ain't been no further than the church pew. This here is all I knows. So this here is where I stay."

"Can't or won't? Don't be dense girl. What options you got? Lil Will is in them streets more and more daily. Is he doing anything to keep you in this place? I didn't think so. You gone make it on pennies now that Lewis gone?"

"I can take care of myself."

"Mony, that's what I'm saying. Take care of yourself. Besides Lewis used to say you got the pipes. He worked this deal for you girl."

"Lewis did not."

"That's why I'm here. He knew there was a chance, that uh, you may need looking after. So he spoke to Henderson about you. Think on it. What harm can come of it? Sugar Hill, no more white folks' laundry, doing what you love, how is that not your dream? I'll watch out for you, you got my word."

"Milo you kept your promise. You've done a lot."

He had tried to protect her. Kept the paying clientele off her, and even withstood Mr. Madden's wrath. There were times she saw more in his intentions. His lingering touches and lust filled looks when she sang. But they never crossed that line and right now she felt ashamed that she knew he understood the lines she would cross for her brother.

"I love you for wanting to protect me. I'll be just fine. I can handle myself."

Milo rose and without a word walked out of her dressing closet. He slammed the door. Harmony jumped at the final message. Her eyes lifted to her reflection in the mirror. She allowed herself no illusions about what the night would bring. "I'll be just fine. Just fine." She picked up her lipstick to dab the ruby gloss across her lips. Her shaking fingers belied her confident words.

CHAPTER TWO
Shall We Dance?

Lenox Avenue at four in the morning wasn't any different than the avenue at four in the evening, except for the congested mix of people. Blacks and whites drove and walked the same streets in the night.

Harmony stood on the sidewalk with her coat on and her grey bell shaped cloche hat pressed down on her head, watching others come and go. Funny how the same white folk that called for an encore just seconds after her last performance, found her invisible as they passed her by. She didn't mind. Who she was at The Cotton should never cross over into her real life. Though she had the sinking feeling this would no longer be true after tonight.

Where was he? Harmony worried over the late hour. Romano should have arrived by now. She hadn't taken that long changing and Paulette said his men were still inside. The cars flew by. She felt a dreaded sense of hopelessness; it dawned on her that he wouldn't show. Maybe the connection she felt when she sang to him was in her head. What did she really know of men, besides what she learned from Lewis? Why did the rejection burn so badly? Was it her pride or did she actually think she could pull this one off?

Her shoulders slumped as she turned to head home. When she crossed over 142nd, a black chauffeured car rolled up blocking her pass. Harmony stopped, leery of the passenger who stepped out. The brim of the driver's fedora shadowed his face, but his eyes were still compelling. He opened the back door and gave her a respectful nod.

Sucking in a breath of bravery, Harmony walked over with steady nerves. The driver took her hand and helped her inside. *Like a lady.* Romano patiently waited for her delivery.

"Hello Songbird," Romano said with quiet emphasis on the last word.

"Mr. Romano." She replied with levity to her voice.

"Vinnie," he reminded her.

"Thank you, *Vinnie* for uh… for agreeing to meet with me to talk about Willie."

Vinnie cut his eyes to the front and the driver nodded, pulling out onto Lenox Avenue. It was warm in the car but her nerves had her feeling ice water in her veins. Milo's words and the spectre of Lewis haunted her, yet she focused. Could be he just wanted to talk. Could be.

She's more fearless than I thought; fearless or desperate. The way she fiddles with her hands surely meant a little of both. Why I never made a move on her was simple. I pretty much stay away from birds like her. Her being a Negress wasn't all of it. It was something about the way she put me at ease with her voice. Not looking for a dame, colored or white, wielding that kind of hold over me.

Romano's gaze dropped to Harmony's lap, her coat covered the tops of her knees, still his gaze travelled up and over her feminine form stopping at her face. Harmony sensed his stare and slipped him a look. He couldn't read the meaning of the challenge blazing in her dark smoky irises, but he got the distinct impression when they found her on the corner waiting, she had entered his car by choice. Her choice. If she decided against his secret desire to touch her he'd have a helluva fight convincing her otherwise. He held her stare and felt a charge of excitement from the bold light of inner strength flickering deep in her eyes. *Who was this dame?*

The night would prove interesting indeed. They traveled out north. Romano saw her visibly tense as the destination dawned on her. He said little for the first half of the ride to make sure she felt at ease in his presence. Eventually the silence felt too prolonged and he spoke. "So tell me about your brother."

"Willie's my younger brother. Like I told you earlier, he works at The Cotton too. He wipes down the tables and keeps the bars stocked, is even a drink waiter on some nights. He also handles small deliveries for Mickey Collins. There's a speakeasy in Harlem that Collins supplies. Willie makes that run. It meant Willie got a little more responsibility."

"He a numbers runner too?"

She struggled with her answer. To confess to all the tricks and hustles her little brother was into would overshadow the claim of innocence she kept shoving his way. He knew she thought highly of her brother, but if he was making deliveries between Mickey Collins and that hot-tempered bitch Queenie and her band of thieves, then he was definitely no angel.

Harmony shrugged. The passing street lamps illuminated her face giving her skin a rich copper appeal.

"Need an answer doll. Is he a numbers runner too?"

Under dark upward swept lashes her eyes were magnets to his soul and he couldn't look away. "Yes, he is, or was. He learned that hustle from Lewis."

Romano narrowed his eyes. "What's a Lewis?"

"My fiancé. He dead now. Used to work for Collins too before he died."

"I understand." Romano dismissed the useless information for the more pertinent nugget. Songbird had once been engaged, which meant his silent desire for her to be his was a reality. If she was widowed he doubted another man filled the space. He didn't care about propriety; he cared more of her willingness to see the evening through, to let him finally touch her.

Harmony cleared her throat. "Willie started under Lewis, but now Lewis gone. So he picked up extra work at The Cotton."

"How does Antonio fit into this?" Romano asked. When she arrived at the table she dropped his brother's name. It was the second reason he considered this little meeting. There was no business between the Romanos and Collins.

"I don't think he does. I… I only know that some say your brother and Willie had words. That's the last anyone seen of him."

"My brother and Collins doing business at The Cotton?"

"I wouldn't know these things."

"You sure about that Songbird? Ever hear Willie mention Antonio Romano, the Black Hand?"

She shook her head no.

Romano nodded. "Not wise of your brother to cross up with Collins and Queenie, no one man can't have two bosses. The name of the speakeasy that Collins keeps wet?"

"Red Hots. A guy named Dennis Red runs the door, but it's owned by Madame."

The name sounded familiar. Romano was sure he had heard it before. "Is Willie helping Collins move in on Harlem's turf?"

Harmony sighed. "Mickey Collins gave him a lot more responsibility like I told ya. Not that Mr. Collins did anything wrong, I'm just saying it proves Willie's on the level for Mickey." She shifted in her seat trying to remain collected. "If I could get to him first, before Collins's men do, I'm sure I can find out what he's done or hasn't done. I can clear things up."

"Mickey runs his business as he sees fit. I can drop a line and see if he has the boy. But if he's stealing…"

"Mr., uh, Vinnie, he's not. I can assure you he's not. I'm on the level. I checked the neighborhood and some of his friends think he may have gotten robbed the night he was working. That's why he ran, cause robbed or not if he's short on Collins's whiskey, you know what that means. He don't have many options here." Her defiant stare at last softened and he thought the dim lighting in the back seat revealed her eyes were glistening with the threat of tears. First her voice, now her damn eyes were getting to him. He decided to stop staring in them for the remainder of the ride.

"You care a lot about your brother," he mumbled.

"He's all I got in the world. Yes, I care."

"Little brothers, they can be quite a handful."

They were headed to the Bronx. Harmony mentally calculated how much it would cost her to catch the Jitney back to Sugar Hill. Too much, probably. She'd have to find a way to the Bronx Park terminal and catch the train. Things were going fast and she had come too far to turn back now.

In front of his brownstone the car door opened and she was helped outside. She stepped into the street and stared up at the place. Romano was out of the car as well, his wool coat draped around his shoulders and his black Fedora resting on the top of his head. The smile in his eyes contained a sensuous flame that set her at ease until he extended his offer. "Shall we?"

Harmony hesitated. At what point did he make it clear he would help her? And at what point had she made it clear she'd pay his price for his help? The lines were blurred and her pounding heart didn't help much. Despite the warning signs of danger she saw in his intense stare and the eyes of the men that shadowed him, he drew her in with his unspoken charm. It would be easier not to resist him.

Walking around the car, she gave a small smile and allowed him to lead her to the doors of his home. They climbed the stairs but Harmony fell back on the step when the door opened. A short dark skinned older black woman in a maid's uniform appeared. Their eyes met. There was an arrested expression on her face. The servant quickly covered it then backed away in respect and held the door for them to enter. God help Harmony but it felt like she looked into the eyes of her Grams.

"Welcome home Mr. Romano," the servant said, accepting his hat and coat.

"Mabel." Romano nodded.

"Good evening," Mabel mumbled, her gaze switching to Harmony.

"Good evening," Harmony answered softly.

"Your coat, Miss?"

Harmony nervously undid the front buttons then passed Mabel the coat, her hat and purse. The woman shook her head in disappointment before she walked away. It hurt, but Harmony had grown used to the sting. Singing at The Cotton had cost her the respect of many people in her old community before she moved to Sugar Hill. She could hear the snickers of the young women when she went to church. It got so bad that even the Reverend's wife asked her not to return. So she didn't. Since her popularity and her one night performance at the Lincoln Theater, even men that knew her Grams when she was alive had propositioned her. It was exhausting. But she'd learned to endure. Jazz is about survival, and as long as she kept it to jazz she had nothing to be ashamed of.

In the parlor, her heels clicked noisily over the hardwood floors so she slowed her walk and tried hard to appear less anxious. Romano had many fine things including his own private bar—stocked full with bootleg whiskey and hooch. He stood there pouring from a crystal decanter. When he turned, she saw he had two glasses. *Dammit, I can't drink with him. I need to keep my wits about me.* Harmony only drank hooch with Lewis once or twice and hated it. The Cotton slipped it to its patrons after late hours but never the staff.

"Thank you," she said, accepting the drink. She sipped it but kept a straight face and the pour burned its way down her throat.

"Have a seat."

She did. Thankfully, he chose one across from her.

"When does Willie run Mickey's hooch to Red Hots? What day?"

"I said Mickey Collins has an arrangement with Madame St. Clair so I'm not sure of how often or what days Willie did his runs."

Romano downed the last of his whiskey as if it were water. He didn't bristle at her sharp tongue. Hard as she tried she couldn't humble her speech any lower. She was quite jumpy now being out of her territory.

"Nunzio," he called out.

A man appeared from nowhere, another Sicilian, younger than Romano, but with a unforgiving scowl permanent to his features. She thought they were alone, except for the maid. His presence made her eye the exit once more.

"Yes, Boss?"

"Take a run up East 96th through 125th and put the word out that I'm looking for Little Will."

"Yes, Boss."

"Oh, and get a message to Mickey Collins, that I want the kid alive. He has a problem with that tell him to see me."

"Yes, Boss."

Harmony blinked through her shock. Just like that and it was done. A cold wave of relief washed over her. She smiled at him. "Thank you so much, Mr. Romano. I mean Vinnie. I really don't know how to repay you for this."

Harmony rose. Romano looked up at her curiously. A tense silence enveloped and sealed the room.

"When Willie comes home I'm sure he can clear it all up." Harmony flashed him her prettiest smile. Her gaze switched to the exit once more.

Romano chuckled. His expression stilled and grew serious. "If he's stealing from Mickey, you'll have to. But I think it best you stay until we bring him in, don't you?"

It was his turn to rise and she couldn't help but admire how nicely he filled a suit. The man was tall. Why he never appeared as tall from across the dining room before confounded her. He had Lewis beat by an inch or two. Harmony squeezed the cool glass until spasmodic tremors cramped her hand. She stepped back. Romano closed the distance between them. She was forced to maintain his stare. Her breath solidified in her throat. "I don't know it's kinda late. I can give you my address. You could send word, maybe?"

"I prefer something less formal."

"Like?"

"Sing for me. Here. Now."

"Suga this ain't The Cotton, and I don't see Fletch Henderson's orchestra." *Could he be serious?* His eyes were a tawny shade of brown. Now she knew the color and couldn't remember why she wanted to in the first place. The man made her anxious to leave, to stay, to explain herself to the maid who was somewhere in this house judging her. She felt anxious all over. He was closer now, closer than any man besides Lewis had ever been. And with him standing so close she was forced to tilt her head and lift her chin a bit to maintain his stare. She had been right. There was an unspoken connection between them. A deep soul stirring familiarity would eventually lead them toward the forbidden. Secretly she had wanted a bit of forbidden.

It had been months ago when she first saw him. The nights he came, her eyes always drifted to him, drinking and smoking a cigar or a pipe in his private booth. He had such a magnetic pull on her she questioned her sanity at times when she performed and found herself disappointed he hadn't come. Now here he was, and that strange feeling coursing through her veins wasn't just anxiety, a bit of excitement stirred her heart to fluttering too.

His gaze lowered to her bosom and lingered there. Romano was so close, his touch was certain to come next. She knew it. She braced for it. Because his hands on her she wouldn't allow. No matter what the circumstance, no man touched her unless she said so.

A thick membrane of tension swelled between him. Would he touch her, would he ask to, or would he walk away? Harmony held her breath prepared to deal with either outcome. Romano smirked then walked around her and away. "Saw Bessie Smith a few weeks ago," he said, stopping in front of a shiny copper, mahogany and gold phonograph. "Next to you she's my favorite singer."

"You like jazz?" Harmony asked, realizing immediately how stupid the question was.

"Surprised? I love jazz, thanks to you."

"Me?"

"Do you know her?"

"No." *Did he think all Negroes knew each other?* "I've met her, saw her perform that is, and met her twice after but I don't know her." She quickly answered. Harmony watched him wind the handle of the crank on the side of the player, then drop the needle down on the record. *So he owned race music?* Why was she surprised? If he didn't have an affinity for her talents or her music she would've never gotten through the door. Turning, Romano removed his suit jacket and tossed it to the chair without a thought. She figured money and nice things came easy to him. She figured a woman like her came easy as well.

"My song?" he spoke, the huskiness lingered in his tone. One of Bessie's recent recordings filled the room. But Romano wanted his own rendition. Is this why he brought her here? A private show? Harmony felt a tinge of disappointment. Here she was thinking the man had deeper desires. Or was she looking for an excuse to act on her own?

"I'm waiting," he said, extending his hand.

The symphony that played about them was sweetly enticing. Harmony itched down in her throat to join in the melody. She knew this song, had sang it before. She reached for his hand then stepped into his arms, now humming through the intro. Other than Lewis, she'd never been in a man's arms. She found Vincenzio Romano's embrace oddly enticing. So much so, she began to relax. Soon she swayed to the music, singing softly into his ear. Her pelvis brushed hard steel between his legs and she nearly fumbled over a note in the song. Romano kept her close. When he gave her a slight turn through their slow rhythmic dance she caught a glimpse of the maid Mabel peeking in at them. The look on Mabel's face said it all.

For Willie, everything I do tonight is for Willie, and a maybe a little bit for me.

Her hand barely draped over his right shoulder, because of his height her arm had extended straight. The other hand was clasped in his. Their dance was gentle almost innocent. Almost. One look into Romano's eyes and she knew his intent. Milo had been right, bargain with the devil he'll take you for a ride.

Romano's large hands clasped her hips. Harmony forced a demure smile and ignored the pretzel tight knot in her stomach from having his hot palms pressed so firmly to her. When the tightness of his touch eased and his thick fingers smoothly slipped down and around to her rear, terrible regrets assailed her. She closed her eyes and tried her best not to react, having decided when she accepted his hand that she'd let him hold her. Instead she let her singing keep her calm. Romano responded in the like, he rubbed the side of his face against her cheek, with his body somewhat leaned into hers to keep her close. The gruff on his cheek wasn't rough, the way she imagined it would be. The way Lewis's cheek was.

Harmony softened. So did the knot of anxiety twisting through her stomach since the moment she approached the mob boss's table. Even the maid spying didn't unsettle her. Nothing could touch her when she sang. When the record stopped, she continued to hum in time with the scratch-and-bump of the needle, having no need or use for a melody other than her own. It took her several moments to realize the dance should have ended. Lifting her head from his shoulder, she tried to pull back. But he held her firm. Their faces were inches apart, and she knew he'd see the blush cover her cheeks.

Words he hadn't spoken since he parted the shores of Sicily escaped him. He whispered them forgetting she didn't understand his language. He wanted to stop time. Never in his life had a woman's voice had such an affect on him. Silently he had craved her for months after the first time he heard her sing. He bought all the jazz records he could, trying to capture the calm soothing feeling of her voice that chipped at the iceberg in his chest most would call a heart. The first time he'd seen her she'd caught him by surprise. He had Madden brought to his table immediately to tell him who she was. And weekly no matter the commitment, he'd carve out time for at least one visit to The Cotton to see her perform.

Once he had arrived and found it was her day off. Enraged, he nearly clued his men into his obsession. Now she was here, in his arms, and singing more beautifully than he ever recalled.

"That's the tops, sweet," he smirked.

"Thank you," she whispered, swaying in his arms.

"I've watched you for weeks. Listened to you."

"I know. I've noticed," she said softly. "Thanks for the tips."

"You knew they were from me?"

"I do now," she winked.

His chuckle came from a deep hollow space in his throat. One could easily forget that this man was as ruthless as he was handsome. His humor simmered to a low groan. "Smart girl."

Romano's arms tightened around her waist. She was crushed against every hard angle of his chest, and it felt good. Though she knew it was well past what her Grams would have called appropriate, having a man hold her was near sublime. She took a deep breath and adjusted her smile. The heat of lust spread so fast under her skin she could feel herself vibrate with need. "Maybe I should go now."

"I've always wanted to do this." Romano pulled back and straightened from the way he held her. His hands went to her neatly pinned hair. Harmony stilled. She steadied her breath in anticipation while he pulled the pins out and let them drop to the floor. Her thickly wound pin-curls fell free in frozen spirals about her face. His fingers ran through the coarse strands, and more pins dropped to the floor, raining small metallic sounds. He began to massage her scalp gently with the pads of his fingers. It felt sinfully divine. Her head rolled back slowly and her eyes shut. It was shameful how much she enjoyed the game. Romano then combed his fingers from the roots through her tangles and spread her untamed tresses over her shoulders.

Vinnie. The name buzzed through her skull with such potent force she felt herself go weak around the knees, so her hands lifted to hold his sides. All ideas of how she'd escape a night in his bed dissolved. "I… I thought… I never, uh… Mr. Romano… Vinnie," she stammered.

Realizing how undone she'd become, she snapped out of it. With her locks falling freely over her eyes, Harmony nervously touched her hair and stepped back from him. *What just happened? In an instant she had lost her senses. How was that even possible with a man like Vinnie Romano?* The pounding of her heartbeat made her short on breath. Lewis was a demanding lover. Even in her inexperience she knew her man was a tiger. Most nights she'd have to fight her way out of his bed just for relief, and pray Willie would come home from those streets so Lewis would give her a break.

The loss of her man hurt. It hurt to the core. She never even dared think another man could spark the flames of desire in her again. Romano reminded her of Lewis. His touch firm and commanding, his hold strong, and that look in his eyes had her stomach doing flips. It wasn't just the physical. Lewis said he stumbled into church one Sunday, a bit inebriated he mistook it for the boarding house next door. But he said he first saw her in the pew and heard her voice. Said he fell in love with her instantly. Romano had that same smoldering look in his eyes. She wasn't crazy, she'd lived for that look from Lewis, and she'd recognize it anywhere.

She needed to get out, and now.

"Excuse me," Harmony stammered.

"For?" he asked.

She couldn't answer. All she knew was in a blink, desire had rolled its way up through her with such force she forgot her middle name. Who could blame her? Power rippled off him in sexy waves hitting her with full intensity. Instead of reclaiming her senses that brief connection they shared melted away her defense.

Again he spoke his language and she frowned. He smirked and translated the words.

"Trust me."

Is he serious? Grams always said, with a man trust is a trick horse, turn your back on common sense and get kicked in your head for it. Of course a mob boss like Romano thinks it should be given freely if he asked. Well, I'm no fool. Sure he may like to hear me carry a tune. Sure he wants a little something extra. But he's like any man. Once his appetite is satisfied that maid Mabel is going to be showing me to the door.

Romano stepped back, but continued to hold her hand. Expectation weighed in his gaze. "You always this jumpy Songbird?"

"No," she said honestly, gauging his response. Humor sparkled in his eyes but he didn't laugh. She offered him a sly smile. "I'll try to relax Vinnie, if you keep your hands to yourself."

Romano's brows lowered and leveled over his hot gaze. Maybe he'd appreciate her candor. "Yes, try to relax. As for my hands..."

"It's getting late." Harmony pointed out. "I think I'll leave now."

"Your brother? You going to abandon him?" Romano's gaze sharpened and so did his speech. "When we're so *close* to finding him. I thought you'd do anything for Lil Will?"

The question hit her hard in the chest. Did she have some deep destructive desire to break every personal rule in her life for a fleeting feel of lust? No. But Willie had gotten mixed up with these men and she was his only hope. "I will," she said, then pressed her lips together to keep the rest of her objections at bay.

He extended his hand once more.

For a brief moment she considered his open palm and the consequences of her actions. Could Lewis see her now? What would Grams think? Harmony lifted her hand slowly and placed it in his. Romano pressed a light kiss to her knuckles with his gaze trained on hers. He then led her out of the parlor.

Together they entered the dark hall to the staircase. Mabel had eased back into the shadows, still she peeked at her from behind a door. A stony look of disgust and disbelief turned what were possibly gentle features hard. Harmony held to her pride and made the climb with her head high. Romano took the lead pulling her hand behind him in silence. *For Willie*, she kept reminding herself. Romano stopped at a bedroom door and pushed it inward. Harmony could barely see inside. She didn't have to. She knew what awaited her there. *Should I delay the inevitable and make sure Willie was all right? What do I have to offer him but this, and once it's had, what then?*

"Harmony?" he said her name, noticing her resistance.

She flashed a small smile of her own then stepped inside. The room was dark, but the bed lay clearly visible and even more intimidating than the mobster that stood behind her. The door lock clicked, engaged and she bit down hard on her bottom lip. Apprehension gnawed at her confidence. She forced herself to exchange glances from the bed to him when he turned on a lamp. Again, she was struck by the hard edges that strengthened his handsomeness. Here she was, alone, with this enigma of a man. Most coloreds avoided the Sicilian and Irish crime bosses, though desire had reshaped her fear. Tall, with glossy golden brown hair, he had fiery hot amber brown eyes, and the most delectable mouth she had ever seen on a man. His cool presence excited her just like it did with Lewis. His olive skin in the darkly lit room made him appear a bit more native than the pale faces of the white men he kept company with. She remembered Grams warnings against the excited fluttering in her breast. She didn't listen then, she wouldn't listen now.

"*Grams. That was rude. You barely said two words to Lewis.*" Harmony closed the door and walked back to the kitchen. "*He just coming to see about Willie.*"

"*Mony, take a seat.*" Her grandmother turned from the stove with her fist to her hip and a serious frown creasing her brow. Harmony knew that look. She thought it ridiculous that she would get saddled with the burden of explaining her little brother's friends. Lewis didn't come for her. He was just a nice guy to think of giving her some chocolates every once and awhile.

"*Yes ma'am.*" Harmony said sitting at the table.

Grams had been sluggish lately. She stopped going to Miss Moncrief's and now did laundry from her back room. It scared Harmony to see the woman she knew as her mother so tired all the time. Even now her grandmother heaved and breathed hard breaths from the simplest of tasks. And the tired lines of stress and worry lent a hint of sadness to her round, kind face. Her skin was a nut brown shade, and her hair, streaked grey from the temples, was always worn parted in two plaits. She'd raised them since Harmony was four and her brother a babe. Her mother had run off when their father disappeared. Harmony had no idea if either of her parents were alive.

"*I see the way that man looks at you when he comes to see about Lil Will, knowing full well he done passed that boy in the streets on his way up our step. He not fooling me girl. Showin' up at my door with those sweets, flowers, he courtin' you Mony.*"

Harmony's eyes stretched wide. "*But he said…*"

"*Don't matter what he say Mony it's what he do. You blooming baby. Men like him bound to notice. The problem with Lewis is he in the world, you ain't. You spend mo' time in the church pew singing and in those books of yours than understanding the attentions of a man. But if you keep on acceptin' those gifts he gone expect more. Every man wants somethin', even if what they give you is barely nothin'.*" Grams pulled out the yellow kitchen chair so worn on its legs the paint had all but disappeared in the wood. She sat and wiped at her brow then forced a smile. "*Been saving up for you sweetheart, to get you out of Harlem. Send you South to learn in one of those colored schools. You gone be something baby, a teacher, or maybe a nurse. I can't worry too much about Willie, he got too much of his daddy in him. But you, baby, you special, that voice of yours was sent straight from God. Don't let the desires of a man change who you become.*"

Harmony blinked away the beginning of tears. Her grandmother died two weeks later from her weak heart. And everything changed. Including her promise to be somebody special. Lewis was there for her, comforted her, even paid for the service. But his attentions had shifted from Willie to her solely. Before she knew the name of the new uncharted emotions she felt over his naughty touches and prolonged kisses she was in his bed becoming his woman.

Now she was alone.

Her own woman.

And here with a man who could only lead her down the wrong path. Just like Lewis, the danger and powerful maleness about Romano made her weak. Every time he spoke her name, she felt an insane urge to touch him. In fact, the more time she spent alone with him, the more those urges consumed her sensibility, and she was oddly grateful for it.

Romano walked over to the bed. The surface was bathed in sparse light, just enough to chase away the shadows. Her eyes skipped over to the wall. It was a rich and masculine room with pecan wood paneling. The bed had tall dark mahogany posts and a broad headboard. It was indeed the largest bed she'd ever laid her eyes on outside Pinkleston's furniture store. Why would a single man like him need a bed so big? She and Lewis shared one less than half its size and Willie slept on the other side of a strung up sheet on a cot.

"You're still nervous," he said, approaching.

Harmony opened her mouth and closed it, knowing that a litany of excuses were certain to tumble out. The truth was far simpler. Her heart thundered in her chest and blood warmly raced through her veins, not from nervousness but something strangely enticing. Good, bad or wrong the unknown held promise. When he stopped in front of her she had to look up into his eyes again. Romano traced his finger along her jaw to the center of her chin then with a pinch he tilted her head back. Harmony took in a few quick breaths through her nose, attempting to stop the breakneck pace of her heart. Her body tension slowly began to unwind. Romano lowered his head and stole a kiss. It was slow, teasingly gentle. A brief touch of lips that felt both soft and innocent. When his mouth parted she realized hers gaped for more. Embarrassed she pressed her lips together and double blinked up at him. Heat slid arousal through her body and she swallowed hard. To hell with innocence! She wanted a kiss. A real one. *Should she say so?* One arm held her. The other free hand caressed her cheek.

"You are sexy." He breathed.

"Thanks Suga, you ain't too bad yourself. Hey, slow down. Maybe we should wait for news on Willie. I might have to talk to him." She pushed against his chest tasting him on her mouth. A stall was the only defense she had left.

"I think I've waited long enough, Songbird." Romano's voice hardened and so did his hold. He ran his hand up the center of her spine, stopping at her nape a brief moment then stepped back as if he was getting a good look at her for the first time. He lifted her arm and spun her in a half circle, crossing her arms in front of her and bringing her up against his chest. She thought she heard a deep groan escape him when her backside pressed into his groin. He released her hand and eased his inside her bodice. The front material stretched and his warm palm massaged her left breast. Her eyes flashed upward to lock with his in the mirror. She stood transfixed, almost hypnotized.

"I can feel your heart beating in my palm." Romano smirked, giving her breast a gentle squeeze, then pulling on her swollen nipple until it was tight. "I've always wondered if the skin between your thighs feels as soft and beautiful as your voice. Does it?" he asked removing his hand then reaching between them to pull down the tab of the zipper to her dress.

The slight quiver in her belly drew her eyes shut. The front of her dress lowered but she caught the fabric before it dipped too low. His penetrating stare said he didn't approve. Her hand fell away. The dress dropped down the length of her arms. She had to tug it over the bend of her hips in order for it to fall to the floor.

Now in her full slip and heels, her neck, shoulders, and the tops of her breasts were available for his perusal.

Romano took a small step back to be sure he could see her fully. "I've imagined quite a bit since I first laid eyes on you. Your breasts for starters. I've given them considerable thought." His hoarse accent didn't garble his words. In fact, it only added flavoring to the seductive way in which he spoke.

"Have you?" Harmony let out a shaky breath and moisture gathered between her thighs. She could feel it build and dampen the seat of her panty. If he kissed her properly she felt certain the last of her trepidation would melt away. Should she kiss him? If he was closer she would. Under the heat of his gaze she found herself unable to move or speak. The shadows in the room chased from the bed, were mostly in the corner where he stood. They cast his face in mystery. It was clear that pleasure awaited behind the veil of taboo. No one needed to know, why not indulge until her back wore out? *Sweet merciful Mary I could really go for a bit of forbidden now.*

Harmony pressed her lips together. She reached for the satin strap of her slip on her left shoulder and eased it down. Her actions peeled away the soft fabric from her breast and the chill in the room made her nipple unreasonably tight.

The corner of Romano's mouth lifted in a smile.

Her hand trembled once arousal curled tighter in her chest. Mindless, she eased down the right satin strap and uncovered both breasts. Harmony's hands lowered, both went to the sides of her slip and began to tug. The garment fell from her body in a polyester wave to her ankles, she then stepped out of it. A shiver went through her and her cheeks warmed as she faced his inspection. Harmony stood before him in her panty and gartered stockings, with the heels she'd borrowed from the club. She watched his hand rise, then reach out to touch her, and could feel the heat from his fingers, barely centimeters from her skin. She didn't know what to make of the tease. Her eyes dropped down to where he barely touched her and for long breathless moments just stared until his hand withdrew.

Not even his sweet Annie, who left him when his violent nature became too much, stirred such raw feeling in him so soon. He knew his fondness for Harmony stemmed from her voice. But now, he had to question that reasoning. Like Annie she had a hold on him from the start. He concentrated on the feeling to understand it a bit more. Nothing came. It was simply her. All of her. She could have remained fully clothed and still affected him this way. She crossed her arms over her breasts and visibly shivered. Was she cold? Why couldn't he move on her? *Dammit this is ridiculous.*

"Come here," he barked, his voice hoarse with desire and tense.

Again she speared him with those smoky brown eyes of hers. To make matters worse she didn't move. Not a breath escaped him as he waited. He swallowed a bit of his pride and asked again. "Come to me Songbird."

She approached him slowly, keeping her lovely breasts concealed behind her crossed arms.

"That's better," he exhaled, feeling the tightness in his chest loosen when she responded to his wish. He brushed his lips over the rapid beat of her pulse. Then lifted his gaze and noticed her thawing under his touch. Romano unsnapped her garter belt and fastens, tossing it aside. He eased his hand down her back and the velvet smoothness of her rounded curves. She released the sweetest sigh against his cheek. *Did every sound escaping his Songbird sound so beautiful? What sounds would she purr when he truly claimed her?* Slowly he ran his middle finger down the crease of her buttocks to rub her indiscreetly. "I want you, here," he said giving her forbidden hole a tap. His other hand eased between his bulging groin and her belly to part the crease of her thighs so he could rub two fingers over the seat of her panty that concealed the plump lips of her sex. "And here."

A shiver passed from her soft sweet body and he felt it like a rippling current of electricity. Romano drew his face from the side of hers and looked upon her once more. Her dazed stare connected with his and he found a silent plea in her beautiful brown eyes. *I'll be damn. She wants me to go for it. Take her. It's all over her face. Exactly who is playing who here?*

A door slammed downstairs. Someone had arrived, possibly his brother. Anger began to cloud his mood. He got a report back from Jimmie that Antonio was making moves without his consent. It would be a nasty matter teaching his brother to show respect. He'd deal with it later. No business was of greater importance than what he desired in his bedroom.

He turned her. His arms went under hers causing them to lift in acceptance. Both his palms rested flat against her belly. He smoothly cupped her breasts. She pressed the side of her face to his as her head tilted back to his shoulder. He could hear her sweet gasps soft against his ear as he weighed her bosom in his open palms. Using his thumbs, he ran them across the twin sensitive nubs. She heaved her chest with deep sighs, whimpering for more.

"Please Vinnie…"

"Please what, Harmony? Should we wait for Willie? Should we make it no more than a deal between us? His freedom for yours?"

"What do you expect me to say?"

"I'm hanging on by a thread here Doll. Don't want to rush things, scare you, but… tell me something quick."

"Like?"

"You understand my pleasure is now your only concern."

"I understand."

He caught the distended tips between his thumbs and forefingers, squeezing lightly. His other hand went south between her thighs forcing her feet to part a fraction. Romano wasn't a man prone to exaggeration. He desperately wanted to ravage her. The passion squeezing his groin urged him to abandon restraint and fuck her hard and strong. But the delicate feel of her, the sweet smell of her breath, and the lovely sound of her voice when she spoke tamed his inner beast. His cock twitched and strained against his zipper. "You're remarkable, so sexy and you smell like a flower."

"Do I?"

"Mmhm."

He felt her tense when he pinched her below. Her ass wiggled a bit against his groin. "You're sensitive. I like that." He did. He wanted to know more, feel more. Releasing her nipple he tracked his other hand down into her panty.

"Wait!" she gasped, taking hold of his wrist.

"Don't make me Songbird." He whispered back. "*Selo fidi*, remember?" He smiled. His finger tangled briefly in the short nest of curls guarding her femininity before dipping lower.

She feared he'd tear her undergarments off her and this was her best pair. But his touch was gentle as he caressed her down there with both hands. A door shut again below them. Someone had come with news. Should she ask him to go see? She knew not to. This was the bargain. Whatever news of her brother was to be heard, she'd have to pay the price to get it first.

"Now," he groaned, plying her open with two fingers then using his others to tickle her bud. Her panty stretched and slipped lower down her hips, it was pushed down her thighs. She rolled her hips against the bulge pressing against her. Then his finger pierced her with a single thrust causing her to rise on her toes.

"I like the way you struggle against me." He flicked his tongue at her ear. "Do you like it when I touch you here Harmony? You're shivering between your thighs."

"Yes."

"Good." He inserted another finger and her hips moved in a sinuous rhythm that was all her, all feeling. She released a silent cry for mercy but it came out as no more than a soft hiss of pleasure.

Again her heart started beating faster due to his mesmerizing presence, she couldn't utter a word. Her throat went dry as her temperature spiked another degree, and the man was just using his fingers. She felt her inner muscles below constrict and release so she grabbed his hand and forced his fingers deeper. "Yes!" She wailed then shuddered through another warm sweet release. She moaned louder as her head thrashed against his shoulder.

It had been over a year since Lewis died. So very long since she'd been touched. And Lewis was such a powerful lover. No part of her was left unexplored. Would this be the same? Probably not. He'd ride his desire out until her back was sore and legs were weak. But the pleasure would be solely for him. Men were selfish pigs. Vinnie Romano was probably like the rest of them. Though from the moment she entered his bedroom he'd given her a taste of the sublime.

She grew weaker as he loved her with his hand. Slowly her channel adjusted to the sweet invasion. Now responding bodily she began to work her hips even more and indulge in the sinful sensations.

"You think I want to rush this? I don't," he breathed. "Slow down, you aren't ready." He grunted against her ear. "I'll tell you when you're ready."

Romano released her. Harmony turned to him and her panty dropped down her legs. She was sticky with her own juices between her thighs. Here she stood, her undergarments at her feet, her sex throbbing for him and he was neatly groomed, tailored, not a strand of his thick hair out of place. He smelled of whiskey, tobacco, and a mossy rich maleness, part aftershave and part him. There was no point in denying even to herself that she wanted completeness with every inch of him.

The brush of his lips was electrifying. A jolt of self-control, an unyielding power washed over her. She felt her own potency in his kiss, and how slowly he was slipping under. Romano's warm, strong, tongue swept over hers. The exchange left her breathless. Her hands lifted to his hair grabbing the silky strands and they slipped through her fingers. She felt their connection, felt his need and returned it, devouring him with her kiss. His passion, slow and controlled, had her desperate and demanding more.

Next her feet left the ground and she wrapped her legs around his waist, prepared for the journey. A few short steps brought her to the bed, and he placed her there delicately. That was the shocking contrast of who he was for her now. All gentle touches and sweet kisses. Was she to believe this behavior change was part of the man who evoked fear in many?

Harmony watched him undo her shoe buckle then toss it, then the other. When he lowered her foot she scooted back into the lush pillows in nothing but her garter stockings rolled to the cusp of her knee.

Romano opened his cuffs and then the collar of his shirt, before he unbuttoned it. His gaze hard, pinned her to the bed. Harmony swallowed another dose of nerves. Shrugging off the shirt he dropped it aside. She was left a clear view of his broad shoulders and his long lean arms, slightly muscular but not massive. She was taken aback by the knife cuts and healed scaring where he was either stabbed or worse. Is that what life in his world meant? A life that stole her Lewis away. She cast her gaze away, but again was compelled to look his way again.

When he dropped his pants, she was caught by surprise by the way his penis sprang to attention. Romano let his gaze travel along the line of her body with an unspoken command. Harmony rose on her elbows. Neither of them spoke. Sucking down a breath of courage she scooted to the center of the bed, parting her thighs for him. He dropped a knee on the bed, his hand lowered to her bent knee and pushed it down to the mattress. In the dim light she caught the swirl of desire in his irises.

"My pleasure is yours." He whispered, and then said more, but in his language and low enough to be mistaken for a growl. To her delight his head lowered and he kissed her below. The kiss he gave her below was soft at first then demanding and scorching with intensity. His tongue swept in deep then withdrew masterfully.

What a wonderful way of saying things. Harmony squeezed her eyes shut and suppressed the giddiness that caused her smile to spread wide across her lips. He blew his cool breath over her hot wet sex and she shuddered. Inside her core heated, melted. She felt dizzy with lust. "Ugh!" She panted in response. It was too much, too powerful, too sweetly gentle.

She arched her back with the heels of her feet resting on the center of his spine, as his face remained buried between her thighs. Her head tilted all the way back burrowing down into the pillows.

Romano's tongue plunged into her channel and then swiped out under her folds to tease her sensitive bud so swiftly her pelvis shook. Her breaths grew shallow, chopped apart by the swift thrusts of his tongue. His breath against her feminine core came faster too, accompanied by manly grunts. To her delight he grabbed hold of her wrist and brought her hand between her thighs when she neared climax. Lifting his head he studied her as he forced her to play with herself then lowered his face to lick, suck, and plunder her with kisses and dizzying swirls of his tongue.

Harmony did as she was instructed, plucking and twisting her clitoris while throwing her hips up into his face for more. It was so sinfully bad, she knew she'd be damned for sure, but she couldn't stop. She wouldn't stop. Then he knocked her hand away and took her jewel into his mouth sucking it hard. She exploded! Her inner walls clamped down on his newly inserted fingers and she gripped his hair tightly before releasing a scream.

Never in Harmony's wildest dreams since the death of Lewis, had she thought she'd experience such beautiful intensity. Letting go of his hair she gripped the sheets. She was mortified by her lack of control. Her eyes shot open when he rose and eased over her. Their gazes locked. Her sight narrowed, constricted until she saw only his taut features. He positioned the head of his shaft at her entrance. Without warning he bore down with his hips, sinking, giving her inch after inch. And she felt every ridge and vein, as her tender walls were crowded, filled with his thickness.

His face came in close and she turned from his lips coated with her essence. He pressed those lips to her cheek and she closed her eyes.

"You are a Goddess," he groaned.

Harmony gasped, Romano delivered thrust after thrust in slow yet forceful succession. Her orgasm built, it pushed higher by the motion of his tunneling cock and the rub of his granite tight thighs. Everywhere their skin touched she burned with fever. She turned her head back to look into his eyes and the sly devilish smile he wore nearly made her climax. She brushed her mouth over his wet lips and he forced her to receive his tongue. Blinking rapidly at the salty flavor, she had to close her eyes once more. He licked at her tongue and lips, smiling while moving inside of her.

Taking her by the lush mounds of her ass Romano pumped his cock into a hot clenching channel that set his toes to curl. Harmony whimpered and moaned beneath him. He wanted to fuck her hard, but he knew she wasn't ready for that. Not in the way he really wanted to take her. So he forced himself to slow, willed himself to behave. But Harmony moved one time too many and despite his restraint he thrust harder and faster. The warmth of her silken walls sent his mind to spinning with foolish thoughts; *I want her to be mine, only mine, it's done.*

Romano shook away the delirium.

Her nails scored his back and he winced. He blinked at her and she gave him a wicked smile. Romano growled dropping his face to her neck while pumping the ache of his cock in and out of her with fierce determination. They bounced on the bed. He pinned her wrists down and she fought to be free. Nothing, not even the sweet sounds of her pleas could stop him. He was lost.

Harmony cried out in his ear and he kept going. Romano thrust long and deep, their bodies sweating and gliding over each other. Her hands now free, they rubbed his back. She dug her nails in and he kept going. He kept going until his muscles locked and he let go every ounce of his seed.

Romano fell on top of her, listening to her rapid heartbeat, his ear against the comfort of her bosom. He kissed her sweaty breast and held on to her, too spent to do much more. But the night had promise, and he would enjoy her over and over again.

CHAPTER THREE
Something in Common?

Harmony opened her eyes. She lay perfectly still. There was no sound, no movement, just the uneven pace of her breathing from a dream she couldn't quite remember. The fear was there. The deep sadness of being trapped and alone covered her mind like a black fog blocking out the source. It hit her with lightening clarity. "Willie," she gasped. Her brother was in trouble and time was short.

She closed her eyes and opened them again. This time the shadows didn't linger. The ceiling clearly came into view and her body bloomed with remembrance of her actions. Shame curled up inside her and made her tense. Did she seduce Vinnie Romano and was she in his bed? Her head dropped over to the left. She was alone.

Clutching the sheet to her chest she rose. She glanced to the door. It had been left partially ajar. She listened for Romano. Silence greeted her.

"Vinnie?" she said softly.

Harmony lowered her sheet and her gaze dropped to her breasts. She could see the raised red patches of skin from the love bites he left after his ravishment. Sex with him had been different. Exhilarating and exciting, it was very different from Lewis yet the feeling remained the same. Paulette called it 'soul ties'. She warned that women like Harmony couldn't lay with any Joe. She wasn't built for it. Sex and all the tendrils of emotions that came with it anchored a woman like her to a man. It would be wise to save it for a lover that would wife her, give her babies, and stay away from the wolves in Henderson's band or the Negroes sending her love letters and poetry in Sugar Hill. Harmony had heeded that warning until tonight. It frightened her how much she ached for more of Vinnie Romano now.

Girl get it together. No. Get your stuff and get out. Her mind shouted several warnings. Harmony couldn't leave now. She'd gone too far. She needed to know what, if anything, Romano knew about her brother.

Quickly she threw aside the sheet. Her clothes were everywhere, dress, stockings slip, all scattered on the floor. Harmony released a deep sigh.

"Do you ever get tired?" She asked and tried to roll from his embrace.

"What man can sleep with you in his bed?" Romano hooked his strong arm around her waist and pulled her back to him. She was forced to roll toward his chest and hold him. The intimacy between them had surprised her. She didn't mind when he took charge, from his first touch to now, he'd never been selfish. He intrigued her.

"Vinnie?"

"Mmm," he answered. He rolled on top of her and thrust half his length inside of her. Her breath caught. Her heels dug into his back.

"Breathe," he said in a voice made hoarse by his own desire. She'd forgotten how. She clutched his shoulders and pumped her hips upward to receive all of him. Soon she found and matched his natural rhythm. The coil of pleasure in her belly unwound slowly.

"Vinne?"

"Yes?"

"This is the third time."

"Mmm," he groaned sinking his teeth into her shoulder as he thrust faster and deeper.

"It's just that...we... we can't do this all night." She half-kidded.

Romano's head lifted. He focused on her face, trained and locked his gaze with hers with such intensity she didn't dare break the exchange. For long torturous minutes they didn't speak. Both released unsteady breaths as their bodies did all the communicating. She hitched her legs high on his waist and raised her arms to press her hands to the headboard to steady their motion.

"Tonight, you're mine. In fact Songbird this is only the beginning. This body, pussy, your voice, all of it belongs to me." He turned over bringing her on top. She sat up and worked her hips to keep the momentum as he gazed up at her with heavy lidded eyes. She felt him deeply and her body was afire with the renewed control she had over him. She worked her hips to and fro harder and Romano groaned, his chest rising and falling rapidly. Harmony smiled. Nothing this wrong ever felt so good.

"Belong to him? I don't belong to anyone. Not Lewis, not Milo, the band, and not even Willie. After it's all said and done I will be also. Hell, I already am." The rebellion swelled in her chest inflating her pride. She didn't know who the target of her anger should be, herself or her little brother. Once she found him she wanted out of this life. She'd leave Harlem for good. The mere mention of leaving the city had been considered blasphemous with Lewis. He kept prophesizing the rise of the Negro in Harlem. He laughed in her face when she brought up the teachings of Marcus Garvey and the UNIA.

"Are you for real Mony? There's no Africa the Negro belongs to. We here now. Here is where we stay. Harlem, the city where a colored man could be his own man."

Lewis loved the good and bad dealings he had with those bandits that ran with Grease Man. And where did all the hustles and big talk get him? Dead. God help her but Romano could end up the same way.

Anxious to escape the room and the flood of memories returning, Harmony felt as if she walked a tightrope. The sex with Romano took her down an emotional spiral. This had to end before she became too stupid to remember the danger lurking behind his smoldering brown eyes when she climaxed on his face, against the wall, on her knees on the bed, and even the floor.

In the middle of a stranger's bedroom, with her life a shadow of what her Grams prayed for, Harmony's wants became clear. She loved to sing. Whether sad, happy or nostalgic, singing made her complete. Jazz was all she had left. But she didn't need Harlem to have jazz. No. It could be wherever she brought it. Heartache and regret is all that she had left in this city.

Harmony eased on her undergarments. A man's voice barked loudly from below. Whoever it was sounded angry. It came from beneath her and echoed up through the empty rooms along the hall. Harmony grabbed the robe on the chair and covered herself. Carefully she crept from the room to the hall then down the hall to the stairs. She kept going along the shadows until the sounds of men could be heard clearly.

Romano struggled to accept the news delivered to him. But the messenger was a hundred percent trustworthy. Jimmie was a large man. With big farmer's feet and hands he looked like a man used to hard labor, born for it. Under Romano's employ, he wore a suit and enforced his wishes with his fists. He wasn't the brains of the crew, but he was loyal and honest. His intimidating presence usually got the information Romano sought without much argument. Tonight what he had to share disappointed and saddened him.

Another matter pulled on his attention. His gaze once again shifted to the shadowy stairs beyond his parlor and his chest tightened with need for the woman who waited for him in his bed. The sun would be up soon and he struggled with why he dreaded the idea of parting ways. Had she awakened?

"I need more from you Jimmie. Is that all?" Romano asked.

"Word is Mickey Collins now deals with the Negress Queenie, supplies her speakeasy. Suddenly Mickey has enough hooch to supply all of Harlem. And this ain't the can shit. It's top of the line Irish whiskey too. Leftie is coming in. Maybe he can shed more light on it."

Romano accepted the truth. He fumed over his brother's absence. But he'd blown his top once already. It was best not to set Jimmie on edge.

"I understand. My booze is missing. We have Mickey bootlegging with the coloreds and Antonio offering protection from the cops to the coloreds. And a missing colored boy in between them all. None of it ties together."

"That's how it figures boss."

"The boy? Did Mickey accuse him of stealing?"

Jimmie frowned. "Not sure what the kid did. My guess is it ain't the booze boss. Maybe he handles the payment. Yeah. That's it. He came up short on the money. No way to know really because the coloreds aren't talking and Mickey, well he's suddenly held up with his crew down near Five Points. Quiet. The streets are too quiet."

45

Romano stroked his jaw. He shook his head and sipped his scotch. How the fuck did his brother think he would get away with this?

"Stay on it. I'll deal with Antonio. I sent Nunzio to find the boy. He's late with news. Find out what's keeping him. I want the kid first. I suspect he could shed some light on where the fuck my booze is!" Romano threw the glass to the wall and it shattered. Jimmie didn't flinch. Romano's angry gaze cut his way and he nodded his huge head that he'd do as he was told.

No! No Willie what have you done? Harmony withdrew with her heart in her throat. Could her brother be stupid enough to steal from the Romanos and not Collins? And to add to matters, bootleg the booze to Queenie of all people? Many revered her as a healer. Others said she practiced old customs, akin to witchery. One thing they all could agree upon was she didn't take any mess from the cops, Sicilians, no one. Now she was in the mix and her brother didn't stand a chance between them all.

A door closed. Harmony heard the approaching steps of her lover and dashed back to the room. She began to dress as quickly as she could.

"Going somewhere?" Romano asked with annoyance in his voice.

Harmony smiled. "Sure am, it's late. Best be getting to my side of town before the sun catches me. You understand."

"The agreement was you stay." Romano closed the door. He sipped something dark from a glass. She thought she heard a glass shatter against a wall down below. Did he go around breaking glasses for sport? She could smell its potency from across the room. Harmony dropped her hands to her hips. She had managed to put her dress on. It remained unzipped.

"You hear anything on my brother? Any news?"

"Nothing new. Kid's either lost or dead."

Harmony's smile dipped. She never considered for a moment that Willie could be dead. Romano's hard edge seemed to soften over her state. "I'm only saying that he's not easy to find. We don't know anything yet."

Harmony nodded. "Right. Like I said. I best be on my way." Now that Romano thinks Willie is tied to his missing hooch he was no longer an ally. This she knew as plain as she knew the nose on her face.

"Stay."

Harmony grimaced, but kept her expression free of the tension building inside of her. Suddenly she wanted distance. No. She needed distance from this man and what they shared. She tried to run up her zipper and stopped. "I'd rather not. I... sun will be up soon. I need to get home."

Romano set his glass down. "It's a long walk back to Harlem." He stepped to her and took her hand. "I can have a car take you home... after."

"After?"

"After."

A soft chuckle escaped her. "Sounds tempting. But how would that look? You sending me home in a chauffeured car in broad daylight. I don't need no trouble."

"You make it hard for a man to be nice Harmony."

She pulled her hand from his. "You have been nice." She replied, her voice tight and firm. "You agreed to help me. I'm no fool honey. I know you didn't do it for my singing." She cleared her throat. "I also know that you have no intention on flaunting some colored jazz singer around your nice tidy white neighborhood. I'm saying it's best I leave on my own terms while the leaving is good. The *after* will have to wait for another time."

Romano stood silent. She turned and he stepped forward and ran her zipper up. Harmony didn't figure him for a man to beg. Though she did consider he'd force his will. Instead he withdrew and watched her with a piercing stare. She collected her stockings and garter and wished she had kept her purse. She caught a glimpse of her tussled hair in the mirror and averted her gaze. She'd pull her hat down low on her head. Sugar Hill didn't sleep at night, but dawn was relatively quiet.

"And if I hear anything on your brother?" Romano asked? His gaze tracked her every movement. *Would he stop staring!* It made her nervous as hell, and clumsy.

"You can send word to the club. Right?" Harmony headed for the door. When Romano didn't move from the window she stopped. "Thank you for... everything. Your help, I appreciate it."

He dismissed her and returned his attention to the window. She couldn't catch her breath until she was halfway down the stairs. To her dismay the maid waited for her by the door. She held her purse, coat and hat out to her. Harmony accepted them both avoiding the older woman's eyes. She barely crossed over the threshold before the door slammed behind her. She fast walked down the steps to the street. There was no way she'd catch a cab or anything in this neighborhood. She looked down the sidewalk realizing the walk ahead of her with the sun rising to her back wasn't quite wise. She really hadn't thought her exit through.

"Mr. Romano wants me to take you back into Harlem. To The Cotton." A man appeared out of the shadows. Harmony nearly jumped from her skin. *Was he there the entire time?* She stared up at the tall bulky figure. He blew out a long smoky stream from his wide nostrils and then flicked his cigarette to the sidewalk. He stepped on it and squashed the ambers before he headed to the car.

"Who are you?"

"Name's Jimmie, ma'am."

Intentional or not she felt crowded when he stepped from the car toward her. She took a cautious step back.

"I work for Romano. This way." The giant said, a snide smirk to his face.

He held the door open for her to enter. Harmony glanced back over her shoulder and her gaze scaled the three-story brownstone. She could see the silhouette of Romano watching her from the upstairs window. He had to have known she'd make a break for it. That's why he stood at the window the entire time. He had a man outside waiting for her. *Guess he wanted me gone too, figures, he got what he wanted.* Though what they shared would never be spoken between them again, the effects of his touch still made her doubtful to dismiss the memory. He stepped away from the window and was gone.

She turned and met the stare of her escort.

"We leaving or what?" The man asked.

Harmony straightened her back. She needed to get the hell away from these men and home quick. God help her, where was her brother?

***

The sun bled warmth and slanted slivers of light over his face. It was dawn. The sounds of the chapel bell reminded him of the hour. Two weeks in the cobblestone walled in cellar, sleeping on a cloth cot Father Michaels gave him had been a new form of torture. Slowly he sat up, placing his bare feet down on the cold slab of concrete. He dropped his head in his hands. Even the light from the single window above didn't chase away enough of the grey. Shadows covered him. A cool empty feeling had settled in his hell and left him without hope. He didn't want to die. To live he'd have to survive this nightmare. At night he had the run of the sanctuary, but in the day he had to remain quiet and wait.

The sound of the heavy door being forced open didn't surprise him. Willie didn't bother to look up.

"I brought you breakfast." Came the familiar grunt from his visitor. "And a bottle of hooch to pass the time."

Willie chuckled deep in his throat. He was only a month shy of his eighteenth birthday but he'd been drinking hooch with Lewis since he was twelve. Mony didn't know. Grams suspected but never said. Now the mere idea of drinking any of the whiskey made his chest tight with anger.

"How long?" His head lifted from his palms and he narrowed his glare. "You said things would be resolved now. When is it done?"

"It's done when it's done Will. You know how this ends. Now eat. I'll stay awhile…"

Willie tensed at the offer. "You staying?"

His visitor smirked. "For awhile."

***

The last of his favorite imported scotch dripped on his tongue. He groaned and dropped the bottle to the side table. He'd finished it off in the parlor listening to Bessie Smith. She was okay, but she wasn't his Harmony.

Romano had avoided his bed since she left. He had Mabel change the sheets and clean out any remnants of the night, and still the soft sweet smell of her lingered. Damn, he wasn't lying when he said she smelled like a rose. He could have forced her to stay. It was his right dammit. She came up here tempting him, seeking favors, knowing her brother was tied to his missing product. He'd been the bastard that would have, many times before. But something was different about her and him when they were together. Alone he had to admit the reasons and understand the guilt that trapped him in loneliness. Annie was enough. No dame was worth the trouble.

"Everyone said you were bad. But I didn't believe them. Teek didn't believe them. Now look at what you've done." Annie wept.

Romano dropped his head in his hands and prayed she went for the door. She'd packed and left him. He hadn't seen her since he had to tell her and her mother Teek was dead. But his grief made him foolish enough to attend the funeral. And one look at Annie and he succumbed to the old familiar self-loathing. Nothing in life ever came to him easily. Not even the exile his father cast upon him, or the burden he carried for his dead mother and the little brother who wanted to be like him. Why should the end of them be any less tragic?

"Answer me Vinnie! He loved you, he and Antonio both, they worship you and look what happened. He was my brother damn you! My only brother! What did we ever do to deserve this?"

"Ann-nie. I never meant for it to happen. Never." He lifted his head and pleaded with his weary gaze for her to just leave him to his misery.

She leveled an accusatory finger at him. Her eyes were red and swollen from a day's worth of tears, her hair, a tangled knotty mess of curls. It hurt to look at her so he averted his gaze. "I put up with your drinking, your meanness, and the violence. Vincenzio Romano, the leader of the Black Hand has half of the Bronx terrified and the other half out for revenge. And here I am thinking I know better. I was wrong. It's in you, the evil and meanness is who you are, and like a poison it destroys anyone around you. I put up with it. Do you know why? Because I love you, I have always loved you. Three years and you won't be seen in public with me, I can't even get you to marry me when you yourself said we should, and still I loved you. You said nothing would happen to him. You promised to protect us all. But it was a lie wasn't it Vinnie? All of it a lie. I know the truth."

He finally met her gaze.

She nodded, her face flushed and tears flowing. "You never gave a damn about his life. I know it's your fault! You did this!!"

"Stai' zitta! Shut your fucking mouth!!" Romano slammed his fist down repeatedly on the table. The small plotted centerpiece rattled then tipped over. *"Vattene! Get the hell out!"*

Annie looked on horrified. Romano rose bringing the table up in a flip sending it to the floor with its legs pointed north. He glared with nostrils flared and fists clenched. What did he need with the constant bitching, the constant tears. He had a war on his hands. And she didn't know the whole story. Antonio had done this, taking the kid out on rides with him. He'd done everything possible to separate them. Hell they even joined separate gangs. The blood and violence of their lives wasn't all his fault. He warned them both to stay off the streets during the turf wars, but they didn't listen. Now the kid's death and his brother's devastation were on his soul. Couldn't she see it? He would give his life for them all. How was he to prevent this?

"My brother is dead. Dead. And so is my love for you."

"I don't give a shit…"

She plucked her coat from the back of the chair and grabbed her purse.

"Annie, wait, I'm drunk, I didn't mean it." He raced after her and grabbed her arm. She'd pushed him too hard, the liquor and grief had him losing control. He didn't want to lose her too. Touching her had been a mistake. She unleashed on him instantly and struck him so hard he blinked out of awareness for a moment.

"May God have pity on your black soul Vincenzio, because the devil won't. You belong to him now. Stay away from me and Mama! I don't ever want to see you again!" She ran for the door. Ran from him. He closed his eyes and reigned in the man who would chase after her. Fall to her knees and plead his case. She and her mother had shown him kindness when he arrived in America, destitute. Teek was a kid and followed him everywhere. When Antonio arrived only a few years older than him, they both became his shadow. She was right Teek didn't belong in his world but he had been selfish, blind to the dangers. It was the nature of who they were. He'd avenge his death but he fucking wouldn't apologize for it. Even though he knew he'd never be able to wash the blood from his hands.

Romano opened his eyes. He stood in the kitchen alone. He walked over to the table and turned it back over. He grabbed a broom and swept up the shards of glass from the broken pottery and cast away the flowers. He went for his hooch and last cigar. Before he finished his grief for a dead kid of barely eighteen, and a lost girlfriend would be over. Then he'd find Antonio and the rest of his men. They'd hit the streets and teach the Five Points Gang a lesson. Lucky was no friend of his, not any more. He'd make them all pay.

The liquor seared his throat after another swig, and fogged his brain. It was working already.

"Fucking dames, who needs them." He grunted. He rarely thought of his Annie. She ran off with some shipyard worker and went West. According to her mother they were happy and having their first child together. The time she shared with him was probably something she chose to forget, until she had to explain the absence of her slain younger brother and why she stayed away from her mother. Blood and death was all that was left between them.

"Mabel!" Romano roared. He tried to rise but dropped back down in the chair. "Mabel!!" he shouted until his throat burned.

"What is it?"

"Scotch, get me some from the basement."

"Let me fix you some breakfast. You should eat.

He shot her a withering glare. The old black woman shot him another. She'd cared for him from the beginning and lost a lot because of her affection. He was grateful to Mabel for staying despite his surly, troubling ways. She reminded him of his own mother, the way she forgave him and Antonio. There wasn't a woman in his life he hadn't failed at some point. "Fine, fix breakfast but bring me another bottle."

Mabel turned and walked off.

Romano closed his eyes. He dropped his head back. The record came to an end. Harmony's sultry voice filled his memory and he began to smile. When he felt his worst he summoned her voice. A secret no one knew. And last night he'd had her in his bed. The hole in his heart from scars so deep they'd never heal made him weak for the sunshine he heard in her voice. For her. Romano groaned.

"What a fucking mess."

He'd get the answers he needed from his brother. The hard way.

CHAPTER FOUR
Missing Truths

Showered and rested Harmony removed the pot from the flame on the stove. She poured the boiled water into her cup. The mint fragrance of ground tea leaves and sliced lemon edges wafted up to her nostrils. She inhaled deeply. It was a special mixture that preserved the sweetness in her voice. A routine she frequented. Every bone in her body felt battered by fatigue. Maybe the tea would work. She prayed so. If not she'd crawl under the covers and not open her eyes until sunset.

Cupping the mug in her hands she walked over to the kitchen table to sit and think. Her evening with Vinnie Romano had brought her no closer to finding her brother. However, she did learn more about herself. The man awakened feelings and emotions in her she never thought possible with a stranger. Part of her craved the attention he showered her. She couldn't help but remember the reason by every delicious ache in her body. God help her, she was losing it.

Willie was in trouble. She did learn a few interesting things. For one, she now knew that the rumors of Antonio Romano being a snake were true. If he'd steal from his brother it made him stupid as well. Vinnie Romano didn't look like the kind of man you'd cross, blood relation or not.

Repeated knocks at the door stole away her private thoughts. She almost regretted summoning the company. Harmony set the cup upon the saucer and hurried, tightening the sash to her robe. Paulette flashed a warm smile as soon as she opened the door.

"Got your note." Paulette sang waving the small letter in Harmony's face.

"Come in." Harmony said.

Paulette sashayed in. She looked fresh, vibrant in her lilac purple dress. Paulette was tall for a woman, but shapely. She had mocha skin so light and creamy that if she really worked at it she could pass for white. It's why Madden had no problem hiring her and making her a cigarette girl at The Cotton. The club's strict rules on what they referred to as 'tans' required the women to be mulatto or of very fair skin. Paulette also dyed her hair blonde and with her clear hazel eyes she turned many heads. "Morning Mony. You look like shit."

"Thanks." Harmony mumbled, she returned to her seat and cooling cup of tea. Paulette had devilment in her smile. Harmony knew she was probably off to see one of her suitors, and guessed Paulette wanted to flaunt it. Inwardly Harmony sighed. Being a colored woman with a taste for something other than making babies or wiping the asses of some white woman's children, made a girl's options slim. She knew Paulette did what she had to, to survive. It didn't justify Harmony's actions with Romano last night though.

Paulette sat across from her.

"So what's the emergency? I was on my way to Sophie's, she opening her boutique for me early today. Need a new hat."

Harmony glanced up from her sip and lowered her cup to the saucer. "Why? It's early."

Paulette chuckled. "That's for me to know and for you to figure out."

"Whatever," Harmony shook her head. She wasn't in the mood for jokes. She almost said as much when a hand reached across the table and covered hers. She looked up at Paulette once more.

"Still ain't heard from Lil Will? Huh?"

The answer was far more complicated. Not only had she not heard from Willie but she may have made matters worse by going to Romano for help. She had to add new worry to her list if Willie did steal from him. She wiped at her brow. Her head was a teased crown of frizz after her bath, and her lids felt as if they sagged with her misery. She knew she looked a sight.

"It's nearing two weeks. If he was alive he would have sent word to me."

"Mony, stop, he alive. You know it."

"Do I?" Harmony asked. "I don't know much of anything anymore. For starters, I didn't know Willie had gotten into bootlegging to the speakeasy Madame St. Clair run under Romano's nose." Harmony watched her friend's face. None of what she said seemed to surprise Paulette. "But you knew didn't you? You holding back on me?"

Paulette drew her hand away. She blinked at her with curious round eyes. "Not true. I'd never…"

"Save it. I'm no fool. Okay!"

"I just work there. Like you just sing at The Cotton. I wouldn't know the dealings of men out them back doors." Paulette averted her gaze and cleared her throat. "All I can say on the matter is Willie shouldn't have gotten between those men and Madame St. Clair."

"Well, finally we agree on something." Harmony said with a bitter chuckle.

Paulette shrugged. "Your brother don't know his place. He was always trying to mix it up with those men. I warned you. Things got serious when Antonio Romano started showing up. He took interest in Lil Will. I've seen them together."

"How often?"

"Often enough." Paulette snorted with distaste. "He used Lil Will to get him to Madame and offer her protection from the cops. I don't think Lil Will stole from these men. I think his problems are because of Antonio Romano. Something ain't right about that maggot. I hear tell he got a Negro boy killed during those riots."

Harmony bristled. The night of the riots cost her, Lewis, and changed her life forever. "So I'm right back where I started?"

"Started? You ain't thinking about going to those Sicilians are you? Antonio Romano and his brother are worse than Mickey Collins. You know the Five Points Gang terrorizing folks? Well Vincenzio Romano used to be big boss over the Black Hand, they rivals. Not sure why the gang split but they the worst kind of men Mony. The very worst."

The knocking at the door startled them both. Harmony frowned over the early morning visitor. It was just after nine. Most people she knew besides Paulette were still in bed. Wednesday night at The Cotton was one of the busiest. Slowly she rose.

"You expectin' someone?" Paulette asked.

Harmony hushed her with a wave of her hand. She crept to the door prepared for the worst. Next to the door was a bat and she picked it up. "Who is it?"

"It's me Mony. Open up!" Once the door parted Milo charged through like a steam engine. "How late before you get in? I was up waitin' on you all night. Please tell me you didn't go through with it. Did you leave with Romano last night? Did you!" he demanded. Before she could answer Milo turned and saw Paulette rise from her chair. The two shared a tense exchange and then their eyes turned to her. She caught the look of disbelief, curiosity and what she thought might be a tinge of jealousy in her friends' eyes. Milo openly glared. He looked mad enough to spit.

"I want both of you to go." Harmony held the door open.

"You were with Antonio Romano?" Paulette asked.

Harmony slammed the door. "No. I was with Vinnie. And yes I stayed the night. I have to find my brother and neither of you can give a damn. Before you stand there and judge me, hear what I got to say. I will do any and everything I have to, to find Willie. And I don't owe either of you a damn thing."

She marched into her room and slammed the door. The vibration went through her and she placed both hands to her mouth to keep them from trembling. Angry at the world she dropped down on the bed. "I don't owe any of you a damn thing."

***

After a fresh shave Romano bounded down the steps of his home pulling up the suspenders on his trousers. He had time to sober up and clear his head. He sent word for Jimmie to pick up his Songbird. He hadn't forgotten the terms of their agreement, even if she had. In fact he couldn't stop thinking of her period. He'd allowed her to leave because he didn't want her pissed off if he forced her to stay.

Now sobered on his bitterness he wasn't as soft on the idea of releasing her from their deal. The only cure for this ailment was to have her returned to him. He'd work out the rest of the details after. Though he convinced himself his interest would fade soon enough, he had no intention of letting her walk away before it did. Especially since he suspected her brother's disappearance and his brother's disobedience were connected somehow.

The front door opened and his brother staggered in. He looked greased with sweat and it wasn't even noon yet. Antonio's glassy red-rimmed eyes glanced upward and snagged on Romano's disapproving scowl. "Morning Vinnie."

"I want a word." Romano marched down the three remaining steps turning for the parlor.

Antonio followed.

"Sure thing, I was just about to look for you…"

Before another word escaped his brother's lying mouth Romano's fist connected with his jaw. The blow knocked Antonio's head back and he crumbled. Romano caught him by the ear. He twisted flesh and cartilage until his brother squealed in agony.

"Don't Vinnie, let me explain. Please!" Antonio begged.

Romano pinched and twisted the ear harder. "Stay on your knees!" He growled. "Do you think I'm a fool?"

"Vinnie stop!"

"Answer me!"

"No. I don't."

"Then why are you gaming me like one? Huh? Huh?"

The entire right side of Antonio's face flamed red and Romano yanked upward on his ear. His brother howled, but his suffering mattered little when he was dragged and lifted with his free hand clenching his throat. Antonio choked and gagged on his pleas, kicking his feet. Mercy had left the room. Raw rage consumed Romano and pushed him closer to the darkness he carried in him thanks to his father. What he couldn't live with was disloyalty, especially within his own family.

In fact the more his brother struggled the more enraged he became. He pounded his fist into Antonio's face until his brother's nose sprung a leak and blood soaked his knuckles and the front of his shirt. Mabel ran in behind him and screamed for his men. He could hear several of them charging into the room like a stampede. But his vision was singular, his anger so consuming he couldn't stop himself. Two men grabbed him by his arms and dragged him away. He saw his brother roll off the sofa gasping while Mabel wept trying to assist.

"Boss, calm yourself, it's Antonio. Christ!" Leftie shouted.

"Hands off me!" Romano snarled. He threw off the hold of his men and glowered at his brother. "Let him up. He's man enough to cut deals in MY name! Steal from me! It's time he answer for it."

***

Harmony's hands ran smoothly down the front of her dress. It was white with tiny yellow and green flowers. She had sewn it herself. The puffed sleeves and shifting hem reminded her of the girl who lived her young life through books and sang for the Lord. *Where had that girl gone?* Harmony rolled her eyes at her own reflection. Who cared where she went, the memory of her existence faded each day. She picked up her purse and coat, and headed for the bedroom door. And immediately she was shocked to find Milo patiently waiting for her at the kitchen table. She thought he left an hour ago with Paulette. "What you still doing here?"

"Had to talk to you." Milo said his voice almost remote with sadness. He rose. "I'm sorry Mony. I shouldn't have… forgive me."

The apology did soften the hurt. After all he'd been a rock for her during some of the toughest of times. If it weren't for him she'd still be scrubbing floors and living in her one bedroom flat with her brother. Now she had a two-bedroom apartment in Sugar Hill. And it was his friendship that brought her through.

"Can we talk about it later? I have somewhere to be."

"Where?"

Did he just ask that question? It irked her to no end how territorial he had become since Lewis's death. She didn't bother to answer. Instead she slipped her arms through her coat.

Milo trailed her around the small living area. "I promised Lewis, Mony."

"Lewis dead. Willie alive."

"You sure about that?"

"As sure as I am that it's up to me to bring him home. He ain't a responsibility or a burden, he blood. My blood. I don't give a damn if he stole from the Sicilians or Collins. I don't care what he done. I will bring him home, because he all I have!"

Milo's eyes stretched. "Do you hear yourself girl?"

"Damn right I do."

He stepped toward her. "And how you plan to do that? Forget finding Willie, how you plan to keep them men out there from lynching his ass? Sleeping with Romano brought you home empty handed." He closed the space between them and forced her gaze up as he leaned in to speak soft words of appeal in her face. "You planning to spread your legs for Mickey Collins next?"

She slapped him with such force her palm burned hot. Milo didn't blink.

Harmony turned to show him the door but Milo reacted swiftly. He took hold of her arm and swung her around to face him. "Get your damn hands off me." Harmony demanded.

"Listen!" He grabbed her by both arms. She struggled but he brought her to his chest and hugged her so tight she wheezed a strained breath. Harmony tried to break free but his embrace held her still. She tired of the fight. Closing her eyes she didn't bother with tears, they never got her anywhere in life.

"Sweet Mony, do you know how I... I care about you. I can't see you hurt. I won't." His hand went up and down her back in a slow rub. She tensed under the caress; it felt too intimate, too familiar. "Willie done got himself in a mess but I won't let you be dragged into it further."

"Too late." She gently pulled away. The look of desire in his eyes was one she often ignored. She'd seen it when Lewis was alive, and for Milo's sake he better be glad Lewis never did. Men often looked at her that way. Vinnie Romano did, which is why she was in the big mess she was in now. Milo had been a friend. She needed a friend, not another man trying to seduce her to be his. "I don't need your protection."

"Then let me help." Milo pleaded. "I'll pay Grease Man a visit. Find out what I can. You stay away from Madame. No good could come from you meeting with her."

She smiled at his attempt to protect her. "No. It's my problem."

"Let me see what I can do." He took her hand and kissed it. She removed it before the gesture turned to more.

"We don't have to be to rehearsal until six. I'll stay. Promise you will come for me as soon as you know something?"

"I promise."

Harmony waited. Milo stood as if he were caught between leaving and expressing something more. The silence between them lengthened, impenetrable for verbalizing a thought. He gave her a faint smile, picked up his hat and headed for the door. Harmony released her breath and sat on her small sofa. She waited until her heart stopped racing and gathered the strength to do exactly what Grams taught her. Fend for herself. She waited on Lewis, even for Willie to figure out that life was what they made it, and choices had consequences. She wouldn't bury another person she loved by sitting down and waiting.

**

The room had settled into a still quiet. Romano closed and opened his fist. The ache to his raw bloody knuckles didn't compare to the one in his heart. He hated being violent toward his brother; it reminded him of the cruelties they both endured under their father's rule. But Antonio's impulsive actions when left unchecked could bring harm to them all. Even now he could never really get the truth on what happened the night Teek died.

The rage had passed. The settlement of cool detachment made it easier to save face in front of his men. Betrayal usually awoke something sinister within him. He glanced at Leftie, and their eyes met. One word from him and blood or no blood Antonio would have a bullet between his brows.

Antonio spewed hasty apologies and angry denunciations of the accusations hurled at him until his voice went hoarse and he shook with caged anger. When he caught a breath, he pleaded for a chance to be heard—in private. Romano knew his brother had ambition. But just an hour ago he learned his kid brother had balls the size of Mount Everest.

"I didn't put it together at first. Your interest in Harlem, your constant negotiating for more time before we move the booze. Then I hear that Mickey's dry. Or should I say Mickey was dry. The Five Points Gang cut him out with the Irish. Now he has a new connection?" Romano leveled a finger at Antonio. "Deny it?"

"No. It's true. I was forced into it. I was trying to avoid a war. To fix a mistake."

Laughter exploded from Romano until his eyes teared. "A war? Try the apocalypse little brother. After I'm done with Mickey Collins I'll…"

"Wait! Vinnie Just hear me out. I was set up I tell you. You put me in charge. I handled it, I really did. But there was so much booze somehow the word had gotten out."

"We have Capelli, Marlo and Slim on watch. Where are they?" Romano glanced around realizing he hadn't seen the men in almost two weeks.

"Dead." Antonio said, in a hollow voice. "Mickey had them killed. A *moulignon*… seventeen or eighteen, not sure, he sold us out to Mickey…"

"I told you not to use that word in this house! What if Mabel hears you!" he shouted.

Antonio lowered his gaze in shame. "I'm sorry Vinnie. I am."

Romano's brows dented. "You trying to tell me that a boy killed three of my best men?"

"No. Mickey killed our guys, but the kid tipped him off to where we were."

"How?"

Antonio didn't answer.

"How dammit!"

"The Cotton. Turns out the kid works for The Cotton. The night it went down Mickey caught me on my way back here. Run me off the road. I was cornered. Next I know I got a gun in my face and Mickey telling me how he plans to take you out."

Romano paced.

"Don't you see Vinnie, this was my chance to prove myself. My chance. I screwed up so much I had to do this my way. So I cut a deal with Mickey. Told him if he let me in on Harlem I'd sell him the booze at a low cost. He knew he really couldn't take from you Vinnie. And I didn't want a war, not after what happened to Teek. You seen The Cotton, the booze is flowing. Then we got the coloreds too. If you hear me out Vinnie it makes sense."

The rising wrath in his chest surfaced once more. Romano drew his gun and paced with it in his hand. He wanted to unload it. He felt like such an idiot, hell he was one. Two weeks and he didn't know shit. Now he had over twenty thousand dollars worth of booze stolen, and a brother who made him look like a fool in front of his men, everyone. "Let me get this straight. You have us in a partnership with a man who stole from me? What the fuck makes you think I'd supply him to run his bootlegging just for a peace of Harlem? Territory I can give a shit about! Huh?"

Antonio swatted his hand at Mabel who tried to tend to his bleeding nose. She had returned to the room in a fluster, weeping, and trying to tend to his brother. Antonio snatched the hanky from her and pressed it against his face. "The problem isn't the deal. He hadn't unloaded the booze yet. My plan was to get the boy to take me to where Mickey stashed it. Come to you on my knees Vinnie and tell you where the booze was. But the boy's missing. I know Mickey is making deals to sell the booze next week. I was working on a lead to find the kid. I wanted to give you leverage, a sure thing."

Romano narrowed his eyes. "What's the name of this Negro?"

"On the street they call him Lil Will. Works at The Cotton. The jazz singer's brother. Mickey couldn't negotiate with Queenie and Grease Man so the boy was the go between. Problem is Mickey went dry just as the deal fell through. Then there come a night me and the boys were at The Cotton getting drunk. The kid was nearby. Didn't pay him any attention but I remember him now. He was in earshot when he talked about making a drive back out to the shipyard. He flipped us to Mickey. That's how this all began. So I knew the kid was the key to finding where the booze was moved to."

Antonio sucked down a deep breath. Mabel handed him some water. Every man in the room was silent and watchful. Antonio swallowed, which looked like it pained him, then started again. "I had to find the kid and I figured the coloreds were hiding him. So I had to work my own deal. Got the Forty Thieves a little protection from the harassment of the cops and now they're indebted to you Vinnie. She'll give us the kid. It's a solid plan. I was going to bring it to you, but I had to cover everything see?"

Romano's cheeks felt fiery hot. Tight-jawed and restrained he advanced on his brother. His men, eight of them remained inside the room, six were outside the doors, all braced for the confrontation. Antonio's eyes stretched and he tensed as well looking around for support.

"The way I see it little brother, you stole from me too. What am I supposed to do about that?"

"I was wrong, but I can fix it. I can get every dime owed to you. I know the warehouse where the hooch is stored. Every last drop. All of it. I just want Harlem for me. Give me Harlem Vinnie. I can run it. After we get rid of Collins and Queenie."

Romano sneered. "Jimmie, make a run. Let Mickey know I want compensation. He either has my money for every bottle that passed between him and Antonio or he deals with the consequences."

"Got it boss."

"Vinnie. There's more." Antonio struggled to rise. Mabel stepped back but looked as if she wanted to assist him. "The boy. He knows Mickey's business. When you strike against Mickey you need to deliver one swift deathblow. We follow my plan and do this quietly, you can settle things, take Mickey out and even have Harlem. Give me the okay."

"No."

"Why? Harlem is ready. We can set up our own numbers bank and…"

"This is my business. My *famiglia*. You don't get an empire for lying and betraying me, you understand? You fall in line." He shot Leftie a look, and his top gun put down his drink and stepped from the bar. "Find this boy. Put the word out I have his sister. He'll reappear. Then pick her up."

"Where should I take her boss?"

"Woodbury. Keep her there while Antonio and I get my fucking booze."

Antonio shook his head in defeat to the order. "I swear to you Vinnie I didn't know how else to handle it. Let's figure it out. If you do it this way it'll be war."

Romano dropped the barrel of his gun and checked the chambers. "There's always a time for war."

***

The day had been frigid from the start. She felt spring would arrive soon, but she saw no evidence of it. Instead she wrapped herself up in her coat and hurried along the slanted sidewalk. A four-story building with duplex homes on each level towered above her. Harmony headed inside and continued to the back. Whether a person received an invite or not, everyone knew where Madame St. Clair lived.

She found the door partially opened and quickened her steps along the narrow hall to speak to the man who turned from closing it. He was mean and powerful looking, his shoulders thickly muscled, he nearly filled the doorway. His black-layered irises fixed on her and watched her approach.

"I need to see Madame St. Clair." Harmony rushed in a single breath.

No sooner had the words escaped her mouth than another person bumped her shoulders and hurried in front of her. The menace at the door accepted what looked to be a payment and allowed the young woman with a baby on her hip to enter. Harmony didn't recognize the girl, and didn't bother to try. Instead she kept her eyes trained on the Goliath of a man now blocking her pass. She sensed his distrust of her and tried to manage a smile.

"Who are you?" He barked.

"Harmony Jones. Tell her I'm Lewis Hill's old-lady."

She never evoked Lewis's name amongst the people he kept her away from, but she wouldn't be turned away today and she had no money to pay her way through the door. The mean giant before her glanced back over his shoulder into a home that smelled of frankincense and burning lamp oil. His gaze returned to her. "Come back tonight. After you finish at The Cotton. She'll see you then."

"Tonight? Why not now? How did you know I work at The Cotton?"

Another young woman pushed past him and out the door. Harmony had heard tale that during the day Madame saw the women in Harlem for whatever ailments they had. Her home remedies and blessings made many believe she had mystical, or divine powers. A reputation she found to be a stark contrast to the ruthless way in which she handled the numbers game from the back doors of her speakeasy at night.

"You don't have an appointment. Now you do. She'll see you in the evening."

"But you didn't ask her? Please could you ask her?" Harmony pressed.

The man sneered through his reply. "Don't have to. She knew you'd come."

He closed the door shut in her face. For a long pause she stood there staring at the worn wood planks. She could bang her fist on the surface and demand to be heard. Raise the roof of the duplex. If she agitated the woman it could make matters worse. Harmony chewed on the inside of her jaw. She turned and marched down the hall out the front doors to the sidewalk, lost in her fears. Time slipped from her. There was no place in Harlem that Willie could hide and not have been seen by now. Either people knew where he hid, or the worst was possible. Willie was dead.

No one cared enough to clue her in, and nothing she did brought her closer to the truth. She had to wonder if Milo even bothered to meet with Grease. Harmony chewed on the inside of her jaw. Would Grease see her if Madame wouldn't? Maybe he'd help her if she tried? A cold sense of dread spread through her gut like ice crystals. Lewis always forbade her from entering his world. Harmony glanced up to the men she passed on the sidewalk glaring at her from under the low bibs of their hats. Suddenly Lewis's warning surfaced and she had to consider her foolish actions and the consequences if she pursued this further.

64

"Mony, it's not a problem babe, I promise." Lewis eased his hand under the covers and squeezed her breast. Her nipple pushed between two of his fingers and he immediately took hold. Before she could answer Lewis lifted the sheet and eased his head under to swipe his tongue over the peak before covering it with his mouth. Harmony rubbed the top of his head.

When her Grams was alive Willie had started slipping into the streets. Before her Grams' death Lewis would often drop by to counsel her little brother against his path. Now she feared Lewis had Willie in training to be just like him, and they were both working for Grease Man.

Harmony winced at the tug on her nipple and pushed on his shoulder until his head lifted. "Honey, I hear that they are hiring coloreds down at the shipyard for some of the unloading work at night. It pays. Maybe you could send Willie there to start looking for work. He need to do something positive don't you think?" Lewis rolled on top of her. Harmony gripped both sides of his pelvis to prevent him from entering her. "You hear me baby?" she pleaded.

Lewis's dazed lustful look cleared. He hovered above her while staring down in her face. "Willie gone be fine. He with me. Don't you worry about Grease Man or any of them. In fact you stay out of it. You hear? I'm your man now. I'll take care of you both."

"But Lewis…"

"It's done. It ain't for you to worry or to fix. Some things a woman just can't handle."

She opened her mouth to object and his kiss came down crushingly hard. Swiftly he entered her, consuming her doubts. Harmony closed her eyes and her mind, allowing him to awaken her body. She lied to herself, because in her heart she knew Grams was right.

A car swerved then made an illegal U-turn in the street. Several other cars honked their horns. She could hear a few people yelling from their windows. Harmony glanced up to the scene as she navigated the congestion of people on the move along the sidewalk. A man jumped out of the passenger side of the car and headed directly for her. She wouldn't have given it a second thought if she didn't catch the determined look in his eye as he approached. Harmony quickened her step, bumping one person and the next to put distance between her and the man following. She turned the corner and walked faster. Glancing behind her she nearly panicked when she realized the man on foot kept pursuit. He was tall, white, in a dark suit and hat. He stood out amongst the sea of black people traveling the sidewalk. Many noticed and got out of his way and others were shoved aside as he hurried after her.

The courage she summoned to visit Madame St. Clair unraveled and her instinct told her to run. So run she did. Right up against the chest of another man. He grabbed her elbow and forced her to the side of the sidewalk, staring down at her. "You Harmony Jones?"

Startled she wrenched her arm free of his hand. The sun in her eyes prevented her from seeing his face clearly. The other man stopped behind her. Now she stood between them both.

"Mr. Romano requests your presence."

She glanced to the street and noticed the car again. This man must have driven ahead and got out to cut her off. Her mind tried to think of what to say, how to escape, but nervous energy clouded her thoughts. He crowded her.

"This way." He gestured for her to come along.

"I can't. And if you touch me again I'll scream." She bumped into another man and her head swung around to see him crowding her from behind.

"I don't remember saying you had a choice." The man advancing on her answered.

Harmony frowned. "I said no. Tell him no, no thanks."

"Hey Mony! Everything okay?" Paulette walked up. The man before her narrowed his steely gaze on her only and didn't bother to acknowledge Paulette. Immediately Harmony slipped from between them both and hooked her arm around her friend.

"Like I said, thanks but no thanks boys. You want to see me come to The Cotton tonight. You'll have a blast!" Harmony shouted loud enough to draw everyone's attention on the sidewalk. A few stopped and said they knew who she was. That she sang at the Lincoln before. One person asked if she was going to leave The Cotton and switch over to the Savoy to perform. The small crowd of onlookers didn't notice the glare of the two white men, but Harmony and Paulette did. She tugged on Paulette's arm and together they beat a path in the other direction.

"Who were they?" Paulette asked?

"Vinnie Romano's men, are they following?"

Paulette looked back but kept step with her. "No. They've gone."

Harmony pulled her to the train station doors. "Come on, before they come back."

"What the hell is going on? What are you doing over on this side of town?" Paulette pummeled her with questions. Harmony's heart thundered in her chest, she could only decipher a few of her questions. The roaring rush of the passing train drowned out Paulette's shaky voice. Vinnie Romano didn't want to help her. In fact she didn't care to explore what he wanted. That game was far too dangerous to play. Not when her brother's life depended on it. Harmony hurried into the train and checked the crowd for the faces of the men. They weren't in the boxcar when the doors closed. She suddenly found the ability to breathe easy again.

***

"Bless me father for I have sinned. I'm not Catholic, and I'm not sure how to do this right. But I'm here. I need... absolution."

"You are safe here my son. Regardless of faith God hears all. You want to unburden yourself? You're ready now for complete surrender?"

The question almost made him bolt. Father Michaels didn't allow coloreds to attend St. Mary's, yet he hid him in his cellar on the orders of Satan himself. Willie didn't want to confess, but the priest made it clear if he were to stay then he'd have to atone for whatever sin brought him to the church doors. So here he was.

"I've lied. I've stolen before. I've even shot a gun once or twice at another man. But I never... ever killed a man." Willie closed his eyes. The words lodged in his throat.

"Go on son, the path to forgiveness is one of truth. God knows your secret. Confess it and shatter the lies once and for all."

Willie shook his head. If he confessed his greatest sin the priest would surely throw him out the front doors. Faith or not, there would be no forgiveness for what he was and what trusting Antonio Romano had made him become. Before God and all his mighty angels Willie did what he was best known for. He lied again. "I've sold hooch, and other things that I shouldn't have and I've stolen from those who trusted me."

"And you did these things because?"

"It's what I know. It's who I am."

"To atone you must understand sin is a choice, and if you want absolution it is time for you to choose another."

"I understand." Willie mumbled.

The priest began to pray. Willie opened his eyes and stared at nothing, listening to the words of the prayer, disbelieving the power of healing in the words. He repeated the prayer and accepted his order of penance. There was no way out of the hell he was locked in. But at least Harmony was safe. She'd done so much for him, sacrificed everything for him since Grams and Lewis died. He'd find a way out of New York and head North to Canada. He'd miss his sister but she was strong, and a survivor. The best thing for them both is if he took his secrets with him, wherever they led him.

CHAPTER FIVE
It ain't all Jazz baby…

Fletch Henderson waved his hand and the band cued up. Harmony tapped her left foot and snapped her fingers to the swing beat. The scene was jumping after her third set. No matter her troubles, she sang her heart out for release. Coming up on her fourth performance she felt a sliver of elation over her favorite song. The one she and Milo wrote together.

Trouble had come when she arrived at The Cotton. Madden was in full rage. He struck Fletch and cursed the band members before storming off. Harmony was afraid to ask the cause or source of his fury. She soon learned that Milo had not returned. He never missed a warm up. And even now he hadn't shown for their performance. If Fletch didn't cover for him Madden would fire him or do worse over the blatant disrespect. Harmony refused to think of what Milo encountered that kept him away. Twice through her first song her voice faltered and she struggled to keep up. Stickman on the piano cut her a look and she recovered. She had to. At The Cotton mediocre wasn't tolerated.

The men in the club roared with excitement. Harmony strutted around the small floor with her arms flung open wide. She worked her hips and shook her breasts to wolf calls and whistles. She sang of a loose woman who had an insatiable sexual appetite and devoured her lovers. The more she sang the more the dread and fear in her heart for Milo and her brother eased. Near the close of her performance Milo walked out wailing on his brass saxophone.

Harmony spun with relief and excitement spiking warmed adrenaline through her veins. He blew a sultry mix of sexy melodies at her and she swayed singing along. The crowd silenced and every man and woman found themselves transfixed by the sensual direction the music flowed. It couldn't be manufactured or called anything less than magic. Together they climaxed their jam session with him on his knees and his horn raised in tribute.

The applause was secondary to the appreciation in his eyes. Milo rose and she drifted into his arms.

"Where you been? I looked for you." She whispered against his ear.

"I'll tell you everything," he hushed her and spun her back out to the crowd. Harmony blew kisses to the smiling audience and nodded her appreciation to Fletch Henderson before quickly exiting. Milo was on her heels.

She stopped behind the curtain, hopeful. He walked over and pulled her further out of earshot. "There's something bad going down Mony. Romano is on a warpath."

"What? Vinnie Romano? Why now?"

"What did you tell him about Willie?" Milo asked.

"Nothing. I only asked for his help. What is it? Is he looking to hurt Willie?"

Milo glanced around. Two men who worked for Madden approached. "I need you to get your things. I brought Belle to sing the rest of the night. You head home. Gather as much as you can and then go to Paulette's. She's waitin' for you."

"No. Dammit this is insane. Just tell me the truth."

Milo grabbed her by both hands. "Do you understand that these men are dangerous? I know you went to see Madame today. Now I hear people think you know something around the missing booze that belongs to Romano."

"I don't."

"Willie does. Turns out the booze he'd sold to Red Hot's don't belong to Mickey Collins but to Vinnie Romano, and he wants it back. Grease Man and Madame are pissed because they've paid for a delivery and got nothing, so they hunting him too. Looking to cash in on Willie's troubles. Everyone's looking for Willie."

Harmony's stomach dropped. "Sweet merciful God. Willie? They'll kill him. Won't they?"

"Trust me Mony. Leave now, and together we can figure out how we can help him. Go."

Milo released her. She'd never seen him frightened, even with the constant burden of walking the criminal line. Tonight he looked scared.

"Paulette will take you some place safe. I think I know where to find Willie. I'll bring him to you."

"Madden's on the warpath tonight. Did he approve of Belle singing for me? Does Fletch know you making this switch?"

"I'll make up an excuse. Belle got talent to get the crowd going so Madden will be cool. But you need to go."

He walked off and she was left to watch him from the wings. There was nothing more she could do or say. Harmony pressed her fingers to her temples and tried to calm herself. Several girls passed and asked if she was okay. She managed a weak smile and dashed for her changing room. She shared it with the two other starlets performing that week but tonight it was hers alone. And when she opened the doors the most colorful sight greeted her. The place looked as if Eden had exploded in it. Flowers in all kinds of colors were stuffed in vases. She checked them one by one unsure of who they were sent to or from. She located a card and paused over the scribbling.

I expect to see you soon. Our business isn't done.
Vinnie

The door opened. A tall black clad figure, with the front of his fedora pulled so low to his face she saw little of his eyes, walked in. But his intense stare was felt in the silent way he stood before her. She recognized him.

"Mr. Madden don't allow us to have visitors honey, if you wait after my show we can talk."

The stranger reached behind him and engaged the lock with a soft click. With a slow deliberate hand he removed his hat and a sly smile eased across his lips. His teeth, even and white, were a stark contrast over his deep olive skin. "Name's Luigi but most call me Leftie ma'am, forgive the intrusion, however, this won't wait..." There was a hint of mockery in the forced politeness within his voice.

He had thick dark glossy hair smoothed back from his face. Hard angles defined his handsomeness, and his eyes looked cool as black ice. "Now that we've had proper introduction, pack your things. You're going for a ride."

"I remember you." Harmony dropped her hands to her hips and held to her courage. She wore her show dress, a firebomb red clingy number with a low-cut front bodice and long hem with splits up to mid thigh on both sides. She glistened like rubies when the light hit her curves, and she knew it. She noticed how his gaze often lowered to her breasts. "You're that guy from earlier right?" She released a soft chuckle. "If I knew you wanted an autograph I wouldn't have been so rude. Thing is suga, I'm just taking a quick break. The boys are waiting on me. I'm not leaving in the middle of my show."

The humor around the man's eyes and mouth faded. She felt her skin prickle with goose bumps, and the air chill around her. She hadn't much use for white men in the past. Besides Vinnie Romano she'd never, ever, ever, spent time alone with one. Now she remembered why. His forced respect was more of a game to him than anything. Like most white men he had an air of entitlement, and her blatant defiance challenged it on many levels. She had to think of something quick to diffuse the irritation flaring between them both. With less sass in her voice she spoke to him clearly. "Vinnie, wants to see me? Okay. I understand. Why don't you wait out back while I change? I can't go to him dressed like this now can I? Tell you what I'll do. I'll meet you in a few minutes. A quick change and we're on our way."

He didn't respond.

Harmony took a brave step toward him. She saw his gaze drop to her hips when she did so. She almost rolled her eyes at how predictable this one here was. "Aww c'mon suga. Give me a minute please."

The stranger situated his hat on his head. "Either you pack something or I'll drag you out as you are. This is happening toots. Decide. We do this the hard way or not?"

If she screamed for help it would worsen matters. Madden would gladly hand her over to end the drama. He'd probably punish Milo and Fletch for ruining the night. And if she went with this man to Vinnie Romano what then? Milo said Romano believed Willie stole from him. Did he think the night they shared had been a setup? She was trapped.

The man before her looked as if he would enjoy forcing her to do his will. Harmony nodded she would obey. She quickly gathered her street clothes (two dresses) into her cloth bag. With her back to him her gaze fell on her half eaten dinner. A knife lay across a sandwich glistening up at her. She leaned forward as if reaching for the scarf on the chair next to the plate and discreetly slipped the knife under her hand. "I guess Vinnie's a bit impatient tonight huh?" She said, placing the knife in her cloth bag. She turned with an innocent smile. "All done."

The guy hadn't moved a step.

"Okay, take me to Mr. Romano."

He opened the door and held it for her to walk out. She followed him to the back doors and passed some of the kitchen staff. Many eyes trailed her, both from black and white faces, but she ignored the questions in their stares. She kept her hand in the cloth bag and on the knife.

Once they entered the alley a car awaited. She was forced inside. Her kidnapper joined her in the back seat. The driver drove off before the door closed. She rode silently, playing out her options. The stranger never glanced her way. He never spoke and the silence was the worst. She thought if she breathed wrong it could set off some deadly reaction. When they travelled north out of Harlem she realized they weren't headed back to Vinnie's place. The city disappeared behind them, a dark forested road awaited ahead.

"Where, ah, where are we going?" she asked.

"You'll see soon enough."

Harmony gripped the knife tighter. Lewis once told her a drive out to the country was a one-way trip. She'd be damned if she'd let it be so.

***

The shipyard, remote and eerily isolated despite it being only a few miles north of the harbor, was the best lead the men had. Romano understood why Mickey would choose this spot. Prohibition had bootleggers creatively handling the drops and storage of imports from the shores of Sicily, and as far as Ireland. Not that the cops wouldn't hand over the product if it were seized, but that too could be costly for business. He'd received word Mickey Collins wanted a meeting in another hour. However, the messy matter of locating Mickey's pirated stash would need to be done before any meeting occurred. He cast his gaze to the window as his car and those escorting him rode through the shipyard with the lights dimmed.

Antonio sat to his left fuming. His bloody nose had been tended to by Mabel. He wouldn't allow a doctor to examine him. The evidence of their brawl was brutally evident. Purple and red bruises spread from his nostrils and extended to his swollen eyes.

The car stopped.

"If this isn't done tonight, I expect you to see it to the very end." He cast his gaze over to Antonio. "You still want Harlem?"

The question took his little brother by surprise. Antonio tried to mask the interest in his eyes when he nodded his answer. Romano understood his brother's need to be his own man. The others had overlooked Harlem, but since Madden opened The Cotton its allure had spiked the interest of a few.

"Then earn it."

Romano's door opened. Jimmie held it for him. "Boss we should go in first. Make sure it's the right drop spot…"

Gunfire exploded in the quiet night. Several windows from the warehouse lit with fiery blasts of bullets that rained down on Romano's caravan. Jimmie was hit in the back. His eyes bulged as blood sprayed from his mouth. Antonio grabbed Vinnie back in the car. The others returned fire. But Antonio jumped to the front of the car. The windshield shattered. "Stay down Vinnie. We'll get you out of here."

Romano had no intention of staying down. He grabbed the Thompson submachine gun, what he and the boys called 'the chopper', from the bottom of the car and began to blast bullets in the direction of the fire-fight. His men would have to retreat. There was no advantage to claim. Romano however, wouldn't relent no matter the mortal risk he placed himself in. Half of his body was out the window as he sprayed bullets in retaliation. He'd be damn if he did it crouched down like a coward.

The car swerved in a semi-circle and raced out of the open lot. Romano didn't withdraw. He leaned out the car window with no regard to his own safety and fired until the gun clicked noisily emptying and he and his men were long away.

"Fuck!" he shouted.

"Mickey laid a trap. Oh shit! Oh shit! They got Jimmie." Antonio half shouted, half whined. Romano breathed hard and heavy. He'd never forget the glazed look of shock and pending death in his friend's eyes before he dropped. He shuddered with black rage.

"How many cars behind us?" He asked Antonio, as he reloaded.

"I counted about six when we drove out but I don't know who was hit and who wasn't."

"Head east. To the cabins in Woodbury. I need to see the men. Mickey Collins is a dead fucker. In fact every motherfucker he cares about is dead as well."

In the country, at the dead of night, anything could happen. Harmony's mind had played tricks on her since they dropped her off. She waited until her kidnappers left to venture out the front doors, and her heart sank. Dark black-forested acres of land surrounded the tiny cottage. A quarter of a mile up was a huge log house. She saw a car parked out front and wondered if Vinnie were held up there. Part of her wanted to march right up to the front door and demand he take her home. The smarter part of her prevailed and she went back inside.

The cold became too much. After an hour she searched the back and front porch for the woodshed. She found a measly supply and tied her showgirl dress up at the thighs to bring the logs in. She'd been to the country several times with Grams and knew how to start her own fire. Soon the heat blazing in the brick hearth warmed the chilly dread she felt herself wrapped in. For the remainder of the night she sat on the modest tan cloth sofa and stared at the fire, thinking of Willie and how terrified he must be.

Harmony heard cars. She jumped upright. Beams of light flooded the front window of the cottage. *Could the bastards who stole her away be returning?*

The roar of the engines passing the cottage drew her. She remained closer to the shadows as she approached the window. When she eased aside the curtain she counted seven cars in total. Two of them had missing windshields.

"What the hell is going on?" she said aloud.

The men parked and several got out. She watched as two men carried someone wounded from the car inside the other cabin as the others gathered around. It was too dark to make out one man over the other, but the way they circled she guessed Romano was among them. Now what should she do?

Harmony paced. Milo would be looking for her. Paulette probably alerted him when she never showed up. Neither would think to search for her here. And what of her brother? If she went missing Milo wouldn't look for Willie, he'd waste energy on trying to rescue her, which most possibly would get them all killed. Harmony stopped pacing. The only way out of this mess would be through Romano. Though her first encounter with him had been unexpectedly nice, she had no delusions of his intentions now. She would have to fight and fight hard to survive. Harmony clenched the knife, sat, and waited.

Romano watched two of his men and his brother drive off with his orders. He and Leftie were all that remained. Inside the cabin Nunzio was most certainly bleeding to death. If the boys didn't return with the local doctor they'd have to bury him by sunrise. The blood on his shirt wasn't his. Jimmie's assassination was splattered all over him. The memory of the night's events burned hot in his mind. His throat was tight and constricted as his chest. But he remained perfectly still. The cool night air had no affect on him. Neither did the large silver full moon.

"Mickey had the jump on us boss."

Romano nodded. "Tell me something I don't know."

"Maybe an inside man. First he knows Antonio is in charge of the shipment and now he knows we're going for his booze before the meeting?"

"Interesting how everyone talks peace since the truce with the Five Points Gang. Yet Mickey was prepared for war. "Romano agreed.

"And Antonio? You sent him back into Harlem?"

Romano had to consider the fact that his brother had been meeting and conducting business deals between the coloreds and his greatest nemesis behind his back for longer than he confessed. It was a hard truth to swallow. Since they entered America, loyalty was never a question between the two of them. Did his brother forget the rules? Maybe. He doubted Antonio was brave enough to start a turf war. "I want you to go after Antonio, keep an eye on him. And before this war is over every enemy, every schemer, every man, woman and child that has plotted against me will know my wrath." Romano's gaze cut over to the cottage. A faint light shone in the window with flickering luminance. Possibly from a fireplace. "Is she here?"

"Yes boss. Been quiet as a church mouse since we dropped her off. She's a feisty one. Got a mouth on her."

"She give you any trouble?"

"Earlier she slipped from me. She's quite resourceful. I wouldn't trust her. I made it clear that you would not be denied. She came along without much of a fuss."

Romano smirked. "No one is to disturb us tonight unless it's news of where the fuck my booze is. I'll get the answers I need and meet with the boys in the morning."

"And Nunzio?"

"Save his life if you can. Spare no expense. Reach out to my friends, invite them all in. It's time for a reunion."

Leftie spat phlegm. "So the gang's coming back? They'll want more than leadership."

"It's time we secure what's ours. I'm sure I can convince them of our new purpose." Romano turned and began to walk through the tall grass toward the cottage. He was fond of his songbird still. Before his brother's deception was revealed he had intended to help her, and help himself to her soft body and sweet angelic voice. Now in one night everything had flipped to shit. Ironically it was Songbird's runaway brother who could give him the leg up on the situation. And if she'd played him for a fool all along she'd be sorry. He was done with niceties.

The porch step creaked under his foot announcing his arrival. The cottage was unnaturally silent. Not even the sounds of the night animals followed him. His hand closed in on the doorknob when a car drove across the grass. Romano's head turned and he expected to see Leftie leaving. Instead he recognized the town doctor in the passenger seat with one of his men at the wheel. *Maybe Nunzio would have a chance after all.* He heaved a deep sigh. Jimmie's death burned his gut and if he lost Nunzio too he wasn't sure how he'd keep perspective. Leftie said Dan, Vego, Twin and Big Boy Stevie were all dead. They'd haunt him like the other fallen men he called brother, just like Paulie.

Darkness greeted him, sweetly doused in her floral scent. It had been quite some time since a woman's fragrance filled the air in this place.

The partially opened door blocked his view of the rest of the cottage. He stepped inside and turned his head as he did so. The brief distraction was the only savior between him and a knife to the throat. She flung herself at him with her weapon ready to take another plunge. Romano grabbed her wrist and threw her back into the door forcing it shut. Harmony fought him with her free hand, the knife noisily dropped to the floor. Romano put his hand around her slender throat, tight. She gasped, and her eyes stretched with fear. She kneed him hard in the crotch and his knees buckled but he held to her throat and managed to keep standing. "Motherfuck! That hurt!" He wheezed. She struggled clawing at his face. He had to lift her with one hand up the wall. "Don't move! Don't!" he seethed.

She stopped struggling. She held his stare. Fire blazed in her dark eyes, her lips drew back from her teeth and revealed how clenched they were.

"You behave, understand me? Hit me again and I'll snap your neck!"

She nodded that she would obey. There was a sad decline in the brilliance of her soft brown eyes. *I'll be damn, crazy broad tried to off me.* Romano nearly chuckled at the irony, but the pain in his groin made the humor fleeting. He'd always figured he'd die from a bullet, not a dame with a kitchen knife. Surely she knew taking a swipe at him would be a costly mistake. In a warped kind of way, he liked the spunk she'd shown. He never played it safe in life, never shied away from the impossible. She was a dame after his own heart. He ought to let her go to see what she'd try next.

"Will you be good if I let you go?"

"Yes," she said and he loosened his grip on her throat. He lowered her and she slid down the door several inches to land on her feet. He studied her, lingering on the swell of her bosom lifting with each staggered breath she inhaled. Her steady gaze bore into him with silent expectation and he had to avoid it to keep revealing how much the violence excited him. Instead he knelt and picked up the knife. Holding it up to the sparse light cast about the room from the flames of the fireplace, he could see the silver carved handle and engravings. *It came from The Cotton Club? Leftie brought her in and didn't bother to check if she had a weapon?* He snorted in disgust.

"Wh-what are you-you going to do to me?" She croaked in a hoarse brittle voice, her hand to her throat. She glistened like rubies in her scarlet red dress. He'd seen her perform in it before. The only thing missing was the orchid from her hair.

"Sit down." He ordered.

Rebellion swelled in her, evident by the defiant scowl she gave. He was in no mood to ask twice. His brow arched and she did as she was told. Could he blame her for her actions? He did bring her against her will. Still he had her pegged as smarter than this. His judgment had been slipping lately.

"Where's your brother?" Romano asked, rubbing the ache from his groin.

"You know I don't know." She said under her breath.

"Songbird, you won't get many chances tonight to convince me to be patient after trying to stick me. Take your time and think carefully before you speak. Where's your brother?"

Harmony crossed her arms over her bosom, refusing him his answers. Romano exhaled nosily through his flared nostrils. "You are one stubborn woman! Fine. I'll fill in the blanks for you. Your brother played games with people who are far less dangerous than me. Now he owes big. And I intend to collect. When he finds out that I have you I'm sure he'll reappear." He pointed a finger at her. "And by then the time for negotiations between you and me will be over."

"Willie didn't know it was your booze, if'n he took it at all."

"So we agree he stole from me? I thought you said he was a good kid?"

"He is. He got mixed up with men like you that ain't. He never mentioned his dealings to me."

"Too bad for him, too bad for you Songbird. Willie has information I need. The money he stole is the least of his problems. You need to let me bring him in before Mickey does."

"I told you I don't…"

"Careful." He warned. "Think about what I just said before you answer again."

Romano walked over to the small wooden kitchen table and drew back a chair. He sat in it wearily. The night had taken its toll on him. Fatigue settled in his bones. He craved sleep.

Harmony exhaled a breath of relief when he sat down away from her. The bastard had almost strangled her. She touched her tender throat and grimaced. The knife was a desperate act on her part. She hadn't really thought killing him through. Hell she wasn't even sure it was him. When she heard the door open her survival instincts kicked in. His reaction caught her off guard. Wasn't he some vicious mob boss? She expected him to strike her, or do worse over the attack. He seemed quite at ease with people trying to take his life. Something in his aloof manner over the matter soothed her fears. Harmony lowered to the sofa never taking her eyes off him.

Is that blood on the front of his shirt?

Together they sat in silence. After several insufferable minutes with no words between them he rose. She watched as he slowly removed his suit coat. There was something stiff about his actions, he looked to be in pain. "Are you hurt?" She jutted her chin toward the evidence of his violent night on his tweed vest and white shirt.

Romano glanced down, seeing the blood for the first time. Harmony felt a bit of panic rise in her. *What if he is hurt, and dies on me? What then? It'll be the death of me and Willie for sure.* "Where are you bleeding?"

"Not my blood." He said dryly. He loosened the button to the front of his vest and removed it. When he shed his shirt she noticed his arm. Harmony squinted at the bruise on his bicep. She rose and approached him.

Romano looked to his arm curiously and didn't object when she got closer and began to inspect it. "You need to keep it clean. I'll…." She glanced to the kitchen and the sink. "Is there a well?"

He didn't answer. He seemed more focused on the scar than her. The sink did indeed have running water. Harmony located a cloth and doused it in the cool water, then returned to him. She wiped his arm.

"You cut me," he said, a bit bewildered. "I'll be damned."

The accusation hit her hard. "I did this?"

"Apparently so." His dark gaze swung back up to her face. He seemed amused by it. She felt her stomach sour over the implications. She really didn't want to hurt him.

"Vinnie…ah Mr. Romano, I'm sorry. I didn't know it was you coming through the door." She lied. His gaze narrowed. She heaved a deep sigh. "I lied. I did know it was you, or I thought it might be you. I was afraid. I had to protect myself."

"From me? Have I done anything to hurt you?"

"I heard at The Cotton that you and Mickey Collins are going to war. Everyone's talking about it. I also hear tell you think it's my brother's fault and I don't know what the hell to do about this mess he in. For you to come after me…"

"After you came to me." He corrected.

She nodded. "You right. I did come to you, for help. And you promised you would help him, after… after I gave you what you wanted." She looked up into his eyes. "And I fulfilled our bargain. You didn't."

"Is that so?"

She couldn't bring herself to remind him of the things he said when he was between her legs. Even now she was uncertain of the forbidden urges the memory evoked. It was lust, a sin, and she wished she'd never crossed that line. "If you let me talk to Willie I can clear this up Mr. Romano."

"It's Vinnie. Back to me hurting you, not in the cards Songbird. I'd never strike a dame, even one after my own life." His voice sounded calm, maybe even a bit concerned when he corrected her. "I deserve your distrust." He grabbed her hand to keep her close. Harmony maintained his stare. "I didn't bring you here to cause you harm. Our business isn't done."

"It is…"

"It isn't," he said firmly. "And now that your brother is between us, it's up to you and I to see this through—to the very end." He drew her closer. She tried to resist but his pull was insistent. Her feet did a short scuttle and she was forced to stand between his legs. With her heart thundering in her ear she stood perfectly still before him. Harmony shivered. She wouldn't have much of an escape if he made a move on her.

"I wanted to see you again." She forced a smile. "It's not a wise thing you know? Me and you are different, we come from different worlds. If we didn't maybe… I would think we might try to be friends."

"That's not quite true is it?" This time there was a hint of steel edge to his voice. She shrugged her shoulders. She had lost her taste for bad boys after Lewis died. If it were up to her she'd date a factory worker or farmer and return to singing in a small church. He released her wrist. Harmony remained still. His hand eased into the spilt at the side of her dress and stroked up the back of her thigh. She was only marginally aware of his touch. Her mind had split over fleeing, or using his desires to gain freedom.

"Thing is…" he began, "black or white I wanted to see you. And it's not all about business Doll."

Harmony moved away from his reaching fingers before they found her most intimate spot. Romano stood. He wore his undershirt and his suspenders were down around the waist of his trousers. "

"So what's your plan Vinnie?" she asked, trying to put more space between them by returning to the sink and rinsing the blood from the cloth rag. "You think keeping me here is going to bring Willie out of hiding? He won't know where to find me. And if'n he do he won't be smart enough to help you. He's young and foolish, dumb enough to think he could get away with stealing from you I suppose. He'll be dumb enough to think he can rescue me on his own. And what then? I'll tell you what." She shot him a pointed look over her shoulder. "Those men with you will put a bullet in him. That's what."

"Maybe. Not if you're smart and we do things my way. You trust me Songbird and I will spare your brother. You have my word."

"Like I had your word you'd help me if we laid together? You mean that word?" She sassed, wringing out the rag she then laid it flat on the edge of the sink. She turned and he was just a breath away. *Dammit why did he come so close?*

The corner of Romano's mouth kicked up. If she were honest the fluttering in her stomach wasn't nerves, it was something far more primal. The man had an irresistible appeal when his focus was solely on her. But she couldn't trust that feeling or him.

"I'm cold." She announced. He paused and gave her a curious look.

Harmony laughed softly. She turned and pointed to the dying fire in the brick hearth. "We need more kindling for the fire. Can you get some?"

Romano's gaze finally switched to the fireplace. He nodded and left. Harmony could breathe again. She slumped down on the sofa and exhaled deep breaths. A five-minute reprieve wasn't a lot of time but it was enough for her to check herself. *Think, think, think, what you gone do now?*

She heard him enter and glanced over to see his arms loaded with logs. Now she could observe him without the heat of his brown eyes spearing her. The bruising on his arm centered around a thin scratch. A pang of regret pierced her heart. He cast his gaze to her. "Are you hungry? I don't think there's food here but I can go up to the house and get some."

If he returned to his brother and those other hoods his mood could sour. "No. I'm not hungry."

The pointed end of the iron rod poked the fire and got the red-hot ambers twinkling upward in a cloud of black smoke. She cleared her throat. "You know, if you really want me to find him you should let me go. I had a clue, a real one. In fact I was going to..." The truth had no limits on her tongue and she quickly silenced herself remembering she told him only minutes ago she didn't know where Willie was.

"Finish." Romano said. He straightened in front of the fireplace and approached her. "You were saying?"

"I was going to go to East Harlem, to some of his old friends and start there. He has to be hiding around those boys he was often with. They won't talk to no white man. But they'd talk to me."

When he sat next to her she tried to scoot discreetly over. But the small sofa made the fit a bit snug. And with him so close she could see him clearly. The changing light from the fire patterned his face. She, however, could not deny the firepower in his stare. "You don't trust me." He stated.

"Can you blame me?" she half-chuckled.

Humor twitched his lips. "That's the weird thing about you Songbird. I can never blame you." He touched the side of her face with the back of his hand. She lowered her gaze against the feel of the light brush. "You're beautiful."

"I must be a sight," she answered. And she knew it was true. Her hair had come out of the bobby pins and was frizzing at the roots. The dress she wore had been torn along the splits and tied in knots at the hem. She had her street clothes in her cloth bag but in her nervousness she forgot to change into them.

His reply was hushed, "If you want your brother to live then you have to trust your instincts, the same instincts that brought you to my bed."

"What if I do," she said softly maintaining his stare. "If I trust you, believe in you, what then? You gonna make me your girl?" she teased.

Good Lord did I just say that?

He lowered her sleeve, and brushed his lips against her bare shoulder. The soft pair trailed up her neck with the gentlest of kisses. Instinctively she put her hands against the solid wall of his chest to push back. His mouth brushed upward and stopped at the inside curve of her ear. "Yes. Give me what I want and I'll set your brother free... after."

As independent as she had been after Lewis's death, there had been many times when she craved abandonment. If she kept her heart out of this and remained focused she could probably get her and Willie out of Harlem for good. She just needed to ignore the soft flutters of her heart that competed with the heat between her legs when he was this close. After all it was nothing more than lust. For Romano she represented the forbidden—possibly. He probably loved living his life on the edge, taking the hard road in every thing he did. Keeping time with a colored woman definitely would be off the beaten path for any of the men he associated with. She'd seen the way he watched her at The Cotton and even now he panted like a schoolboy when she allowed him to touch her. His obsession could prove to be dangerous to toy with. What choice did she have?

He reached behind her, with his cheek pressed to hers. She felt his warm breath escape his nostrils and cover her ear as he lowered the zipper to her dress. "Lie back. I want to be inside of you—again," he said in a gruff commanding voice. She did as he asked putting the middle of her back to the side of the sofa. The man was all hands. Her leg was lifted and she heard her dress rip a bit more along her right thigh as she obediently dropped it over the back of the sofa. Harmony was so grateful for the darkness. Here she was holding to the front of her dress to cover her bosom with her legs spread to high heaven.

Romano shifted on his one knee. The scrape of his zipper sounded. He grabbed at her panty until the nylon tore from her hip and came away in tatters. Her thighs felt warm and clammy in her garter stockings and she wished she could remove them. Her body was burning with feverish excitement. But Romano wouldn't be denied. With his stare locked in on hers the blunt head of his cock stabbed at her center then plunged inside. His free hand lifted and gripped the side arm of the sofa and the other held to her hip. He braced her for the short hard strokes he delivered.

It felt uncomfortable at first and a bit awkward. But his thrusting was steady, measured, drilling for her liquid lust. She dropped her head back allowing herself to enjoy it as he ran his tongue over her throat and nipped her chin.

A quick pounding at the door startled her and she tensed, pushing hard at his shoulders. Romano kept going driving himself deeper into her being, working his hips in a circular motion forcing her toes to curl. *Did she hear knocking, or was that her heart beating in her ears?* It came again more insistent.

"Vinnie, wait, someone's here." She grabbed his hips to still him. Halting his rhythm made the insides of her thighs quiver. But she feared someone peeking in the windows and seeing her spread on the sofa with him piling into her more than she craved their shared lust. He looked up dazed and confused, then he heard the knocking too. His head swung left and he peered at the door. The knocking persisted.

"Fuck!" he grunted.

Romano's cock slipped slowly from inside of her. He rose and ran up the zipper to his trousers as she lowered her leg from the back of the sofa and gathered her torn panty from between them. She could barely get the front of her dress up when he threw open the door and glared down his visitor. Then he walked out of it with a slam.

Harmony tried to gather her senses. Her breathing was so fast and strong she almost felt as if he was still inside of her. She went to the oil lantern near the fireplace and with her breasts freed and the dress gathered around her waist she plucked a long matchstick, ignited it in the open flames of the fire, and lit the lantern. She glanced around for her next move.

The bedroom door was the first she tried when she arrived but it was so dark inside she abandoned it as an option, and decided to remain to the front of the cottage to get a jump on anyone arriving. Maybe it would be a great escape from him if she went inside and locked it. She carried the lantern in front of her to keep the light steady and went inside. With the door firmly closed she found no lock to keep herself safe. She sighed and turned with the lantern. Her breath caught in her throat. She lifted the yellow flames in the glass casing and cast the light everywhere. And her eyes stretched in shock at what was unveiled.

"Sweet Jesus. What is this?"

CHAPTER SIX
Things Remembered…

"This better be good!" Romano hissed. He paced. His dick remained semi hard behind his zipper and his arms, chest, legs all felt uncompromisingly tight. She was making him crazy! His Songbird had tried to slice his throat. Nothing he said or promised quelled her resistance, unless he was worshipping her body. And the more she fought him the more he craved her.

"Sorry boss." Leftie answered in a voice void of remorse. His friend hadn't said it but he noticed the way he sneered whenever he was distracted by Harmony. If Leftie had objections to his desires for a colored woman he was smart enough not to say it to his face. However, Romano gave him an order, and Leftie always walked a straight line of obedience with him. Apparently he didn't consider this one worthy of the same respect. That too incensed Romano.

"Well? What the fuck is it?"

"The boys have about four of Collins's men, questioning them in the barn." Leftie said.

Romano glanced toward the red and brown barn isolated to the east of his property in a field of three-foot tall grass. The full moon above cast silvery blue light over the roof and surrounding trees. "That was quick." He frowned.

"I saw them coming up the highway and turned around to follow. The boys have a couple of saws, nails and hammers to use on our friends. After we're done, what do you want us to do with the bodies?" Leftie flicked his cigarette and exhaled a long stream of smoke.

Romano itched in his throat for his tobacco and smoking pipe. It would calm him. Behind him he heard a door slam inside the cottage. He glanced back over his shoulder and imagined she'd found the bedroom. *Shit, I forgot about the bedroom.* He burned in his gut to return to her and explain away what she would find. "The boy? What about him?"

Leftie frowned. "I don't know… we haven't…"

"Make it a priority. I want him alive." Romano's voice boomed over Leftie's half-ass explanation. "Put Antonio on it. He knows Harlem. Make sure he understands I won't tolerate failure on this." Romano could see Harmony's reaction if he granted her wish and delivered her brother. The idea of her being grateful to him made him soften a bit.

"Got it, and Collins's men?" Leftie pressed with a hint of irritation in his voice.

"Get what you can out of them. Drop what's left on Mickey's door." Leftie backed down the steps and turned away. "And Leftie?"

"Yes Boss."

"Don't fucking interrupt me again, unless you got Mickey Collins's head as my trophy."

Leftie tipped his hat and sauntered off. Romano wiped his hand down his face. He watched Leftie drive out through the grass toward the old barn and nearly decided to join. The violence he'd done and witnessed since he was a boy was the blame. Annie warned that soon it would consume him. Still he could no more deny that part of him than he could deny an arm or a leg. Without his detached temperament he'd never have survived the mean streets of Bronx and the turf wars.

Turning he went back inside. She was gone. The fireplace blazed so hot it boiled the air around him. He needed a release. He needed her. Romano opened the door to *his* room. She looked up at him, her eyes bright with curiosity. It was to be expected. After all he'd brought her here with little thought to the room he kept for himself. She had to wonder why.

"I thought this was a servant's quarters. What is this place to you?" she asked rising from the bed. The room was plainly furnished, and windowless. A person would find it quite ordinary if it weren't for the wood carvings of people, sculptures that were exquisite in detail.

"Vinnie?" Harmony spoke. She pointed to the shelf. "Did you do these?"

"No. Yes. I did."

"Oh," she said softly. "They're beautiful. I'm surprised."

"Why? You don't think I'm capable of creating beauty?"

"No. It's just. I guess you're such a tough guy I didn't think... Look at the detail. These, look so real. Like people."

"Let's go Doll. This room is off limits." He said, loosing his nerve to reveal more.

"Wait." She pleaded. He returned his gaze to her and found her smiling. It was the first genuine smile she'd given him since he captured her. Yes she laughed with him and he suspected at him, but she never smiled at him like this.

"I want to know about the people you sculpted. Why do you create them?"

"What do you mean why?" He tossed back at her. He didn't mean to sound harsh. The pressure in his chest and head had him by the balls. He didn't discuss his carvings or the compulsive desire to make one of every person who has come and gone from his life. Ever.

"C'mon Vinnie. Start with her. This little girl." She picked up the bust of a child's head carved in detail down to the curly locks that framed her face. Harmony held her gingerly in her hands. "Who is she?"

He released a deep sigh and closed the door once more. "My cousin."

Harmony. "How old is she, four, or five?"

"She died of consumption in Lercara Friddi when she was three."

"Where is *Lercara Friddi*," she pressed.

"Sicily. A very long way from here. When I came to America I lived on the streets, until I met Annie and her brother Teek. She had her mother take me in," he began, "I kicked around until I formed my own... family." His gaze lifted to meet hers to see if she fully understood what *family* meant to him. She didn't.

"Your gang?" she said.

Romano blinked. *She did understand.* Harmony nodded for him to continue.

"I made money, enough to send for Antonio. When he came I bought a place in the Bronx, and this place. The main house is where the boys hold up, but this cottage is mine. No one comes here."

"I'm here," she said.

"Yes you are."

Harmony picked up the iron ring at the top of the lantern and lifted the encased flames causing shadows to dance over the faces of the sculptures. The light bounced off the wall to a painting. "Did you do this too?" she asked.

He nodded.

She raised the lantern before the single painting in the room. He'd done it after Annie left him. He couldn't sculpt her image, it would hurt too bad to look upon her face and know she'd never return. The same with her brother Teek, Antonio's best friend and a kid Romano considered as close as a brother. Instead he put down his carving tools and painted instead. This one was filled with cliffs and fields of red flowers. The painting was indeed his favorite. He would carry Antonio on his shoulders through the olive patches to the open fields for him to play when he was a tot. Romano would get a kick out of how his brother's chubby legs pumped as he ran and chased butterflies before tiring out.

"I've never seen any place this beautiful. Sicily must be a slice of heaven." Harmony said her voice low and soothing. The anxiety drained from his limbs. Instead of focusing on how vulnerable he felt he focused on what Annie's love inspired in him.

"Sicily can be paradise for some. Not my family."

"Really? Why? Who is your family?"

Romano walked over to her. He took the lantern from her hand and captured it with his free one. He led her over to the only sculpture in the room that filled him with dread. A large bust carved from a block of wood. It stood a foot tall from neck to head. She gazed upon it curiously. Before her was almost exact likeness of Don Giuseppe Romano.

"This man *is* the family. My Papa."

"He looks… mean," Harmony said. "Did you mean to carve him with such an angry face?"

Laughter exploded from Romano and Harmony smiled. He was grateful for the levity. But it only lasted a moment, and faded altogether when his gaze fell upon his father's image. He felt her hand slip from his. Had he dropped it? He wasn't aware. Instead he stood transfixed by the hard glare of his father, remembering life as his son until he could stand no more. Don Giuseppe looked like a Neanderthal. He was a big stubble-bearded man with black malevolent eyes. His mother's bust was next to him. She wore a sad smile, like the one on her face for most of her short life. He'd taken time with her bust. Even painted her carved long locks black, which he'd had, fall about her face in thick waves. He believed she was no more than thirteen when her family gave her to the Don, and fourteen when she gave birth to him.

"He is more than mean. For the people in my village he is like a god. Children pray to the saints for him to be blessed before they pray for their own famiglia's well-being. Men offer their daughters to him no matter how young just to show honor and respect. The town officials all seek his council before any law or decision is passed."

Harmony's hand went to his back. She stepped closer to him, staring at the detailing in the sculpture. "And your mother? Is this her?"

"Yes, her name was Rena."

"Was?"

"She died giving birth to Antonio."

"Must have been hard losing her?"

He gave a single nod. "I remember the peaceful smile on her face when we buried her. She was happy to be free of him."

"That's awful. Why is your father so important?"

"He just is, and so was his father and his father before him. He owns the land, the creeks, the air everyone breathes. But he doesn't own me." Romano stepped away. He set the lantern down on the tiny wood dresser. She walked up to him and put her arms around his waist blocking his ability to turn. Her hands went up his chest with her palms flat. She nuzzled her nose to the center of his spine and it felt heavenly. Romano closed his eyes thankful for the serenity he found in her embrace. The intimacy surprised him. Yes, he'd made love to her body, but she never willingly touched him.

"You are no different than most men, full of regret and pride, but unable to see your blessings."

"I've never been blessed."

"Not true. You're alive, you survived whatever happened with you and your father and started again. You found a life and name of your own. You didn't do these things alone. I think it's courageous."

"I'm no saint Songbird."

"Well, maybe not. But you're no devil either Vinnie Romano." She pressed her face to his back. He stood silent for a minute staring through another sculpture, one he did of Antonio when he was a small boy. She withdrew and the separation was a disappointment. "What was that for? The hug?" he asked casting his gaze back at her from over his shoulder.

Again she smiled. "Because sometimes a girl needs a hug."

"I can take you up to the main house. You'll be more comfortable there, more rooms and space, until we work our agreement out."

Harmony shrugged. "I kind of like it in here." She spun then pointed at the small carving. "What is that, a schoolhouse or church?"

"Schoolhouse." Romano nodded. "We all attended together, me, Antonio, and then my mother. She wanted to learn to read and write her name. That was until my father discovered she had been and was angered. The school was burned to the ground."

"Jeesh. Why would he be angry that she wanted to be educated?"

Romano yawned. "I don't remember. Look Doll, I'm tired, you have to be. Like I said, let's go to the main house. Do you have something to change into?" he swept his gaze over her ripped ruby red dress. Though she zipped it up in the back, it hung on her now like a rag with the bodice stretched revealing more of her bosom, and the split to her right torn all the way up to the bend of her hip. He didn't want to march her up through the fields and his men to see her disheveled state. Hell he didn't want any man looking upon her treasures, ever again.

"Can we stay here? Tonight. This room?"

"Why?" he struggled to keep the discomfort from his voice.

She didn't flinch. She walked over to the bed that slept two barely, "Because I'm comfortable here, and so are you. If I have to stay out in the woods with a bunch of mob boys I'd prefer to do it in a place they can't reach me."

"You think you're safe with me?" Romano smirked.

Harmony let go a sweet peal of laughter. "I think this is the one room none of those bad boys come into. So yes, I'm safe."

"I wouldn't hurt you Harmony. You do believe me, don't you?"

She blinked and didn't answer. He understood her reluctance to accept his good intentions. At best they were half-ass to this point. His promise to her was true. Dame had a way of making him at ease. He'd never shared the story of his parents with a female. Annie though a sweet tempered woman, preferred the city and rarely visited.

"This room is you Vinnie. I'd like to know a little more about you."

"And why is that?" he pressed, his gaze narrowing her into his single line of vision.

Harmony rose again. She batted her lashes at him and he knew he was in trouble. The tables had turned. He felt vulnerable, trapped by the gleam in her eyes and the sexy curve of her smile. She slowly lowered the zipper to let the dress drop away. She stood before him in her stocking and round toe shoes. The melting softness of her body was evident in the golden brown flawless skin covering her flat tummy, round hips, thick thighs and slender legs. Her bush lay over her sex like black velvet. Her up tilted breasts were absent of age, or the weight of suckling babies, and were large enough to fill his hands.

She extended her arm with an upward turned palm. "You're not going to leave me here by myself are ya?"

His lips drew away from his teeth in a tight smile as he approached her. His hand cupped her gently behind the neck and her lashes lowered until her eyes closed. "Are you playing with me Songbird?"

She nodded slowly and breathed lightly through her soft lips. "Maybe."

"Before the night is over your answer will be yes." He dropped her back to the bed. Memories of home, good and bad, would normally render him incapable of the emotions she drove through him now. Tonight he felt charged, exhilarated, a bit of happiness to have her so willing to be his without his threat of harming her brother. Yes, they had a bargain. Her body and a bit of her soul for her brother's life was fair trade according to her, for him he'd need more, much more.

The tension drained from his body as he eased over her. He lifted on his elbow, positioned with his erection pressed into the mattress and her thighs closed around his hips. With his free hand, he framed her face, and placed his thumb under her jaw while his fingers pressed to her cheek. "I'm having a hard time keeping things straight Doll. You... you do this to me."

Her dark lashes lowered but her gaze never broke from his.

"The first moment I heard you sing I thought of home, what I've lost, what I miss."

"Why? There are other singers, other girls."

Why indeed? He refused to voice the answer. He'd had another woman, a lovely woman, and when she rejected him it did burn in his gut. But in his most intimate moments with Annie he never felt the fire that he felt through his loins whenever Harmony was near. He never felt free to be who he was with anyone but his Songbird tonight. The truth was, he never felt much of anything but bitter regrets until she slipped in his arms.

"Let's just say you're the tops kid."

She ran her hands up and down his arms. He winced at the sting slicking up to his left shoulder.

"Does it hurt?" she asked touching him there.

"It doesn't hurt anymore." He answered. His head lowered to press his lips against hers. He found them soft and giving, molding to his. She moaned softly, her hands reaching between them to lower his zipper and push his trousers down off his hips. Romano didn't have the patience to fully undress. He needed to be in her now. She was so warm and soft beneath him. He couldn't decide if he wanted to suck her nipples or lick her pussy dry. He reached and grabbed his shaft giving it a long stroke between them while devouring her mouth with a hungry kiss. He centered the head of his cock on her slick entrance. He found her opening tight with heat and nicely swollen before he took the plunge.

Harmony released a muffled cry into his mouth and he kissed her harder. She clutched his undershirt drawing it up higher across his back as he flexed to drive himself deeper, again and again. His arousal sharpened under the clenching constricting spasms of her inner walls.

The currents of pleasure were so strong he cursed in his language and shuddered. The slippery heat of her channel caused him to sink deeper and he felt his cock expand until the skin stretched and his balls were hard as stones. She swirled her hips beneath him and clung to him refusing any release. Romano dropped his face in her neck and pumped his clenched ass cheeks harder and harder until he was groaning and jerking his seed into her. She cried out in that beautiful voice and they were both done.

For a long breathless moment they couldn't speak, and even when he managed to he couldn't bring himself to move off her. Romano blinked, beads of sweat clinging to his lashes from his eyes. She grabbed both sides of his face and forced him to look at her. There was no judgment, and no pity in her expression. Only the quietly intense stare of hers that captured him from day one. Her legs cinched higher around his waist and kept his waning erection firmly planted in her core. "You are a strange man Vinnie Romano." She drew his face down to hers and kissed him. He knew it then. He knew the truth one hundred percent. He was lost, and it was all for a dame named Harmony.

***

"What is it?" Willie shot up from his cot. "I know something is going on. Where have you been?"

"Shhh, keep your voice down. The nuns will hear you."

"I could hear people on the streets." Willie pointed to the windows above them that reached the sidewalks before St. Mary's. "They're saying there's going to be a war. And then you didn't show today, I got worried. What the hell is going on?"

"He took her, he has your sister."

The news hit him like a brick to his heart. The mere idea of his sister being dragged into his mess shattered his control. He lunged and swung, connecting his fist with the target. His companion fell back a bit stunned, but recovered enough for the next blow. He grabbed Willie's arm and pinned it behind his back. Willie roared in pain and anger until his attacker's forearm went chokingly tight around his throat.

"Calm down! Now!"

He nodded he would. After a painful second he was thrown free and landed on his hands and knees. He quickly rose and turned on the man equal to him in height. His hands clenched to fists but he didn't try another swing at the bastard. "You swore she would not be part of this. You swore it! You said we'd take down Collins and make him pay for Lewis's death. Now he has my sister!"

"Not Collins. Vinnie took her."

"No. No fucking way. That's not what we agreed…"

"I'll get her away from him." The shadow advanced on him, covering him in the dimly lit basement. "I'll make sure we get everything we want, revenge, justice, power. You have to trust me to let it play out. Mickey Collins and Vinnie will kill each other. And when it's done we're free."

The soft kiss of his lover's lips to his cheek did calm him. Willie pushed at his chest forcing him away. "Don't do that. It's sacrilegious. We're in a church."

His lover gripped his groin and Willie blushed at the erection he felt forming. "You're mine. Nothing we do can be wrong…"

CHAPTER SEVEN
Lies and Broken Promises...

Harmony turned over to her side and found herself face to face with a sleeping Vinnie Romano. Soft breath escaped his nostrils fanning her face. He slept with his leg thrown across her thigh. She stared up at him in the pitch-black darkness. The lantern had long gone out. But even in the shadows she could see his handsome features. The man was full of surprises. She didn't think Lewis had one single mystery to him. His needs were simple, and his dreams big, but there was never anything as mysterious and complicated as the man before her now. Vinnie Romano was unlike anyone she'd ever known. And she could feel her heart softening toward him.

She closed her eyes and tried not to think of Willie. But alone in her new lover's arms the sadness crept in. What had her brother done to these men? Why would he be so foolish? Lewis had taught him better. Now they were in hell and she had no real answers. Willie was always secretive. But he was her brother and she needed him. Maybe the bond between her and Vinnie would help his plight. Maybe?

"Stay awake." The low growling texture of his voice made her stomach flutter. He hooked his arm around her waist and pulled her closer so that their noses touched. She blinked in the darkness and focused on what she could see of his face.

"I thought you were asleep." Harmony whispered.

"Why aren't you?" He whispered back.

"I don't know."

"Mmm, come closer."

She eased her arms around his waist and he lowered his leg from her thigh, his palm slid down the curve of her hip and lifted her leg to bring over his. The maneuver allowed his erection to slip between the folds of her sex.

"Talk to me Harmony. I love the sound of your voice."

"I don't know what you mean." She gave a nervous chuckle, then soft sigh when the thick head of his shaft nudged her and nearly slipped in.

"You do know. I want to know why you would risk your life, everything for a brother who ran from you without a word."

The answer was something she hadn't considered. Why did she do any of the things she'd done since Grams died? "I love him, he my blood. It's that simple."

"It can be Songbird. A woman's love flows deeper than what we men can understand. Isn't that so?" He brushed his knuckles across her face. Her sight adjusted to the cave black darkness and saw more of him. A kiss landed on her nose and it was so comforting.

She cleared her throat. "Yeah. I suppose."

"Where's your fella? Someone as beautiful as you shouldn't be alone. Do you have a man?"

"Not anymore." Harmony said, her voice cracking with emotion. It felt as if he were peeling away skin from her bones. She didn't want to talk about her feelings, or her loneliness. He kept her close.

"What happened to him? The guy, you said his name was Lewis."

"Why do you think something happened to him?" she asked softly.

He brushed his lips across hers. "I get the feeling it had to. I know I would have never gotten this close to you if any man loving you were alive."

Was he serious? Did he mean the sweet words he said in the dark? She wished she could see more of his eyes to be sure. Harmony's gaze fell then her lids closed. Her voice was tight when she spoke of Lewis. "He was murdered. I don't know why or by whom. The night he died Willie come to get me out of bed. He was in tears. He said someone had shot him. He'd dragged Lewis to our steps but couldn't bring him no further. I got downstairs and…" Tears filled her eyes, and she didn't bother to keep a few from falling. "I got downstairs and he was bleeding so bad. There was blood everywhere. He… he told me he was sorry. He broke his promise. He said he loved me. And he died."

Romano pulled her head down to his chest and held her. She released her grief and sadness in a staggered sob that pitched high and fell to a low whimper when she was all cried out. She hadn't cried since the night she washed blood from her clothes and fingernails as they carried a dead Lewis away. She saved her tears and did what was expected of her. Even when Willie disappeared she didn't cry. Tears never gave her comfort until now.

He stroked the back of her head and held her through the last of it. "What are we doing? Why did you ask me about Lewis?" She wanted to put all the pieces together regarding the tough-guy who many men feared, created life-like sculptures from wood when he was alone, and now had started seeking the embrace of a colored woman. Why? Ceaseless inward questions hammered at her.

Two fingers pinched her chin and lifted her face. In the darkness she could see the earnestness in his eyes. He rolled on top of her. She felt his hand slip away to take hold of her wrists and pin them above her head. She could sense the shadow of him hovering close. "Do you have anyone else in the world? A mother, father? Anyone besides your brother?"

"No," she said.

"Is it wrong of me to say I'd be jealous if you did?"

"Wrong? Yes. Why would you be jealous?"

"Because. The idea of you belonging to any man makes me that way."

"That makes no sense, we… we aren't anything, really."

"Your happiness is a new priority for me Doll. I care about Harmony Jones… I've had this thing for…you… you make me…" Romano dropped his forehead to hers and started to breathe shallowly.

She waited.

When he couldn't finish and his grip tightened on her wrist revealing his restraint she moved under him to soften his heart again. Passion for him radiated from the soft core of her body where his erection once again pressed down. She felt the slight shudder of his chest pressed to hers. He had said as much as he could. Like most men, pride cometh before the fall. "You don't owe me anything, Vinnie. I'm here now, and right where I want to be. You hear me? This here is a bargain between us. I know the rules. I'm okay with them."

His head lifted and she knew he was staring at her. Then he lowered it again and spoke against her ear. "Things may have started as a bargain between us Songbird, but I think we both know the deal serves another purpose now. *You're mine.* And I'm going to show you how sweet my feelings for you can be. No more broken promises. My word is solid on this."

Shock flew through her. Her response wedged in her throat. This man rarely gave away a weakness. Not by expression or word. But tonight she'd seen and learned so much of who he was she found herself wanting to know more. Was he really saying that they could… no he couldn't possibly think they could be more than this. He kissed her and released her wrists to press his palms flat against hers and allow their fingers to intertwine. He kissed her again. His lips and tongue were more persuasive than she cared to admit. Could it be possible that she was starting to fall for this man? Their kiss was slow and exploratory. His tongue would sweep deep then chase hers in the most tantalizing way. She found herself humming. His lips pulled away from hers and began to graze over her chin, teasingly slow down her neck as he released her hands and went lower.

At first he brushed her pert nipple, flicked his tongue at it, then nipped the swollen bud and enveloped her areola in his mouth. She gripped the sheets and her back bowed from the bed. He sucked hard, soft, slow and moved his tongue in circular motions until her hips were thrusting upward into his pelvis, demanding more.

Nothing prepared her for where he'd take her next.

Romano lifted bringing the sheet with him. He grasped her ankles and pulled her legs apart. She held the position for him remaining perfectly still. He took his pillow and eased it underneath her lower back to cause her pelvis to tilt just a degree higher. He positioned her legs, spread with knees bent. He again lowered, the shifting of the mattress indicated so. She wished there was light. She would love to see his head go below. He slid his tongue between her folds and made it flutter, tickling her clit. His thick fingers parted her outer lips.

Harmony groaned.

He pressed his nose, chin and mouth down there and seemed to rub them all against her wetness. "Oh my…." She cried out and heat tremors rippled between her thighs igniting her core to liquid. He tunneled his tongue into her, swirled his lips, sucked her clitoris painfully slow. It was killing her. Every time the tension built in her pelvis for her climatic release he'd change tactics.

"Please... Please...," she begged.

Romano shook his head, which rubbed his stubble cheeks against her inner thighs and burrowed his face deeper. Harmony breathed deeply to slow down the quickening flutter of her heartbeat. She feared her chest would explode. He bit down lightly on her clitoris. A shudder racked her body. Her breasts heaved, the tips grew impossibly tight. He licked her from bottom to top and her thighs trembled. Deep in her core, tension was winding, tighter and tighter.

"PLEASE!!!" she nearly screamed.

He was on her in a flash. His penetration so swift he nearly collapsed on top of her. It took a brief second but he began to move. "Breathe, beautiful, breathe...." He instructed and she realized she had forgotten how. He gave her several thrusts with his hips working in circular fashion. She clawed at his back and licked the sweat from his broad shoulder. Not only was she breathing but she was loving him back with everything in her. Surrendering completely. For weeks she watched him, watch her. Some nights she felt the invisible ties through her singing. With him in her arms, she believed in the connection she could never truly conceive. Vinnie Romano had made opening her heart again, possible.

When she woke she knew she was alone. She felt the loss of his presence instantly. Sitting up in the darkness she listened to her surroundings. She didn't hear anything. She crept from the bed and opened the door. Silence greeted her. Harmony quickly found her dress and zipped it up. She had no concept of time but she sensed it was still pretty early. When she returned to the front of the cottage she found the fire was nicely lit. She rubbed heat into her arms, craving a bath.

"Vinnie?" she called out, and got no response. She headed to the door and it was flung open. Vinnie walked in with fish tied to a string. He looked a bit surprised to see her standing there.

"Hi," she said.

"I thought you were sleep." He mumbled closing the door.

"I was, is that breakfast?" she asked.

"Can you clean them?" He headed to the kitchen table and dropped the fish on top. She nodded her answer and her stomach churned. Her Grams taught her many things. Often they would visit the country and have to fish and hunt with her cousins to catch dinner. She most definitely knew how to skin a trout, and her mouth watered over the prospect.

"We got running water here. I've got some heating over the fire if you want to warm your bathwater," he said, his cheeks flushed and eyes cast down. It was very considerate of him but he didn't look comfortable with his generosity.

"Vinnie?"

"Got business to take care of. I'll be gone for an hour or so. Then… I'll come back."

She nodded but he wouldn't see her agreement with his back turned. So she approached him. "About last night."

"You need anything else? I can bring some things in from the main house. Or you could go up and…"

"No. I'll take a bath and start breakfast. Then when you get back we can talk."

His brows furrowed and she had to stifle a smile. The awkwardness between them was new. It was mostly on his part. He didn't seem to know how to address her in the light of day. She decided to take the pressure off of him. "Talk about Willie. How we can find my brother."

"Oh, yes, I might have news soon." He leaned forward and gave her a quick peck to the cheek. But she caught his hand. She pulled him toward her.

"Is that the best you can do?"

The tension in his jaw lessened and his eyes softened. Gathering her into his arms he held her snugly to his chest with his hands locked against her spine. His head lowered and so did his lashes. He recaptured her lips with a demandingly sweet morning kiss. The man needed a shave, a bath, but the velvet warmth of his kiss was near perfect. His lips left hers to nibble on her earlobe before he spoke. "I'll clean up at the main house, do you have something to change into?"

"I think so, yes."

"Good. I'll see you soon."

Romano withdrew and stopped at the open door. He glanced back at her once more. His expression was tense, his eyes dark and probing. She almost spoke to him before he winked, turned and left. She stood there for several seconds waiting for the sweet feeling of his kiss to fade. The thought of his return made her heart kick into higher gear. Her feet seemed to be drifting on clouds when she forced herself to walk away. Harmony recognized her affliction. She was falling for the bastard. Any relationship with him was doomed to end in disaster. Right now she'd focus on the positive fact that he was letting his guard down and just maybe she'd be able to find a way out of this with Willie.

Near the sofa she found her cloth bag. She fished out the clothing she was able to pack and breathed a sigh of relief. She grabbed two of her dresses and underwear. She usually kept a few outfits at The Cotton. Harmony thought of Milo. By now he knew she was missing and it was probably making him desperate. "I might need to get to that main house. If they have running water they may have a phone." Harmony figured she could have an operator ring The Cotton and get a message to him. It was definitely worth a shot.

She found the bathroom and ran her bathwater. Then she added some hot water from the cast iron pot over the fire. It warmed the water a bit but not much. Her bath was quick and thorough. She felt like sex and sweat was embedded in her skin. She even located a brush and managed to style her hair in a manageable fashion, using the few bobby-pins she had left to pin the back locks up from her neck. The ordeal with cleaning the stinky fish didn't go as easy. Skinning and gutting them was quite a chore with the dull knife. She switched to the one she had brought from The Cotton and managed it. She tossed a few logs into the stove and got the blaze hot enough to drop some olive oil in a cast iron skillet and fry up fish coated in Swan's Down Flour.

Romano had kept his promise. He returned just over two hours later, shaven and changed. She had just finished setting the table. She didn't have much to offer with the fish and he didn't seem to mind. Instead he ate, constantly lifting his gaze up to peek at her.

"Good?"

"My Songbird can sing and cook?" He smiled.

She wrinkled her nose and then smirked. "I see you'll have to learn that I have many talents."

"And I will learn them all." He forked a hefty bite and gave her a sexy smile.

"Everything go okay?" she asked. "You hear anything about my brother?"

"He's not my only priority Harmony."

The abrupt reply stung. She forced a smile. "Of course. It's just, I thought he'd have turned up by now."

"We haven't found him. Antonio isn't back yet, so I'm waiting to hear more from him. He went into Harlem last night. He's looking for your brother. I won't give up. He's out there and Harlem isn't big enough to hide him from me."

"What if he's left Harlem?" The thought and words just popped out of her mouth.

Romano stopped chewing. "Do you think he did?"

"I'm not sure, does the other house have a phone? Can I place a call?"

"Call who?" Romano stopped mid-chew. His focus narrowed on her and his lips pressed into a tight line.

"Milo Stevens. He's in Fletch Henderson's band at The Cotton. He and I are friends. He keeps tabs on things. Milo might be able to help. My friend Paulette too, she knows stuff and people."

"What kind of friends?" Romano's mouth took on an unpleasant twist. His expression stilled and grew serious. She took a deep breath and adjusted her smile.

"Huh?"

"What kind of friends are you and Milo?" He frowned with cold fury.

"Why does that matter?"

"The answer's no. Like I said I'll take care of it."

"You can't take care of it. You don't know what you're doing."

He slammed his fist down on the table hard. She jumped. He pointed a fork at her to state his warning but didn't. The utensil was tossed back to his plate and he rose from the table as if to leave. "Don't do this! I'm sorry. Milo's just a friend. He means nothing to me. Vinnie, you said you wanted me to trust you then you have to do the same. He could be of some help."

Romano stormed over and turned her chair to face him. She saw the seriousness set a hard frown to his face and held her tongue. "Let's get something straight. You don't tell me how this works. In fact you don't dictate anything to me. If I say something...."

"No!" She shouted up into his face. A momentary look of disbelief flashed in his eyes. "No! No! NO! You won't treat me like you treat them." She pointed to the door. Her voice now shaky still held a hint of firm determination. "Not after last night. Too late Vinnie, we both know we're beyond it."

He smacked his forehead with the flat side of his hand. "What you think, a few sweet words between us and now you decide on how this works?"

"You said you wouldn't hurt me. You said to trust you…"

"Then do it dammit!"

"It don't work like that Vinnie. It's got to go both ways. I won't hurt you either. I'm not trying to tell you how to do things. I'm trying to help. Isn't that why you brought me here? To figure out where my brother is and get whatever the hell it is he stole from you back?" She stood and dropped her hands to her hips. "Do you want to know what your problem is?"

"A mouthy woman?" he scoffed.

She clenched her fists, but tried to keep her temper in check. "I think you're jealous."

"Bullshit!" he laughed.

"That's it isn't it? Your pride! I tell you I got a friend named Milo who can help us find Willie and you act all tough guy on me."

"Trust me Songbird this is no act."

"Whatever it is I ain't buyin' what you sellin'! This has to end *our* way, and your brother isn't the person to help Willie. I don't trust him." Her stomach sank when his glare narrowed and grew intense. She was pushing his buttons and it could backfire. "I don't trust anybody but you Vinnie. Can't you see that now? If you ain't out there lookin' for him personally he's dead. I feel it in my gut." Harmony placed her hand flat to her tummy and approached him but he paced away. "What is it? What has you so… un-agreeable? Let's not fight. Why don't you hear me out? Or do I have it wrong Vinnie? You ashamed of what you said to me in bed, now that the sun come up? You ashamed of what you feel for me. Is that it?"

"No."

"Prove it." She challenged. "You all talk Vinnie Romano. I ain't seen no action. I've proved it. I give you what you want, when you want, and how you want it. What does it mean to you? Anything?"

"Get your coat." He answered.

"Why? We ain't done talking."

"Come with me. Now. I'll show you how much I trust you. And I'll show them too."

Without delay she did as she was told. Harmony eased her arms into her coat and buttoned the front. Locating her charcoal-grey bell shaped cloche hat she situated it on her head hoping she looked respectable. He waited at the open door patiently. When she joined him he immediately captured her hand in his. "My friend died." he said. "We're going to his funeral."

The idea of him presenting her to others while holding her hand was a terrifying yet exhilarating thought. Hell they could be arrested, though she doubted any lawman within miles would dare try. The rumors and innuendos would reach Sugar Hill and she'd lose the respect of her friends. Paulette would probably be the only one who would dare to be seen with her.

"You got a problem with us Songbird? Going the distance… with me?"

She glanced down at their joined hands. "It's you that should have the problem Vinnie. Us in public, it's illegal ain't it?"

Romano frowned. "Who told you that?"

"Everyone knows it. What we done is against the law. Probably against God. Coloreds and whites ain't supposed to mix it up like this."

"Not true. In New York it's legal for us to mix, hell even marry, Vermont, Connecticut, Wisconsin too."

She was floored. Stunned beyond speech, but she summoned her voice. "How do you know this?"

"Looked it up once," he mumbled, appearing a bit uncomfortable.

"You looked up where it was legal to marry a colored woman?"

"Enough questions, let's go."

She pulled back on his hand. He shot her a look and she lost her nerve. She wanted to know more about what he had just shared. Why would a man like him care where he could marry a colored girl? But she tried another tactic. "What your men think of you is important. What will they think if you parade me around?"

"Fuck them. It's not as important as what you think."

The eyes of Vinnie Romano were compelling, magnetic, but it was his words that reached far deeper. She decided she'd save her questions for another time. Right now he needed her. "You lost a friend?" she asked.

"One of my best men, Nunzio," he answered, squeezing her hand gently.

She reached over with her free hand and touched his face. Harmony rose on her toes to extend her lips and brush them against his. "I'm sorry sweetie."

There was a lethal calmness in his amber brown eyes. "Make it better." His hoarse whisper demolished her doubts of his sincerity. There was a silent plea in his eyes. "Stop fighting me and just let it be. It's going to be a helluva day Harmony."

She nodded. "Sure Vinnie, I don't have a problem."

Romano dropped his Fedora on his head. They walked out into the brisk morning air. Harmony shivered a bit. Despite the temperature, sunlight buttered the land he claimed as his own. They started through the fragrant long grass. Weeds had yellowed during the first frost, but now that they were near the end of winter she could see new blooms budding. He didn't seem bothered by the weather, or to notice anything about the clear blue-sky day. He wore his hat but not his coat. Only his shirt and vest shielded him from the rising winds. She held his hand and the warmth of his palm pressed flat against hers felt natural, almost perfect.

A hot ache grew in the back of her throat. She tried to settle her fears, but with Willie missing the last thing she wanted to do was attend a funeral. "Where are we going?" She dared to ask.

Romano pulled her closer with a tug to her hand. They walked with their shoulders touching. She kept glancing over to his face, looking for an explanation for the path he'd chosen. They were headed away from the main house and cars. The clearing revealed his troop of men. Harmony counted thirteen in total. They gathered, smoking and chatting in small groups as two others piled shovelfuls of dirt on a mound. Every eye lifted and locked on her first. Some of the men exchanged puzzled looks to see their union, by the holding of hands. Romano didn't seem to notice or care. He continued to walk her toward them.

"Are we ready?" he asked.

"Yes boss." Answered her kidnapper, she believed his name was Leftie. He glared directly at her. There was such blatant hatred in his stare she felt her own pride swell in response. She tossed her chin upward and walked at Romano's side with confidence.

"We were waiting for you." Leftie spoke, and then spat a dark stream of tobacco moving the wad in his cheek to the other side of his mouth. He swiped the spittle from his bottom lip with the back of his hand.

"Then let's get this thing over with." Romano grumbled.

Harmony scanned the solemn faces. Her gaze lowered to the mound of earth. One of the men came forward and made the sign of the cross before him. He said a prayer in Italian and she bowed her head in respect. She wondered who Nunzio was and how he died. Half way through the prayer she stole a look over to her guy. His head was bowed and his eyes squeezed shut so tightly his face looked flushed and strained. She covered their joined hands with her other, and stroked it. Romano's eyes opened and slipped over to her. Harmony gave him a sweet smile. He managed one as well. Soon it was done. Men walked off. Romano never let her hand go. In fact he squeezed it painfully tight through the prayer and only loosened his grip when the praying stopped.

"Vinnie! Vinnie I'm sorry." Antonio emerged from the forest. "Aw fuck. Is that Nunzio?"

Antonio removed his hat. He had an old scar on his face that seemed to stretch longer when his features went slack with emotion. However, the most recent bruises were ghastly. Suddenly he was aware of her stares. He looked a bit surprised to see her holding his brother's hand, but he covered it and focused on Romano. "I was out all night trying to… handling business. I thought Nunzio would make it. Damn."

"Not now Antonio. The meeting's up at the house. See me in twenty minutes." Romano tugged on her hand and pulled her away. She glanced back at Antonio and caught the look of irritation over being dismissed.

"Your brother doesn't seem happy."

"Well he can join the club. Today isn't a day to be happy."

"Nunzio was someone you cared about?" Harmony pressed, keeping up the pace and walking at his side. He didn't answer. She looked up to see a caravan of cars driving along the dirt path out of the forested trail. More men than she cared to see. "How did Nunzio die? What happened to your brother's face? Dammit Vinnie, would you look at me!" she snatched her hand free.

"Things aren't as I planned. But they will be. Stop fussing over nothing woman. I want you up at the main house with me today."

"No." She took a panicked step back. She could deal with him one on one, but the idea of being held up in a two-story house made of logs with murderers and mobsters turned her stomach. "I can just wait for you in the cottage. I'm comfortable there."

"I'm not hiding you like some dirty secret." Romano softened instead of hardened to her refusal. She could see him trying to ease her fears, again, and she felt horrible about it. Here it is he just lost a friend and she was behaving like a brat. Harmony cast her gaze to the arriving men. Her fears weren't totally irrational. The only person keeping her safe and alive was him.

"Hey." He touched her chin and forced her gaze to return to his. "What difference does it make now, everyone has seen you? I got some things to settle, and your brother to find. You'll come to the cottage and stay with Mabel. When my meeting is over I'll come for you."

"Mabel? The maid? She's here?"

"She is now." Romano cast his gaze ahead and Harmony saw the old black maid get out of a fancy black car she drove. Her mouth nearly dropped open. Did Romano buy her the car? Why would he buy something that extravagant for a servant? The maid walked slowly up the steps of the main house. A young man at her side aided her as if she were his grandmother.

"So it's done. No more discussion."

"Whatever you say, Vinnie."

He bracketed her face in both hands and forced her to maintain his stare. "Bear with me a little longer. And don't sass me in front of my men. *Capice?*"

"Your men don't want me here. I could see it on their faces."

"My men want what I want. That's how this here thing goes."

"I have a job. Mr. Madden will fire me."

"You're mine now. He'll show you respect."

"Are you serious? You can't possibly mean you want other people to know." She lowered her voice and stepped in closer to him. He continued to cradle her face in his hands, and she placed hers on his waist. "I'm tired of living my life outside of God's law. I just want to find my brother and get things back to normal again."

He brushed his lips over hers. She quickly turned her head to see if anyone saw. The man named Leftie was the only one to the front of the main house. He stood on the third step and flicked his cigarette, watching them. Romano calmly released her from his embrace then pulled her along. He walked her inside. She heard the rustle and grumbling voices of men in the room to the left and silence when she passed through the hall. He leaned in closer to speak against her ear. "Go upstairs. I'll send Mabel."

She nodded. Quickly she climbed the stairs refusing to look back.

The men seated stood when he entered the room. There wasn't a pleasant smile in the bunch. Everyone remained silent and waited for him to speak. The last to arrive was his brother. He noisily stomped in and dropped in a chair, a lack of respect that didn't go unnoticed. Antonio sensed the impatience over his tardiness from the tense silent glares of the men around him. He cleared his throat.

Speaking clear and precise, he addressed Antonio first. "Mickey Collins?"

"He's arming his men. The well's dry from the Irish and the Germans. It's our move Vinnie."

After a long pause Romano switched his gaze to Leftie. The tall brooding man gave a single nod that he delivered the special package to Mickey. He'd paid a visit to the barn before dawn while his Songbird slept. They'd brought the horses back in and cleaned up the blood. He had a full report on the special delivery he sent to Mickey. The gauntlet had been thrown down.

"I called you here because I know you all can be trusted. The time has come for us to join together and take back the streets we divided a year ago. Who among me wants a bit control?"

Several men exchanged looks, however, the first to speak was Ignacio. "A year ago you walked away from us Vinnie. After the truce with the Five Points Gang, you told everyone to be their own man. Now you start a war over a few crates of booze and we're supposed to follow you?"

"It's not about the booze, it's about the respect. I earned it with each man in this room. I honored it by not holding any grudges. New York is a pretty big state. Big enough for each of you to strike out on your own, who was I to tell you not to try? But we all know that's not how this works. No matter who it is, the Irish, the Germans, the Italians, the Jews, even the Blacks, every crew needs a leader. That's the mistake we made. Those of you who want a family can join me and create one."

"Are you talking about a new *Mafioso*? Outside the families?" Gino asked, his Sicilian accent so thick most could barely understand a word. However a grumble of disbelief ripped across the room.

"We're descendants from farmers, fisherman and you…" Ignacio glanced to Antonio then back to Vinnie. "It's your birthright as the son of Don Romano. Why do you think we followed you in the first place? There are rules and sacrifices Vinnie. Are you sure?"

No one spoke. No one dared breathe until Romano nodded that he was indeed sure.

Ignacio licked his dry lips, then swallowed hard. He turned and addressed the room. "Then here it is boys, if Mickey Collins has stolen from Vinnie Romano then he has taken from all of us, and we'll make him pay." Ignacio's head swung left. He bowed it in respect then stepped closer. He kissed Romano on the right and then the left cheek. The others exchanged looks. Gino was next to show the same respect. Romano glanced to Leftie as each old member of the Black Hand came to him and honored his leadership. Leftie tipped his head, signifying that a new reign had begun.

Harmony found the room much lovelier than the dark cramped cottage. To start off she'd never seen so much space given to a bedroom. The bed faced two double glass doors. When she approached and pulled them open, clean air and brilliant rays from the sun washed over her. From every vantage point trees stretched tall to the sky and the landscape flowed beyond the forest to sloping hills in the distance. It was quite stunning, causing her heart to patter faster and faster under her breath. She wished Vinnie had come with her so she could view it with him. The thought of him warmed her inside as she recalled the paintings he'd done of grassy hills and open parkland like the one before her. Maybe this was why he was so inspired and reminded of home.

"Nice ain't it?" A voice spoke behind her.

When she turned she was face to face with Mabel. The woman wrinkled her nose in disapproval and locked her gaze on Harmony. Mabel wore a matronly sky blue dress with a white lacy apron over it. Her hair was smoothed back from her face into a neat chignon, with graying temples that gave a hint of her age. Full in the bust and hips, she had soft features and Harmony could tell probably once upon a time she was quite striking.

The maid glared at her, crossing her arms under her large bosom. Harmony nervously fixed her hair. She didn't look bad. Hell she was positive she looked a hell of a lot more respectable than she did when she was first brought there. Still she felt her cheeks warm with shame under the scrutiny. "Hi. Mabel right?"

"Hmph." The woman said and turned to point to the linens she had brought up. "Fix your own bed honey. I'm sure you know how."

"Wait a sec." Harmony stepped forward. "We got off on the wrong foot. My name is Harmony."

"I know who you are." Mabel spat the words back at her. She dropped her curled fists on her round hips. "Poor Eloise. Poor, poor Eloise!" Mabel put her hand to her heart and raised the other above her head in some type of sad homage. Harmony drew back. The maid's eyes flashed open and locked on her once more. "Eloise is turning over in her grave to see you now."

The mention of her Grams sent her mind spinning. Did she know Mabel? Had they met before? Mabel either sensed her distress or the deep shadow of shame was written all over her face, because she pounced like a spider after his prey caught in his web. "First you start singing at that devil's den, The Cotton. They don't even let colored folk in that God forsaken place. And those yella girls that work there think they some new kind of special brand of Negro cause they can shake their tails for money. Call themselves tans when they nothing but jezebels. And if to make matters worse, here you come, sneaking around at night with Mr. Romano. Up in his room howling to the moon like some kind of bitch in heat, for what he doing to ya. And for what? To become his whore?"

"Who the hell do you think you are? You wait a minute." Harmony stammered.

"No you wait! Your grandmother and my mother grew up in Slimwood, Mississippi barely escaping the sharecropper's fields." Mabel stepped to her and Harmony drew in her trembling bottom lip, trapped, by the raw anger and disgust fixed upon her. "I was fifteen but I remember it all. We damn near walked and swam for six months until we made it here to Negro heaven." Mabel scoffed. "Eloise did the entire trip fully pregnant with your mother in her belly. Do you have any idea what her struggle was? Do you?"

"No ma'am," Harmony said softly.

"Just like your selfish ma. She didn't even bother to come back to see Eloise buried. Your grandmother had her heart and tears all prayed up on you child, and look at you now. Take a hard look at what you done become."

"Now you just hold on there Miss Mabel cause it's my turn to speak. No need to recount my sins to me. I've lived each and every one of them. And there's no need to tell me of my Grams' sacrifices because they're burned here." She touched her heart. "Where were you when I had to bury her alone? I don't remember you or any of her so-called friends lending my Grams a hand or a kind word when my ma run off."

"We all struggle," Mabel said.

"Maybe so. But ain't no need to judge me, because you ain't God. What I do and what I done is my burden, and I owe no one an explanation for it."

"You owe yourself more than to be some white man's whore." Mabel tossed back.

Harmony laughed. The bitter tears dropped from her cheeks, and she wiped them away, smiling. "Is that so? Because being his mammy works so much better for you?"

Mabel's face pinched in anger.

"And for the record." Harmony sniffed, tossing her chin up and glaring down her nose at the self-righteous witch. "Vinnie and I are more than just friends. Wasn't me howling to the moon, that you heard honey. It was him."

"Silly girl, you ain't special," Mabel said shaking her head.

"You ain't my Grams so you can't convict me. You ain't my minister so you can't preach to me. Take your advice and sanctimonious attitude out of here! Get out!"

Mabel turned and walked away. Harmony could barely remain standing. She backed away until the bed hit the back of her legs. She dropped on the mattress shaking with grief. She didn't cry. Didn't know if she could summon tears, and the pain she carried over the painful reminder of broken promises to her Grams wouldn't release her. Now what was she to do?

"Vinnie, I know where the boy is," Antonio whispered in Romano's ear. The others argued over the best tactical advantage they could take with Collins boxed in between South Street and Pier 7. His gaze swung left and locked on his brother's. He'd been waiting all day for news of the boy. He had begun to believe he'd find him dead. Especially, when he considered he was the only missing link between Mickey and where his booze had been stolen away to. If Antonio had found the kid then Romano had every intention of reuniting the boy with Harmony. The idea of the happiness the reunion would bring to his Songbird made him feel a bit of warmth himself. Harmony would be so grateful she'd be his without complaint. He could probably set her up here, and who knew what the future between them could bring.

Romano rose from his chair. A hush fell across the room. "Pay a visit to Chief O'Brien and make sure the night is ours. No cops in or out of South Street. I agree with Ignacio. We will take out his three warehouses first. Burn them to the ground. You must move in quickly, on foot. They'll see cars coming and be ready for them. If you can save the booze try, if not fuck it, it's not where Mickey is storing his supply. I'm sure of it."

"It's not just business now boss." Gio interrupted. "We need to send a message. In blood."

"Find his daughter and her husband. I believe they'll be hiding in Brooklyn. Remember we don't touch the women or children. Make sure the husband gets what Mickey Collins deserves. Understood?"

A few questions were asked and answered before every man in the room nodded in agreement. The room began to clear. Antonio paced impatiently to be heard as others approached Romano and expressed their personal desires within this new allegiance. After several minutes it was just him and his brother.

"Where is he?"

"There's this Negro that plays the horn at The Cotton. He's hidden the boy, tucked him away at St. Mary's. Father Michaels is soft on the coloreds, from what I'm told. I've already paid him and the nuns a visit. He denied knowing where the kid is, but I'm sure he's there."

"His name Milo?" Romano asked.

"That's him. Yes! He's the one keeping him hid. I followed him last night after I got a tip. He disappeared inside the church, but went in through the rectory side doors. Stayed there for a while and then left. We'll have the kid tonight. The services during the day would make it messy if we go for him now."

Romano nodded. "Good. Remember I want him alive. And don't you disrespect Father Michaels, handle it discreetly. Draw no attention to us in this, we clear? On second thought make a donation in my name."

Antonio nodded. "Everything's copasetic Vinnie. Thing is, something this delicate I think it'll go over better if you and I go in and get the kid. While the boys take out Collins. What you think?"

The request made sense. Romano paced a bit thinking it through. He stopped and glanced up. "This Milo person? What's his relationship with the boy?"

"Not sure," Antonio shrugged. "Why?"

"Strange. If he was hiding the boy and he's friends with Harmony then why not tell her?"

"Who the fuck knows Vinnie. We get the kid we get the jump on where the booze is. You're right to think it's not at the pier. The boy knows where it is. Collins will be busy with holding off our guys. It's the best plan."

"Okay. Not a word of this. You and I will take care of the boy."

Antonio grinned. "Sure Vinnie, whatever you say."

Time slowed to a painful crawl, each minute hammered in the memory of the past. She could feel every grievous emotion tenfold. Her breath quickened and her cheeks felt warm with shame. She gulped hard, hot tears slipped and she quickly wiped them away. Harmony rose from the bed on shaky legs. Her embarrassment had now turned to raw fury. How dare that woman say the things she said to her? She never wanted to disgrace her Grams or herself. She just wanted to find a place in a world where a woman like her often had none. Mabel was wrong. Hell maybe even Grams was wrong. Singing at The Cotton wasn't her downfall. Jazz had provided her with a mindless solidity that helped camouflage the deep despair and loneliness in her heart after losing all the people she loved.

Harmony inhaled slowly and calmed herself. At first she'd dismissed the giddy feeling of contentment she felt in the night when she slept in Romano's arms. Not anymore. The man had been straight from the start and he treated her kinder than Mabel and half the others who turned their nose up when she walked down the street. He loved her voice, her body. Hell he even said he loved her feet. Harmony laughed out loud until her spirit broke and she began to sob. To hell with Mabel and any judgmental witches like her. She wasn't going to carry shame over being who she was anymore.

"Hi beautiful."

"Vinnie?" She turned to find him standing in the doorway. She sniffed and wiped under her eyes to make sure they were dry. He walked in and she smiled brightly. "Your business done already?"

"Not quite. I had to come check on you. Mabel get you settled in?"

Harmony nodded. She tried to sidestep him but he drew her into his arms. "Were you crying?"

"Huh? No. I'm just, emotional. Missing Willie."

"That's the second reason why I came upstairs. I got the best news Doll. Gonna make you smile."

"You do?"

He smirked. "I'll have your brother here tonight. Plan to bring him in myself."

A cry of relief broke from her lips. "You found him? You found Willie?"

"Didn't I tell you I would?"

Harmony threw her arms around him and kissed him passionately. She felt the warm glow of joy spread through her within his kiss. She could devour him whole, with her body humming with excitement. Romano chuckled and she peppered his face with more kisses. "Yes! Yes! But how did you do it? Where is he?" She lowered her arms. Romano kept her snug in his embrace. He dropped his forehead to hers when he spoke.

"This Milo person, you sure he's a friend?"

"Milo? Yes, he was Lewis's best friend. Why?"

"My men say he's the one that hid your brother, been keeping him at St. Mary's. Now why would he do that and not tell you?"

Harmony pushed until she broke free of his embrace. "That's a lie. Milo wouldn't do that, he's not that type of guy. He wanted to help me find Willie. Your men are wrong!"

"I got it from a reliable source."

"I don't care! It's a lie!"

"Harmony, listen."

"No. It just can't be. Milo is like family to us both. Even if he helpin' Willie he wouldn't lie to me. Not after he knew I was going…"

She stopped herself. She couldn't look him in the eye and say the rest. Milo knew she would go as far as to sleep with Vinnie Romano to find Willie. He was sick with jealousy over it. She saw it all over his face. He would have never let her go through with it if he had Willie. "It's not true," she said sadly.

"Harmony," he grabbed her hand. "Slow down. Neither of us can be sure of the man's motives right now. Maybe he did it to protect you both. Sometimes the less everyone knows the better. Either way I'll bring your brother to you personally. Keep my promise." He kissed her hand. "Does that make you happy?"

It took considerable effort to keep from squealing with joy then frustration. She couldn't figure Milo on this one. She had no clue what was going through Willie's head either. None of it made sense.

One look into her lover's eyes and she saw how much he wanted to please her so she let the disappointment in Milo go. Her hand went up softly over his chest; her face drew closer to his. "Yes, that makes me happy, Vinnie. Thank you so much," she said with her mouth only centimeters from his.

"I want to take you out on my land," he breathed, his gaze lowered to her lips and he licked his own. "We can have lunch. How does that sound?"

Being so close to him forced her heartbeat to skyrocket. "But you said you'd go get Willie? I need to see him Vinnie. I need to see him now."

"Tonight Songbird," He touched her cheek and all the blood in her body seemed to rush to that spot. "It's best we pick him up after dark. Besides the day is nice, it's warm. We can take my horse. She hasn't been ridden in a while. Mabel has fixed us lunch."

"Yes. I'd like that. I, ah, I need to get some fresh air."

He withdrew and she could breathe with ease again. He walked towards the door then paused and cast her another one of his half-smiles. He really was pleased with himself.

"Are you sure Milo was the one to keep Willie hidden?"

"Positive. I'll bring Milo here myself and make him answer for it."

"I still think maybe I should go with you to get Willie…"

"No." Romano said firmly. "Things are a bit tense on the streets now. I need to know you're safe. You stay here where you belong."

Harmony frowned but nodded her obedience. He winked. "Good girl. I've already told Mabel to fix us a lunch. You pick it up and meet me out near the barn."

"Okay, Vinnie."

She watched him go. Harmony's spirits lifted. The blow to her heart thanks to Mabel's cruel words still stung. But she had hope. That's what she found with Vinnie Romano. Hope. Wrong or right, she'd made her peace with it. Milo's betrayal hurt deeply, but if he had kept Willie safe through all of this she'd find a way to forgive. Her gaze returned to the open doors and the landscape outside. This place reminded her of new beginnings. Maybe after things settled down she'd go West. She heard the frontier was full of Negroes trying to start new lives. A new start would do her and Willie some good. Her stomach fluttered at the thought of leaving Vinnie. He'd never leave New York, not for her. Even if he did, they could never have a real future, though the idea of it did make her smile. *Harmony, stop, the man isn't yours. Not really.*

"Can I have a word Boss?" Leftie asked. He stood at the bottom of the stairs waiting. A tight, firm look of disapproval hardened his features. Romano nodded that they'd speak freely in the room off to the right. When he followed Leftie in, he removed his pocket watch and checked the time. He'd have three maybe four hours with her before he'd leave with Antonio to bring in her brother. It would be enough time.

"I trust you. I always have, even when I didn't agree with you."

"What's this about?"

"Things are moving fast. You got a good two hundred men rolling out on Mickey Collins tonight. When it's done things are going to change. It's a big move."

"And?" Romano lowered to his chair. He didn't see the point of rehashing his plans. He'd learned the ways of leading with a firm hand from his father. Though he'd never be that bastard, he wouldn't explain his decisions to anyone. Leftie was fishing for something and Romano didn't like it.

"So that makes you a leader, and men who lead need to be careful of their image. Careful to remind others of the balance of things, always focused."

"You saying I'm not?"

"I'm saying the Negro woman has been a distraction, almost as bad as Annie was. And we both know how badly that ended. Antonio tells me that you found her brother, and you plan to pick him up personally? Tonight of all nights? What's she really doing here Boss?"

The question caught Romano by surprise. He knew Leftie would be concerned about the ramifications of the war he declared on Mickey Collins. There would be some fallout. If he started taking over Mickey's territory it would rouse the suspicions of the Gambinos, The Five Points Gang. How Harmony fit into his plans should be of no concern to anyone but him. Though the comparison of Harmony's need to save her brother and Annie's heartbreak after he destroyed hers, was not lost on him.

"I mean no disrespect, but it's our business. These men are gong to risk their lives for you, and the lives of their families. You have to consider what your position means. It can't be serious between you two? Right?"

"Harmony Jones is here, she'll be here tomorrow, and she'll stay here for as long as I like." He ground the words out between his teeth. "That's all you need to know. That's all the men need to know."

Leftie paced away. Romano glared, watching him struggle to choose the correct words. It didn't matter. He'd already crossed the line. "All I'm saying is tonight we need you with us. And tomorrow when the gun smoke clears, we need the same. To be with us."

"Harmony is off limits. To all of you! You understand?"

"Perfectly." Leftie said.

CHAPTER EIGHT

The Lion's heart...

Determined, Harmony entered the kitchen with her head high. Mabel had caught her off guard the first time, but this time she was ready for the meddlesome woman. The smell of baked bread, roasted meat and melted cheese made her mouth water. Mabel stood at the stove stirring something in a pot. She didn't bother to turn around. Harmony let her gaze take a complete sweep of the kitchen. Mabel must have spent many a day cooking in this place because it had a homey lived in feel to it.

The walls were lemon yellow and the kitchen cabinets and countertops ivory white. There was a knit dishcloth that matched the tablecloths hanging from the door of the stove. Her gaze fell upon the icy pitcher of lemonade with large round slices of lemons on the table and she started to approach.

"The lunch he wanted for you both is on the counter, I placed a blanket at the bottom of the basket also." Mabel spoke.

Clearing her throat Harmony went to a cabinet and located a cup. She returned to the pitcher feeling completely parched. "I, ah, I want to talk to you," she said as she poured.

"You said your peace girl."

"I need to apologize."

The old woman stopped stirring and cast her gaze over her shoulder. Harmony forced a polite smile to her face. She drank down the lemonade in three deep gulps. "I'm not apologizing for who I am, or for the choices I've made since my Grams died. I'm apologizing because I shouldn't have yelled at you. It was disrespectful."

Mabel dried her hands on her apron and walked toward her. Her skin glistened with beads of perspiration. She had slender hands to be such a stout woman, and a heavy bosom that was proportional to her wide hips. "I'm sorry too. I shouldn't have spoken to you the way I did. Thing is, when I saw you with Vinnie…when I saw you two, it just made me sad."

"Don't be. Vinnie and I are friends. I know that's hard for you to believe but we are."

"You sure about that honey? I heard him in there just a minute ago yelling at his men about respecting his choice in you. Vinnie Romano is a complicated man. Been with him for many years, seen what losing Annie did to him. He hadn't brought another woman home, and never here, until you."

"Oh that doesn't mean anything," Harmony said with a soft chuckle.

Mabel narrowed her eyes and dropped her hands on her hips. "Open your eyes. He's not like the rest of them, and that makes him even more dangerous because he won't play by the rules. It ain't never dawned on you why he ain't bothered by your differences?" Mabel shook her head with a look of disgust. "Besides, a colored girl ain't safe in a house full of these kinds of men! But I see you prancing around here like it's the most natural thing."

"I did no such thing. I didn't plan to come here, he forced me."

"He forced you to hold his hand out in them fields? Force you to kiss him the way I seen it?"

Harmony chewed on her bottom lip and averted her gaze. Mabel released a patient sigh. "The man barely smiled around her, and he stopped smiling altogether when she run off. You been around him for what, days, a week or so, and I hear the man laughing?"

"You think I'm trouble because I made him laugh?" Harmony wrinkled her nose and rolled her eyes.

"I think you trouble because the more you make him feel anything for you the harder it will be for him when this game of yours ends. And a heartbroken Vinnie Romano ain't a man none of us want to see again."

"It's no game Mabel, I'm a hundred percent. And the truth is I do care for him. More than I should I suppose when I think on our short history. I can't explain it, but you know him, like you said he's different. That don't make me dense, I know the score. When this is over we will go back to our lives."

Mabel looked her over. Harmony stood ramrod straight and matched her stare. The silence between them lengthened and for a second she considered the conversation over. When she turned to collect the basket Mabel spoke up again. Her voice absent of judgment was soft and almost pleading.

"He has a lion's heart." Mabel warned. "Showed it to you didn't he? Down in that cottage he don't let nobody go in. You think that soft side of him the true side of him? Maybe it is, maybe it ain't. Don't change what he is and what you two will never be. Thing is Vinnie don't think in those terms."

"This conversation is over. I'm done discussing it with you. What I have to say I'll say to him."

"You'll never be her!" Mabel shouted blocking her pass.

"I suppose not," Harmony said, a bit stunned by the tears in Mabel's eyes. "Thing is I don't want to be her, and to be honest I don't think Vinnie wants it either. Since I'm sure I'm nothing like her."

Mabel managed a smile. "You look like your mother. She used to give Eloise the blues, a stubborn little girl, a stubborn woman. But you different, I sees it. Stronger, I see that too. I never saw it in my daughter. She broke when he needed her to be strong. She took the easy road, when I taught her to be a fighter. She give up, you won't will you?"

"I'm sorry what are we talking about?"

"Annie. She my child." Mabel said.

The revelation flashed hot in Harmony's mind. *Annie is her child?* Romano's lost love was a colored woman? He'd done this before? She blinked at Mabel confused. The woman paled as well, with a lowered gaze Mabel took in a deep breath before she spoke. "Annie is my daughter, and she gone now because of Teek's death. It drove her and Vinnie apart. Now he done gone and replaced her, with you. Not before she run off and replaced him with a man that could never love her the way he would."

"He never said…"

Mabel shook her head. "He different Harmony, more than you know. I'm sorry for what I said earlier. Who am I to judge you? I just, I was surprised when he brought you here. I thought my Annie was special but if he could replace her…"

"She probably is special to him. He and I, well we met under different circumstances I'm sure."

"No. I see the way he looks at you. He romancin' you. Don't deny it."

Harmony had no intention of denying it. He was indeed gentle, passionate, and even caring toward her after one day in his arms. But she doubted his feelings for her could reach beyond a love affair he had with another woman so fast.

"What happened between him and your daughter?"

Mabel waved her hand and dismissed the question. "Here's what you need to know. Vinnie making plans and they include you and this place. Already done asked me to go into town and get some dresses and shoes for you."

"I never asked for that."

"Wants me to open the house up and fill it with the things you like. Even told one of his men to bring up his phonograph and records. That mean he plans to stay here for awhile."

The idea that his feelings for her had grown rocked her to the soles of her feet. He addressed her like she was his woman. Things with men like him moved fast. Hell, Grams wasn't cold in the grave and she was tending to Lewis's desires and needs. But she thought she was special to him. And the feelings blooming between them were new to them both since they were so different. Now she hears she is his replacement? For Annie?

"I'll be careful," Harmony mumbled trying to mask her disappointment.

"Good. Now get going. He's waiting on you."

"I have a question, is there a phone here?"

Mabel blinked. A guarded suspicion clouded her eyes and her lips pressed into a tight thin line.

"I won't get you in trouble but I'll need to use it when I come back. One phone call. Please?"

"There's one in his office, got a direct line into town. Come find me when you get back. I'll let you in there to use it."

"Thank you." She plucked the basket from the table and hurried out of the kitchen through the back door. Harmony sucked down fresh noon air, and cleared her head. She straightened her back and fought back the angry disappointment stirring in her gut like a winter storm, cooling her feelings for him. At the very least he owed her an explanation. Bringing her here, trying to set up house, had all of it been to replace another woman in his life?

The little mowed path zig-zagged off in the direction of the barn and stables, and she could see Romano in the distance. A scrawny man in overalls whose greasy hair shone in the sunlight led a golden brown mare with a white mane toward her lover. The horse trotted along proudly throwing its large head back with a loud snort. She'd never ridden such a majestic animal before.

A giddy bubble of excitement stirred in her and she quickened her pace, squinting against the sun as she tried to see the animal clearly. When she arrived at Romano's side he whispered to the horse in the same familiar voice he often used with her when they were alone. He cut his gaze over and she caught the gleam of mischief in the chocolate swirl of his irises. Romano patted the horse's nose then turned it's head a bit to make sure she was in the animal's line of sight.

"Harmony, meet Mary."

The horse focused her dark eye on Harmony and tossed her head up in greeting. Romano stroked the horse's forehead keeping her steady by the chin grove. "Don't be shy Songbird, before we can ride her you need to introduce yourself properly."

The stableman handed her a carrot. Braver than she believed herself capable of being she accepted the stalk then lifted her hand and raised it. Mary chomped hungrily, gobbling the offering up. The horse snorted and kicked her right hoof, anxious for more. "Shhh girl, don't be rude. This here is my special lady. Show her some respect." Romano cooed.

Harmony blushed as the horse keeper stared on. "I'm your special lady, huh?"

"Don't you feel special?" Romano asked.

"Today I do," she smiled despite her hurt pride.

"Damn right." Romano smirked.

She extended her hand and reached out to rub her open palm over the horses shoulder. The coat on the animal felt soft as velvet and warm under her touch. "She's beautiful."

"She likes you."

"It's the carrot."

"No. She has good taste, just like me."

Harmony found heart-rending tenderness in his gaze, and voice. A shy smile crossed over his mouth. She wanted to touch him, but resisted. It wouldn't be appropriate. He leaned in and kissed her. Harmony lifted her chin to accept the gentle caress of his tongue, and the passion mounted, drawing her into his arms. Every time their tongues clashed her heart turned over and she felt a bit lightheaded. When he withdrew she nearly groaned in disappointment.

"I think we're ready. Sam!" Romano announced, licking the taste of her from his lips.

"Yessir."

The horse keeper hurried off then returned with a block of wood. The man placed it on the ground under the stirrup of the saddle. He then went over and took hold of the chin groove and throatlatch to keep Mary steady.

"Shall we?" Romano asked. He had shed his vest and tie. He looked ready for a day of relaxation with her. His easy manner had been infectious, she saw herself through his eyes and it made her long for adventure. No matter where it would lead them both. Mabel's warnings surfaced and she paused over the consequences of her actions. Her attraction to him was so vastly different than anything she'd had for a man, she doubted the sensibility in trusting it. One look back into his eyes and her doubts drifted away.

"I have lunch for us." She held up the modest basket hooked over her arm. How did he expect her to ride the animal and carry the basket? Romano took the small basket from her and hitched it to the flap over the saddle. He gently guided her with his hand to her waist. Harmony reached between her legs and gathered her dress in the center drawing it up her thighs. The horse snorted at her but remained still. "Never rode on one of them before."

Romano grabbed her by the waist and thigh to steady her. She gripped the handle of the saddle with her free hand and held her dress between her legs with the other as she lifted her leg and was heaved up. Harmony straddled the horse comfortably. "Wow!" she laughed.

He joined her. Positioned himself right behind her. "Hold on. You'll enjoy this."

With the click of his tongue the horse began a mean trot that soon caught the speed of the wind. She bounced a bit but his arms around her kept her firmly in place. They galloped through the tall grass and vast open field to the dirt road that led from his hideaway to the forest. Tree branches arched thickly over them, blocking the sun, making the leafy shade expand and cover them. After several minutes he veered the mare off the road into the forest. A small worn trail was open to them but she felt the sharp sting of thin reaching branches and thorny leaves. The horse maintained an even pace and then slowed to a causal trot allowing her to absorb her surroundings. A colorful splash of flowers blooming about them captured her heart. It was March and close enough to spring to make the flowers come to life. Romano leaned in to rest his chin on her shoulder and press his face to the side of hers. Harmony lifted her hands from the tight grip she had on the saddle and smoothly covered his that held the horse's reigns. She loved the power she felt within his tight grip and the snug fit of safety within his arms.

"Look over to your right," he said against her ear.

The forest sloped down to the right, and the hills glistened with dewy blades of sweet grass. Harmony caught a glimpse of what looked to be a stream with waters sparkling like crystal. It flowed east along the same path they strolled. A baby doe sprang out of the bush and shyly walked over to the bank of the stream with her head bowed. She lapped at the cool water. After a satisfying drink the animal's head lifted and she focused directly on Harmony.

"I think she sees me."

Before Romano could reply the doe turned and fled back into the cover of the trees. "She's beautiful. This place is wonderful. Where are we going?"

The trail curved around a flank of tall oaks and Romano eased the horse to a slower gait as they headed downward. She squeezed her eyes shut and held her breath. Images of them being pitched over and the horse rolling down the hill with them had her paralyzed. Somehow he and the animal managed the descent gracefully. Harmony opened her eyes to a lush green clearing with a calm stream flowing through. "What's this?"

"This is our place." Romano said, and dropped down from the horse. He reached for her waist and brought her into his arms. "I thought of bringing you here last night. I know it can be a bit chilly, but we have the sun today, and I promise to keep you warm."

"It's perfect Vinnie." She brushed her lips over his. "Perfect."

Proud of himself he led the horse to a tree to tie her down and unhooked the basket from the saddle. He returned to her side and she relieved him of their lunch. They started toward the open field near the stream. The chosen spot he pointed to was where the sun burned the brightest. The chill that clung to her from the ride seemed to thaw instantly under the bright warmth of sunrays. "I love it. It's really beautiful here. Do you come a lot?"

"Sometimes when I need to think. Reminds me of home more than the Bronx does."

After a few silent minutes of reflection Harmony stopped. She lowered the basket, and smoothed out her dress. She stared up at him for a moment. The sun burned brightly behind him and his tall stature almost made it appear as if he had a halo. She shielded her eyes from the glare with her hand to her brow. Her mouth fell open then closed. The words were lodged so tightly in her throat she had to swallow hard.

"What is it? What were you about to say?" he asked.

"Mabel told me about Annie and Teek."

The light in his eyes dimmed. A grim tightness locked his jaws and thinned his lips. "You think I'm trying to replace Annie?"

"Are you?"

"No."

"Why did you come all those nights to hear me sing? Did I remind you of her? And when I told you about my brother why were you so willing to help? Is it because of Teek and how he died?"

"No," he said casting his gaze away.

"I believe you. If last night hadn't happened I might not be able to." His gaze returned to her and she stepped a bit closer to him. The back of her hand tapped the back of his. Their knuckles brushed, several fingers moved and gently rubbed against each other. She held his gaze and didn't touch him further. "You never told me she was colored."

"From what I hear she still is," he chuckled.

Harmony had to restrain a smile. He was so smooth at times, but this conversation needed to be had, especially if he was trying to romance her. She needed to know from him if any of the things they said or shared were real. "Be serious please."

"I loved her, but it has nothing to do with what I feel for you." He captured her left hand into his and placed it upon his heart, pressing it firmly there while he spoke. "It's a long story. I'll tell it, I promise. When I'm ready."

"Okay, that's good enough for me." Harmony rose on her toes and gave him a brief but gentle kiss. The smoldering, loving flame of desire shared between them burned in her blood and her lips against his sealed her fate. What a wonderfully complicated man, and oh how she loved discovering new things about him.

Romano reached for her but she found the strength to delay their passion. She stepped back to retrieve the lunch basket and started walking again. They did so in silence for several minutes. "Mabel seems to think you have a lion's heart. Said I ought to be careful around it. Do you know what that means?"

"No."

"I remember my Grams telling a story about the lion's heart. Mabel knew my Grams. I wonder if she said it because Grams told her the same story?"

"I'd like to hear this story." He said, hurrying his steps to catch up to her. She glanced over and happiness filled her as she began to talk. He visibly relaxed. She eased into the telling. "In Africa the lion is the king of the jungle. Every other animal in the forest fears him. It's because the lion doesn't follow, he's born to lead. Being a leader of others is a very important burden isn't it?" He walked at her side with his gaze lowered. She continued. "Lions are predators."

"So are some men."

She laughed. "True. But listen to the story. A lion's instincts are very self-serving, as the king I suppose that makes sense. But he has a weakness, as do any of God's creations."

"What's the lion's weakness? His heart."

Harmony ignored the question and kept on with her tale. Sharing it made her feel the wisdom and strength of her grandmother within her. "There are things a lion cares about. Not just the common things like water, food, sex with his lioness, and yes his babies. He has to continue his bloodline you know."

"And this makes you think of me?" Romano's brow rose, his hand landed on her backside and he squeezed her romp. "The sex with the lioness?"

"Let me finish." Harmony playfully pushed him away. Another chilly wind cut through the forest trees and washed over them. It was hard to explain with him watching her so intensely. The man had the most compelling brown eyes. She veered left and he stopped to watch her stroll away. Instead of acknowledging him her gaze focused on the scattered clouds, and a bird sailing high above. "The lion does what's in his nature, Vinnie. It's the way God made him." She glanced back over to be sure he was still paying attention. He was. "Remember every living creature has a weakness. The king of the jungle has a fragile heart, and his heart is his family."

She loved this story. It explained him perfectly. "Under all that muscle and mean, his heart beats for his pride. If another Lion, his only true natural enemy, comes to take from him the one thing that keeps him strong he will fight back to the death. My Grams used to ask the question at this point in the story." She returned her gaze to him. "Why would God give such a vicious creature a gentle heart?"

Romano wore an amused smile on his face.

"Grams says it's the divine order of balance between good and evil in the creature. The lion leads by example. Do any and everything you must do to protect your family, because family is the most important blessing bestowed upon him."

"Family, is important," he said.

"Your heart is your family." Harmony said.

"Interesting story."

"Mabel thinks that you're that lion. She says I should be careful with your heart. She doesn't believe Annie was."

"Mabel doesn't know what she's talking about. Never been to Africa to meet this lion."

Harmony let go a soft chuckle. "The end." She curtsied.

He applauded.

"Thank you for not lying to me." Harmony said. "And for finding my brother. Thank you for keeping your promise to me. It proves I was right about you. I think Mabel's wrong. This lion knows exactly what to do to sustain his heart." She stepped closer and fingered his collar, her lashes lowered shyly. The scent of his spicy aftershave, the sweet smell of air and wild grass, bloomed in her nostrils. "And you know what I think?"

A deep chuckle rumbled in his throat. "Tell me."

Harmony lifted her gaze from his open collar and locked in on his soft amber-brown eyes. She licked her lips. "Maybe I'm the lioness sent here to claim you."

"Is that so?" he ran his hand down her backside. Her body could barely stand the closeness they now shared. With his strong arms locked around her waist. Heat softened her core. Could he feel her belly quivering against his?

"I've been wanting to get you alone since this morning." He leaned in to kiss her. She dodged his semi-parted lips and stepped away. She picked up the basket and strolled toward a charming spot under the sun for them to lunch.

Romano's gaze tracked the slow sexy roll of her round hips under her dress as she found a thin patch of grass for them to rest upon. She bent forward to lower the basket and her dress climbed up her slender, toned, brown thighs, tempting him. When she removed the white and yellow quilt and flapped it out over the grass a swarm of butterflies were disturbed and several took flight. Harmony laughed, now caught in a shower of fluttering wings. Her eyes stretched in delight as the butterflies fanned out and away from her. Maybe it was time to tell her about Annie? He was ready to come clean about the battle scars over his heart.

"Did you see that?" she cried.

He nodded that he did. From his vantage point he could eye every inch of her frame. The gentle slope of her shoulders, the indent of her narrow waist under her raised bosom, and when she turned the lush swell of her ass held him captive. He burned in his gut to express himself. To share with her all the reasons his desires extended beyond Annie and what they've shared physically. For weeks he'd watched her from a far and his desire for her voice mixed with his loneliness.

To convince her of his feelings he knew he'd have to go at her pace. She had legitimate reasons to doubt his sincerity. He wanted to do things right, make his proposal stand. He'd thought it all through thanks to Leftie's provocation. He was going to ask her to leave The Cotton and her life in Harlem. She'd stay here. He'd visit her when he could, and make sure she had everything she wanted. He had it all worked out even down to the sons she would bear him. Now he had to convince her that his feelings were true.

She flashed him a flirty smile and it forced one to form on his lips. "Come on over here. I know you're hungry," she said.

Romano walked toward her. Having her alone at his mercy seemed to heighten every one of his predatory senses. He should ravage her on the spot. Instead he dropped to his knees and then over to his side, watching her remove Mabel's lunch from the brown paper wrappings.

"Ever been out West?" she asked.

"West? No. Why?"

She shrugged. "Just wondering. They say it's a wild frontier. Coloreds own their own towns, and lots of land. I was thinking when this is said and done I might like to travel out there. See it for myself."

"Stop singing?"

"I suppose. I could see myself teaching, yes, getting me some schooling and being a schoolmarm."

Romano accepted the sandwich. "Maybe I'll take you one day."

He didn't read anything into the nonchalant shrug she gave him. He supposed he should have paid attention. The things left unsaid between them would leave him unprepared for the loyalty and devotion she would show him in the weeks to come. For now he'd been too absorbed with his needs, his wants, to hear anything regarding her desires. He took a large bite and fell over to his back. Harmony removed the bottle of wine Mabel added to the basket then eased down on the blanket and scooted close to him. They both stared up at the sky.

"When I was a little girl I used to dream songs. I would close my eyes like this and see pictures of my ma, my daddy, God, you name it and then I could just sing to them and it would feel like I had them with me. Used to call them my prayer songs."

"You always wanted to sing?" he asked.

"I just always knew I could sing. Did you always want to paint?" she asked.

Romano pondered it for a moment. He too realized that his paintings were something that came from a place inside of him he knew little of. Maybe his mama loved to do it when she was a girl. She never shared much of her desires, only tended to her children and her husband's needs and read her bible. "I suppose I'm like you. It's something that I could just do." His gaze slipped over to her. Her expression prompted him to roll to his side. He popped the rest of the sandwich in his mouth, chewing fast and then swallowed.

There was something wistful that shone in her large brown eyes as she stared up at the sky, and he wanted to understand it. God help him, but she was still a mystery to him. Her energy drew him at every turn. *Have I actually fallen in love with her?* She would doubt him if he told her he had. Who would believe a man could secretly desire a woman for months from afar, then love her after a few days of meeting. At first he thought it was her singing, because her voice was straight from heaven. Now after having her the past few days he knew it was more. *I love her.*

"I want to know about you Vinnie." Her gaze switched from the clouds to his. "I want to know about you and her. Tell me."

It was a simple request. Still the painful memory of his history with Annie soured his gut. He felt encouraged by the understanding and sweet presence of his Harmony. Truthfully the only thing left between him and Annie was his guilt. And that had been enough to keep him immobile over the past two years. It was time for him to let go of the past and move forward.

"If you don't want to talk about her still I understand. It's just that..."

Romano pressed a single finger to Harmony's lips. She silenced. He traced the seal of her full lips then pinched her chin to lift her face to caress her mouth with his. Her eyes closed and she visibly relaxed.

"I'll tell you. I came to America when I was sixteen. I did what I could to survive but this place was so different than home. I spent the first year stealing and eating whatever scraps I could find, catching odd jobs here and there. Then I met Annie and her kindness changed everything."

"How did you meet?" she asked, keeping her eyes closed. As if she could see his tale unfold behind her lids.

"You could say we met by accident. That's how a lot of my fortune came to me, and was lost, by accident."

Romano remembered their meeting. Annie had skin the color of sable, and thick curly hair she wore tamed from her face in a single braid down her back. She would tie a baby blue ribbon on the plait. He used to stare at that soft ribbon for long moments before she ever allowed him to touch it, or touch her. Back then she was no more than fourteen herself, and the prettiest girl he'd ever seen. In Sicily he'd never encountered brown skin people. The dark olive skin of Sicilians was nothing compared to those he saw in America. For some reason the people fascinated him. Their style of dress, their music, even some of the foods he could scavenge out of their neighborhoods.

"The first time I saw Annie she nearly lost her life."

"How?" Harmony gasped. Her eyes remained closed.

"I was running with my friend Lucky. We were looking for a kid who stole from us that day. Lucky took one side of the street and I had the other. We searched the crowds and the stores, thinking we had him cornered. I was the one to spot him first. He ran hard through the outside market darting in and around the street vendor's carts and tables. Annie and others were there, shopping, not paying attention. I went after him. I was faster and closer when he panicked and started to shove people out of the way. Annie appeared from a vegetable stand with a bag of groceries. She didn't see him coming. He crashed into her and she fell toward the street. I got to her in time to pull her back from the cars. If she were to tell the story she'd say I saved her life."

"And you? Do you think you saved her life?"

"If I hadn't been chasing the kid he would have never pushed her in the first place. So what do you think?"

"I think she was lucky you caught her before the front end of a car did."

The praise was lost on him. He'd been the lucky one. Living on the streets and fighting for everything had taken its toll on him by the time he met Annie. He loathed everything and everyone until she showed him kindness. Romano had been blown away by the instant connection they forged. She offered him a ruby red radish from her bag as a show of gratitude. He was so hungry he bit into it as if it were an apple. He was so taken by her gentle sweet smile and almond shaped honey brown eyes, he couldn't leave her side. But his limited English made it hard to express his interest without coming off too forward. Annie seemed to understand him.

"I didn't know English then, but she didn't seem to mind or question it when I offered to walk her home. I guess she could tell by my rags and scruffy appearance that I lived on the streets. When I walked her to her door she announced me to her mother and said I was staying for dinner for saving her life. That's how Annie was."

Harmony rolled in close to him. He lifted his arm so he could hold her and she rested her face on his chest. "Finish, I want to hear the story of how you two fell in love."

" Mabel and Annie didn't seem to care that I was some vagabond. They even let me bathe and gave me some fresh things to wear that were left behind by Mabel's dead husband. The clothes were kind of big but I was grateful. It started from there…"

"What started?"

Romano sighed. "My life with them. My life without them. My wanting to be somebody important. Every day I'd visit Annie, until my presence in the neighborhood became routine. She took to teaching me English and how to read it too. I was able to get a job with a bootlegger named Greco and a room down in Five Points. Soon I began to make deals on my own. Her brother was a kid then, he'd follow me around everywhere. I took to looking after him. He reminded me of Antonio. By the time I was eighteen Annie was my girl and I had enough money to send for Antonio, and while I did the bootleg runs for Greco, Mabel let Antonio stay with her. He and Teek were both fifteen then, getting into trouble. We were kind of like a family."

"What went wrong?"

"I went wrong. Antonio and Teek wanted to imitate me. But the circles I ran in, I couldn't let the others know about my surrogate arrangement with a black family. I kept them away from that life. Time passed and when I made enough money to buy a nicer place, and this one, I hired Mabel. Paid her four times more than any domestic. Antonio and Teek were both eighteen and wanting to strike out on their own. I had to keep everything under control. So I eventually moved them all in with me. Everyone knew Annie was my girl, but it was never officially said. For those that didn't know they feared me enough not to ask."

"Is that why you know where you could marry legally?"

Romano nodded. "I would have married her. She didn't believe me. Thought I was ashamed of her. The truth was I was ashamed of me. I had become my father. It's why I broke up the gang, I had decided to go solo. Two years ago Teek was killed, Antonio barely escaped with his life, and I wanted revenge. The cost of it all was Annie's faith in me. She could stand no more."

"I'm sorry."

"Don't be. Annie was right to blame me for Teek. I knew things were changing between him and Antonio. Teek could never be part of the world Antonio was drawn to. Antonio started to run with small time Sicilian gangs and Teek did the same with the blacks. By the time they were twenty they had separate lives. And when a young Sicilian kid got killed in Harlem it started the race riots."

"I remember. That's the night Lewis was killed. I think he got shot in the middle of the chaos."

Romano sighed. "It's the night Teek died. The cut on Antonio's face came from a knife fight he was in trying to save Teek. Antonio barely escaped while members of his crew ripped Teek apart. Turns out it was the Five Points Gang that killed the kid and dropped his body over in Harlem. So, all of that bloodshed was for nothing."

He stroked Harmony's back focusing on the shifting clouds moving in and blocking the sun. "Annie couldn't look at me after what we'd done. She couldn't stand the sight of me. Mabel tried to convince her that we belonged together but that drove a wedge between their relationship too. I cost Mabel so much, her son and daughter."

"She still works for you?"

"Calls me Mr. Romano when appropriate and Vinnie when she wants to remind me of who's really in control." He chuckled. "She's like a mother to me and Antonio. I've done everything to try to make it up to her but she won't leave, won't take off the apron, won't stop pretending that Annie and Teek are gone forever. And I don't want her anywhere alone. I've given her money, bought her a nice place, but she's stayed."

Harmony's head lifted from his chest. She rested her chin on the back of her hand and gazed at him. "What do you want from me Vinnie? I'm not your Annie."

"And I'm not your Lewis, Songbird."

"True."

He touched her face. "I guess we can't deny what we miss in them both."

"Guess not."

"Just as we can't deny what we found in each other. Can we?"

"I suppose not," she said.

"The truth is I want you, Songbird. It has nothing to do with Annie, though I will give her credit. It's because of her I know what I want. It's why I've not been able to look away since the first day I saw you."

"It's strange, you talk beautifully at times. Like a poet. Like your sculptures."

"Does it scare you? My lion's heart," he asked.

"No. It makes me want… makes me feel warm inside. You could have any girl you wanted. You chose me."

He chuckled. "Trust me Doll you chose me. I would have never been brave enough to approach you. You had no idea how surprised I was when you walked over and sat down at my table."

She snuggled him closer.

"I don't think of our being together as just a matter of choice. Something else is at work here Doll. I wasn't looking for you, and you were looking for help for your bother, now here we are. Thing is, I'm pretty sure I can't let you go. It is what it is."

She nodded, as if his answer made sense.

"Does my answer surprise you?"

"No. Men are like that. They want what they want and don't give thought to the reason." She half-joked. "I doubt you would ever care to explore the reason why a little black girl with a blue ribbon in her hair fascinated you, or why a jazz singer in your arms makes you happy now. Got that lion's stubborn streak in ya."

A deep laugh escaped him. Harmony rose. She crawled over him. Placing her hands on either side of his face she straddled his chest and leaned in almost to the point of their noses touching. "Don't matter anymore why we do what we do. All that matters is that you know you're mine now too."

Romano shook his head, fighting off a smile. He felt like a grinning idiot. "You test me woman." Up close she was even more beautiful. With skin the color of autumn with a sea of swaying emerald green grass around them, she blended with nature encompassing the beauty of Eve.

The tease of a smile on her rose colored lips turned sensuous and a surge of pride swelled in his chest over his proclaiming her as his own. Inside he burned with the need to run his tongue over her succulent pair of lips and draw her bottom lip into his mouth.

At the base of his throat a pulse beat and swelled as though his heart had risen from it's unusual place and lodged there. No words passed between them.

When he could stand it no longer he flipped her underneath him and pinned her down to the blanket. *Oh, she feels so good, so good.* She released a soft giggle and spread her legs so he could fit nicely. A slow aching throb pumped raw desire between his legs turning his groin into granite. Her gaze remained locked on his, daring him to go the distance, as she had the night she stepped to him and they struck a bargain. Beneath her soft breasts he felt the erratic beating of her heart pressed up against his chest.

The needful yearning to touch her upset his balance, and made him fumble over where to begin. Romano's hand began to undo the top buttons of her dress. The tiny pearls pushed through the small slits of fabric and more of her beauty was uncovered. The buttons trailed down to her waist. She lay perfectly still with her knees parted and the hem of her dress gathered around her copper brown thighs. When the front of her dress opened and her bra was revealed he searched her face for a reaction. Her pupils dilated, her breath hitched, but she didn't say a word. He eased her bra up slowly and released perfection.

Twin dark peaks hardened instantly and the swell of her areolas made his mouth water. Romano felt his temperature rise and swallowed hard to suppress his emotion. Her little fable of the lion with the fragile heart had made a believer of him. He failed with Annie and he understood why. He'd do things different with Harmony, if she gave him the chance. Even now with all his gentle words and kisses she only released a bit of a sigh under his touch. Another cool breeze blew in from the forest making him want to cover and protect her.

"I have something to confess," he began. "I wanted to say it to you last night when we… after you and I talked and you told me about your man, and how he died. I didn't. Guess I'm not as brave as that lion." He traced his index finger around her nipple and she visibly shivered and heaved an affronted sigh. Her gaze lowered under a veil of dark lashes and she stared down the line of her body at him. "He didn't deserve you. No man deserves a treasure this fine. Always had a thing for you, Doll. Not just the singing, though it's part of you. It's how beautiful you are inside too."

He pressed the side of his face to her breast, against her heart. There beneath warm soft as silk skin, was the slow melodic vibration of her heartbeat. Romano could be lulled into just about anything listening to the sweet harmony of her breathing. Her small slender hand ran over the top of his head with such love. Romano closed his eyes and tried to focus on what he needed to say. "I'm sure he was a good man. Didn't mean to say he wasn't, Doll. I only mean a woman like you deserves the best. Annie helped me get over my anger about *mi madre* and *mi sorella*, some of it. I have many regrets. We are not one of them."

The images of his exploits through the slums of the Bronx and lower Manhattan flooded him with dread. As the leader of the Black Hand his gang was the biggest rival to the Five Points Gang. The death of Teek had been a set up. The Five Points gang knew a race war would divide his heart. And by the time Teek lie in a street drowning in his own blood he'd lost everything. That suited him fine. The hell he raised garnered such a reputation that doors usually closed to a poor immigrant cast out of Sicily were kicked open. He even had the Irish under his payroll. And it hadn't stopped. Mickey Collins stealing from him helped his focus return. He had his men back. His *famiglia*. He took the sacred vows of the Mafioso, and no one could question him. He could marry her if he chose to. No one would dare question him.

Romano was no fool, and not completely blinded by his weakness. To ask her to become part of his world would mean great risk to her life and her brother's. Just as it had been for Annie. But he had to ask, just as her man Lewis had to pluck her before she was ripe, and so soon after her grandmother had died. Neither of them deserved her. Romano eased his arm around her waist to hold tightly to her. *Yes he had it bad for his Songbird.*

"Vinnie?"

"Mmm."

"Do you still love her?"

Romano opened his eyes. His answer was no, he didn't still love Annie. He'd already told her as much, but Harmony needed more. This he understood. He needed to hear her say she'd be his. Permanently.

"Vinnie? Do you still love her?"

Slowly his head lifted. The appeal in her voice and eyes made his throat itch to shout the word; no. That would prove him weak. He had to keep control over their affair, on all fronts. He reached and pressed his hand to the side of her face. It was her turn dammit. "What do you feel for me, Songbird?"

"I don't know," she answered softly. "I don't understand how I feel, what I feel." She sucked in a tight breath and closed her eyes. "The idea of you loving another woman does turn my stomach with jealousy. I'm growing a bit dependent on your affections I suppose."

"We have time. After all of this is over, can you give us more?"

"How much time Vinnie? What about my job, my place, my friends?"

"I'll take care of it all. I need a chance here Doll, for us both to figure these feelings out. Which means you need a chance too. Stay with me."

A sensual light of understanding softened her gaze and she nodded that she'd grant his wish.

"*Grazie.*" He said his voice low and even. No longer able to deny himself the privileges of being her lover, he rolled his tongue over one plump nipple then the other. He stole a glance up at her before he swallowed the peak of her left breast and caught the pleased emotion softening her features and causing her lids to flutter shut. Romano eased back on top of her and she parted her thighs to accommodate him, her hot core pressed now into his abdomen.

"I—I—I can't catch my br-breath when you do that," she gasped, pushing down on his shoulders. He sucked her breast harder and her nipple swelled against his tongue. Her staggered breathing made the most primal of urges rise in him. Her insistence drove him down. The fabric of her dress gathered in his hands and he pushed it up to her waist. His eyes widened with delight to find she wore no panties.

"I forgot to put them on." She said with a sexy smirk.

He shook his head, smiling as satisfaction filled him to have her so open and exposed beneath him. It had all happened so fast. One minute he was totally focused on growing his business, controlling his brother, building a *famiglia* amongst the men he called brothers. The next he had found himself considering the love of a woman. This woman. How did he get here?

With a slow steady hand he cupped her moist pussy. Holding her gaze he eased two fingers into her tight warm channel. She dug her nails into his shoulders and her sweet round ass bounced up and down off the blanket, her clit scraping his zipper. He thought his cock would burst through over the teasing brush. Her breaths shortened when he slowly inserted, withdrew, and inserted his fingers.

"Jesus!" She cried out then bit down on her bottom lip holding to his shoulder. He kept moving his fingers in and out of her silken walls, getting her ready for him.

"You like that, Songbird?"

"Mmm, yes." She rolled her hips. He lifted a bit, balancing on his left elbow to watch his fingers slip in and out between her dark folds, knuckle deep. He glanced back up to her dark berry nipples and they shimmied with her staggered breathing. She was enjoying it. He couldn't decide if he wanted to taste her or fuck her. He figured he'd do both and more before he let her go.

"Kiss me, there, Vinnie please."

He removed his fingers and her sex released him with a soft suction noise as she rolled her hips. His gaze fell upon the sweet lips of her pussy as his head lowered between her parted thighs. His tongue flicked, rolled, loved.

She gave a shaky laugh. "I can't believe how bold I am with you."

"You were always brave, Doll. You never fooled me."

Harmony swallowed hard when he pushed the backs of her thighs up and apart then stuck out his tongue into her tight channel and licked her there. Her eyes flew open and then quickly fluttered shut. The teasing little flickers of his tongue sent darts of electric pleasure zinging her womb. "Yes! Yes!"

Without provocation he latched his wicked lips around her clit and began to suck so slowly she was thrashing and bucking beneath him. The release was swift, and so was the plunge of his tongue into her pulsating channel. Repeated tongue thrusts and licks had her crying out so loud he could hear the rapid flaps of bird wings as many took flight, fleeing from the surrounding trees.

The moist suction sounds of her cunt were almost obscene in the quiet serenity of the forest. But her cries of passion surpassed it. "Yes Vinnie! Oh yes! I'm almost there! Don't stop, no, no, don't stop, I'm almost there." She reached between her parted thighs and grabbed the back of his head, grinding her pelvis up into his face. Her body came apart as an all-consuming orgasm split her down to her core.

Romano could wait no more. He sat back on his legs to remove his shirt. Harmony, breathing hard, with her knees parted and the front of her dress flipped up, reached between her thighs and covered her quivering sex.

"Take it off, everything," he nearly growled at her.

She blinked awake and looked at him with a dazed, lust crazed stare. When she managed to gather her strength she rose and lifted her dress, removing it. Then she pulled off her bra. Romano stood to shake off his trousers. He glanced around the open forest. There was something primal about taking her out under the sun in sixty-degree weather. She shivered and it excited him. She moaned when he dropped back down on her and it excited him. Damn everything about her had him turned on.

"You cold?"

"A little." Her eyes were wide and her expression taut. Her bottom lip quivered so he sucked on it until she mewled for release.

"I'll warm you soon enough," he whispered.

Her thighs eased opened and he licked along the seam of her lips before he captured her juicy mouth into a loving kiss. "Yes," he breathed, stroking his cock between them. He angled the tip at her opening. Her belly undulated when he hesitated and stroked her sex against the bulb of his cockhead. "Ready?" he teased.

"Now. Do me now, Vinnie."

He plunged into her and her breath seeped into his mouth sliding in on a satisfying sigh. "Mmm, you're so wet, so ready." He said unable to thrust his hips. She clung to him rolling her cunt around his shaft and he shook off the melting urge to release and he began to pump his cock in and out of her lovely tightness. Her inner muscles clenched as she pumped upward with her thrusting hips. She clung to him, her entire body shivered.

She wants this as bad as I do, damn I know it's crazy but I think I'm in love with this woman.

"Top. Let me. Get. On. Top." She wheezed under his hard thrusts. He paused then rolled to put her on his lap. She shivered hard and a renewed breeze washed over the open field. But she never broke rhythm. She fell forward with her hands pressed to the tops of his arms. His gaze latched on to her swaying breasts and her ass bounced on his length, swallowing and releasing him. He lowered his gaze lifting his head a bit to see his thick long cock appearing and disappearing between the lovely lips of her pussy. She rode him. Up and down she went on his shaft with tight wet heat taking him deep.

It was Romano's turn to shiver. He rubbed her thighs and moved with her but she was in complete control. The internal heat their passion generated made them writhe and moan in pleasure. He rolled her again to her back and threw her leg over his shoulder opening her deep for him. He beat his cock in and out of her and she clawed at him for more. She was taking him under with her bottom maneuvers, his entire body shook hard before he grunted and dropped his head near the edge of losing control.

"Give it to me baby, I can take it, I can," she said cinching her legs around his waist tighter. He knew she was close to exploding because her moans were tightening, her voice pitched higher and higher.

"I'm not going to last much longer," he groaned through hard thrusts.

"Me either!" she cried out.

He thrust, harder and deeper and timed his explosive release with hers. Together they were shattered under the sheer power of their union. Vinnie dropped on her exhausted.

Maybe it was the sweat cooling along her spine from the temperature dropping around them. Or maybe she just knew deep in her spirit that this man was made for her, and loving him was right. All she knew for sure was that sex had little to do with the warm flow of joy filling her heart. She had fallen in love with Vinnie. Harmony snuggled closer to him. He'd rolled them up in the blanket. They lay with their arms and legs wrapped around each other. She pressed her face to his chest and listened to his heartbeat. It was strong, like his embrace. She felt safe, and loved.

"Vinnie?"

"Yes."

"I think I might want to stay, keep time with you. To see where it leads."

"Mmm, that makes me happy."

"Me too."

CHAPTER NINE
Dead Time…

The murky water rippled with rising steam drifting up from the surface. Harmony sneezed. She couldn't shake the chills from their day out and hoped she didn't come down with a cold. Even now in her warm bath she felt a slight quiver tickle along her spine. All she needed to do was think of him and every bone in her body melted on the memory as she slipped deeper into the belly of the clawfoot tub. Her lids sagged, then closed and she eased into the memory of their time by the stream.

They talked until they were hoarse. She and he shared the wine and it made her giddy and long winded. He didn't seem to mind. He made love to her twice, and they lay under the cooling sun until it began to drift away and the chilly weather covered them. He asked her to be his. She said yes. He asked again. And she said yes again. She'd say yes to anything now. Her dreams of becoming more than a jazz singer were still there. She'd focus them now with Vinnie included. Together they'd figure out the details.

Harmony discovered some truths about herself. Lewis had blown into her life and swept her into his. When she reflected on it she never chose him. She never had a say in where her heart went. That was the difference between Lewis and Vinnie. This time every beautiful moment had been one she allowed, to some extent. And falling in love was brand new and full of promise, just as she had always dreamt.

"Harmony?"

She opened her eyes to see he'd returned dressed handsomely in grey tweed trousers and a matching vest. He'd bathed and cleaned up as soon as they arrived. She spent her time plucking grass from her hair and looking over the dresses that he had brought in for her. "Yes?"

"The boys and I have business to tend to. Afterwards I'll go for your brother. It might be late before I'm back," he said, walking over and sitting on the edge of the tub. She grinned up at him.

"Okay. I understand. I'll be here waiting."

"About that phone call you asked Mabel to let you make Doll." He said. Harmony blinked in surprise, though after hearing how close he and Mabel were she shouldn't have been surprised at all. She doubted the maid would ever keep something from Vinnie. "I told her to open up my office. You aren't my prisoner Harmony. I'm sorry I made you feel like one."

"Thank you, Vinnie."

He leaned forward and their lips met in a brief accepting kiss. She nearly reached to pull him into the bathwater but he rose and drew away. "I'll try to make it quick. Okay? I know you want to see your brother."

"I… I'll miss you."

He glanced back at her. He winked and was gone. Harmony closed her eyes relaxing. She would miss him. But now she had the ability to dream a bit. Where could it all lead? Marriage? Her? Grams must be having a real good chuckle over her now. As she would say; *girl you always take the hard road, but somehow you manage to find your way.*

After a long soak, she rose from the cooled water and dried herself. In the room she and Vinnie would share she found Mabel had left her oils for her skin and some sweet smelling fragrances to dip behind her ear in pretty crystal bottles. She changed and prettied herself up. When her brother arrived she wanted to greet him as normally as she could, before she beat him to death for worrying her so.

The house was still. She descended the stairs expecting to see a few of Vinnie's men. She saw no one. "Mabel?" she called out. Harmony poked her head through the swinging door to the kitchen but didn't see her. *Maybe she went down into the cellar?* Harmony decided against the search. Instead she explored the lower level rooms. When she found a door closed she opened it. On the third try she located Vinnie's office. Harmony nearly turned away when she saw the phone.

Harmony entered his office and closed the door. She went to the desk and sat behind it. The chair's leather was as soft as butter and had a large back fit for her prince. Picking up the listener ear to the phone she dropped her pointer finger in the circular dial and rung the operator.

"Operator, how can I help you?"

"Ah yes, can I have The Cotton Club in Harlem please."

Nightfall had come in and stole away the sun. She knew the hour had eased into rehearsal time at The Cotton. Paulette would be there early. She could talk to her and locate Milo. He owed her an explanation.

"One moment please." The operator said, and the line went silent.

Harmony waited on the connection, thinking over how she'd get Paulette to the phone. To her surprise Charlie the doorman answered. She pleaded with him to bring Paulette to the phone after he said Milo and the band weren't there. Lucky for her Madden hadn't arrived either. She doubted Charlie would have bothered if he was there. Harmony glanced around Vinnie's office while she waited. There was nothing personal in the room. Just books and furniture she knew he never touched. Nothing as revealing of his other side as the room at the cottage.

"Mony? Is that you?"

"Hi. Yes. I…"

"Sweet merciful God it is you! Oh girl, oh Lord, I was so worried."

"I'm fine…."

"Where are you? What happened to you?"

"It's a long story. Look, I don't want to get you in trouble. I need to speak to Milo. Can you get a message to him?"

"You don't know?"

"Know? Know what?"

"Milo dead."

Harmony gripped the chair with the phone pressed tight to her ear. "What do you mean… he dead?"

"He dead Mony! They killed him. I thought they killed you too…"

"Who dunnit?"

"They found his body yesterday. Oh my God Mony it's horrible. Everyone's upset."

"Paulette! Stop! Who killed him?" she gasped, tears welled in her eyes and the room around her blurred. "Who dammit!"

"That evil ass gangster! Vincenzio Romano. He killed him."

"That's not true!"

"It is Mony. He had his men do it. Stickman say they saw them roll up hanging out of the windows of the car and shoot him up on the sidewalk. Everyone is talking about it. Mony, where are you? What the hell is going on… where have you been the past two days?"

She dropped the phone and shot up from the chair. Paulette called for her on the other line but Harmony raced out of the room in a full on panic. She ran for the front of the house. Though she knew Vinnie was gone, she prayed someone was here. Paulette had to be wrong. Something was terribly wrong with her accusation. Why would Vinnie kill Milo?

"What is it?" Mabel said carrying a wicker basket of fresh laundry.

"Where's Vinnie?"

"Gone? What has you in such a state girl?"

"I have to find him. No. No." She shook her head furiously and wiped at the tears on her cheeks. "I have to get to my brother. They're going to kill him. Oh Lord I'm so stupid. I believed him! The bastard was lying to me!" Harmony cried.

Mabel lowered the basket and looked at her with open shock. "You aren't making any sense.'"

"My friend is dead and Vinnie did it!"

"If he did then he had good reason!"

"Shut up!" Harmony shouted at her. Mabel crossed her arms defiantly under her bosom. "Vinnie is going after my brother. Do you hear me Mabel? I might have handed Willie over to his death!"

"Vinnie is a good man, and if you don't know that by now I was right about you all along."

Harmony closed her eyes. In her heart she believed in Vinnie. But Milo was dead and now her brother might be next. Could she really put all her faith in a mobster she'd only known for a few days? Calming her voice she opened her eyes and tried to speak reasonably. "Please Mabel. Your son was murdered because of the violent wars of these men. My brother will be next. I have to get out of here and try to find him. I don't know if Vinnie has anything to do with it, but I can't sit back and not do anything. Can you help me?"

"I…" Mabel stammered.

"You have a car. I saw you when you drove up." Harmony spun and searched the front of the cabin through the large picture window. There were no cars. "Where is it? Where?"

"The men park the cars behind the barn. Vinnie wouldn't hurt your brother. If he said he was going to help him then he will. Believe him."

"I don't have time for this! Give me the keys!" She turned and grabbed a vase and threw it hard to the floor causing it to splinter into shards of glass. "NOW! Or I'll break every damn thing in here!"

Mabel hurried for her purse. Harmony was hot on her heels. She accepted the keys from her and ran for the door. Mabel said something behind her but she didn't bother to listen. Hell she forgot her coat. She ran across the open field toward the barn. Mabel was right. Vinnie's men parked three cars behind the red and grey barn. What she hadn't expected was the man left in charge. Leftie opened the door to the black Packard and eased out of the car. He eyed her suspiciously.

"Where do you think you're going?"

She hid the keys in the palm of her hand and closed her fist. "I was looking for Vinnie."

"Well he ain't here. Left me behind to watch over you. Now take it on back up to the house."

If she turned and left then she'd have to follow Mabel's advice and believe in Vinnie. But what if it wasn't Vinnie, what if someone else was out there set on killing her brother. It could be Mickey Collins that killed Milo or Bumby Man. She just didn't know. And if Milo knew where Willie was hiding then it's most likely his murderer did too.

"Problem?" Leftie said. He eyed her with unmasked suspicion. She had to get around him but how.

"You don't like me do you?"

"Not my type." He spat.

The feeling was mutual. He wasn't a bad looking man, but the raw hatred and smugness he exuded when she was near him made her skin crawl. "I'm sure you don't want me here. Right?"

Leftie didn't answer.

"What if I leave?"

He snickered. "Not going to happen."

"What if I do? I could drive out of here and keep driving. You'd be free of me."

"He'd just find another one like you." Leftie sneered. The comment burned her pride. She tried to keep her face clear of emotion.

"Maybe not. Fool him twice, maybe, but I don't think he'd trust any woman again. It works for everyone; Vinnie would not be distracted anymore. That's what you want. For him to get rid of his fascination for my kind?"

She stepped boldly toward the car. "I have Mabel's keys. I'll get in the car and drive off and it's done. You won't see me again. I swear it. No harm no foul."

She turned her head in hopes he would agree but he grabbed her arm painfully hard. "Nuff games you mouthy bitch, go back up to the house now!" he grunted. She tried to yank away but he started to drag her by the arm from the car. Out of reflex she swung and hit him in the face. Temporarily stunned he released her and staggered a step back. He recovered too quick. A sharp back handed slap that sent her to the ground immediately blinded Harmony. Harmony blinked hard to keep from losing consciousness.

"Fucking hit me? *Una bella, fica! Puttana!* I got a better plan. It's time I show Vinnie what type of whore you are!" he snarled. She barely heard him from the ringing in her ear. He really hit her hard. When she struggled to rise he yanked her to her feet. She struggled against him only able to see out of one eye. Dazed she could barely land her fist or get her bearings before he grabbed her by the waist and lifted her from the ground.

"Let me go!" she screamed.

Leftie half dragged, half carried her into the barn.

***

The map of the shipyard covered the entire table. Gio pointed to the east and left flanks that his men had scoped as a targeted entrance the day before. The torture session with Mickey's boys in his barn confirmed this is where he'd hold up after two in the morning. Neither men knew where Mickey kept the stolen bootleg booze but both confessed that they'd definitely moved it to the shipyard after they were sure Romano's men had been dealt with.

"Does this sound right, Antonio?" Romano asked his fidgety brother.

"Sure Vinnie. It sounds right. We go for the kid and while they box Mickey Collins in we can find out where the booze is kept. Sounds like a plan."

Ignacio and Gio exchanged looks. "What boy?" they asked in unison. The rest of the men fell silent. Romano considered the danger the kid would be in if anyone other than him brought him in. He promised Harmony he'd see to making sure her brother was safe. Still he found it hard to send his men off to war and not take on the General's seat.

And there was something unnerving about his brother. Antonio seemed too jumpy. He kept wiping the sweat from his face and brow with his hanky. He nodded to Antonio that they'd follow his plan. He gestured for his top men to follow him away from the others. The trio walked with him through the warehouse. They passed troops of his men loading guns that he'd brought in for the raid. Antonio hung back but Romano noticed how his brother kept tracking him with his eyes. He wished he felt a hundred percent about Antonio's advisement on things, but his gut said otherwise.

"Boss? Care to fill us in? You got a lead on the booze? Where Mickey keeps it?"

He stopped and faced both men. He wished Leftie had come but he thought it best to leave one of his toughest hired guns with Mabel and Harmony. At least that way, if Mickey was fool enough to track him down at the cabins the women wouldn't be defenseless.

"There's a boy, colored boy, who runs booze and numbers for Mickey Collins. He's been hiding since this jumped off. I know where he is. Antonio and I will take separate cars. When we get to him and question him Antonio will meet you both down near Pier 7. Have a truck and six of our strongest men on standby. While the others take down Mickey you will get my product."

Ignacio nodded as if impressed but Romano noticed the questioning doubt in Gio's eyes. "Trust me, this is a good plan. And when it's done I'll cut you both in on the Atlantic City deal."

The offer set them at ease. He heaved a burdened sigh. Every bone in his body was tight with tension. Again he felt a sense of dread. He worried about Harmony and Mabel as well. He needed to hurry things along and get back to the cabin with the kid. And soon. "Now. Let's get to business boys."

***

Leftie threw her into the stall. She could hear the neigh of panic from the horses as they bucked in their stalls.

"Fucking bitch." Leftie shouted. "He and his brother can't stay the hell away from you niggers."

Harmony scrambled away. She searched the straw hay scattered about and found no weapon to aid her. A hand gripped her left ankle and dragged her back toward the front of the stall. She dug her nails into the wood planked floor, breaking three in the dragging. Kicking back at him wildly she connected with his chest and heard him howl in pain. Harmony flipped to her backside and scooted away from him as he stalked inside the barn raging in Italian. The side of her face throbbed and she could taste blood in her mouth. Other than her heart slamming into her ribcage she wasn't panicked. She seethed with anger over his attack, and calculated the best move. She needed to be calm to think of how to strike.

"He'll kill you when he finds out you touched me. Kill you! What concern is our relationship to you?" she shouted.

Leftie paused. He glared down at her. "What concern is it of mine? Who the fuck do you think cleans up the Romano boys' mess?" he undid his belt. Harmony glanced to the wall of the stall and noticed some rusted tools hanging off the hooks. She returned her gaze to him as he ran the belt through the loop of his pants. "He doesn't even know what the fuck Antonio is!"

She shook her head not understanding and scooted back into a pile of straw hay.

Leftie released a peal of laughter. "His brother is a queer! Has been since he came across the water."

"Queer?" she stammered.

He swung the belt and the leather strap struck her across the legs. Harmony howled in pain. Leftie hit her with the belt over her arms and chest before she rolled out of the next strike. She couldn't process a thing but her escape. Leftie snarled and cursed her again as she tried to run past him. He grabbed her arm so hard she thought he'd pulled it from its socket. On reflex she turned and shoved her fist as hard as she could into his throat. His knees buckled and he let go of his hold on her. The release was just enough for her to reach the pickaxe and hit him on the side of his face. He staggered back with blood gushing from his cheek. He roared like a madman covering his face, a crimson stream seeped out between his fingers. Harmony raised the pickaxe in her hand ready to slam it into the top of his skull, "You fucking bastard!" she shouted, blinded by tears. Then her eyes caught a glimpse of his gun. Before he could recover she dropped the weapon and went for the Colt. She put it on him, kept it trained on him as she backed out of the stall. Leftie glared at her with his good eye. He stopped wailing, and the raw hatred she saw there almost prompted her to pull the trigger. Instead she turned and ran.

On her first try she found Mabel's car. She turned over the engine and pumped the gas with the Colt resting on her lap. The car started and she shifted gears reversing away from the barn at a dangerous speed.

Thank God Lewis had taught her to drive before he died. He had Grease Man's car and used to steal her away to give her lessons. When she backed up she saw Leftie staggering out of the barn. Harmony threw the car in drive and gassed it directly for him intent on running the bastard down. He jumped out of the way just in time and she ended up side swiping another vehicle busting a headlight. No more time to waste she crashed through the field and drove hard toward the road. "Bastard! Rot in hell bastard!" she screamed, her body was ablaze with pain from the attack and part of her wanted to turn around and even the score. Instead she drove at breakneck speed. She had to get to her brother, and now.

***

"Before we leave. You and I need to clear the air." Romano approached his brother who paced impatiently by the car. Antonio masked his annoyance and agreed to hear him out.

"After tonight things are going to change. No more fuckups. No more mistakes. I want you to focus Antonio. Do you understand me?"

"Vinnie I made mistakes, but tonight fixes it. We get the boy and he will tell you what you need to know. Then we start fresh."

Romano cleared his throat. He glanced back at the trucks driving out of the warehouse under the silver moon. "There's something else. It's about Harmony."

"The jazz singer?" Antonio asked.

"She's my lady now." He returned his gaze to him.

"Like Annie?" Antonio asked, his lips tight. Whenever they spoke of Annie it always made them think of Teek. And if they thought of Teek the shared guilt over his death made it impossible to finish any discussion. Today he'd see it through.

"Not like Annie. It's different for us. I'm not that man anymore, and neither are you. We learn from our mistakes."

"The men aren't going to take well to you and a black mistress."

"They have no say. You know how this works."

Antonio shrugged. "What about her brother?"

"That's why I agreed to your plan. We do this clean. When we have him you return to the boys and get my booze. I'll take him to his sister. Do this right Antonio and I'll let you be your own man, give you your own turf. Fuck it up and we're done little brother. Do you understand what done means?"

He vowed to his dead mother he'd see after his brother. He failed with Antonio. Excusing his behavior and reckless actions, had cost Teek his life. Now it was time for him to grow the fuck up. And he intended to see that transformation to the end.

"I get your meaning Vinnie. Let's go deal with the kid and be done with this."

Romano glanced to the full moon looming in the distance. It had turned into a cold white orb glowing bright against the dark, starless sky. A foreboding feeling of consequence was the only shadow cast over him and his brother. He couldn't shake it, and he always trusted his gut. He shifted his gaze to Antonio who started his car and nearly stopped him. Something was amiss. Maybe he should dig deeper into whatever it was that had them divided so much lately. Antonio glanced up at him. Their eyes met through the windshield. They were brothers, blood, and ultimately he trusted him with his life. He decided to shelve the talk they needed to have for another night. Harmony was waiting for him. Romano needed to be sure she was safe. He almost dawned a smile when he thought of the future he and his Songbird would have. Almost.

***

"May I help you child?" A morose looking nun with the clear blue eyes and pursed lips asked. She shuffled toward Harmony with her robe sweeping hauntingly about her feet, and met her half way into the vestibule of the church.

"Days of worship for coloreds are Tuesday and Wednesday only." The nun said.

Beyond the petite woman, the sanctuary was silent. A few people sat scattered in the pews with their heads bowed, lost in prayer. A woman with a white lace shawl draped over her head knelt before an altar of flickering candles. Harmony glanced up to the large marble statue of their savior with a head ringed in thorns and a sad look of grief upon his face while pinned upon a wooden cross. Did Jesus intend for such a divide between coloreds and whites? When her gaze lowered to the pristine look of scorn the nun wore she knew that the woman before her believed so. Still Harmony couldn't help but remember the story Vinnie shared with her of his life, and the beauty of hope she found with him. She struggled with her heart now. How could he kill Milo? Had anything been real between them?

"I need to see Father Michaels."

The nun frowned, her gaze swept Harmony from head to toe. She inwardly cringed over her outward appearance. Her bruised face and torn dress had her looking more like a stray than a parishioner. She kept the Colt tucked inside the front of her dress with her arms crossed over it. If the nun suspected she carried a gun she didn't indicate so. Harmony opened her mouth to explain her intentions when from the corner of her eye she saw the shadow of the priest materialize. He entered from a side door that most certainly led to the rectory. Harmony marched straight for him. She recognized the man, he was a few years older than her with piercing blue eyes and coal black hair. He'd donated several times to the local shelter and was rumored to have a hand in keeping the girls home for unwed mothers opened. His cool gaze fixed on Harmony and never wavered during her approach. In fact he paused and waited. He wore a long dark robe with a white minister collar, and a golden crucifix hung from his neck. He gave the nun trailing her a discreet nod, and she was dismissed.

"Father Michaels? My name is Harmony Jones and I know my brother is here. His name is Willie, they call him Lil Will. I need to see him please. Now."

"I don't know any Willie. Now if you don't mind, I'm afraid you'll have to leave."

"In a minute mobsters are going to storm this church to drag Willie out of it. I'm his sister. Either you help me, or be responsible for his death. You can't protect him anymore. I don't have time to argue. I have to see my brother. Now please!"

The priest gripped her elbow and pulled Harmony through the side door. "Lower your voice. This is not the place for your hysterics. I've told you, young lady that I don't know your brother."

Harmony imposed an iron control over herself. She fought hard against the tears that kept welling in her eyes. If she didn't convince the priest to help her soon she'd be helpless to save him. And everything in her being warned her that Willie's life was in this man's hands. "I'm sorry for barging in here. I'm grateful to you father. Very. I'm not lying to you, and I know the only reason you're standing here now lying to me is to protect him. I have to help him, and I'm the only person besides you that wants to. Take me to him."

"I can't. Leave."

"Can't? Or won't? Why are you keeping him here?" She stepped in his face when he made to turn and lead her out of the back doors of the church. "You know he's a small time street hoodlum. Why protect him? Huh? Someone made you keep him here. Who? Was it Vincenzio Romano?"

Father Michaels physically paled and Harmony's heart stopped. It was true. Vinnie did betray her trust. She didn't understand why, but the revelation hurt worse than Leftie's violent act of aggression towards her. Harmony blinked away the tears clouding her vision and swallowed the lump lodged in her throat.

"Father Michaels?" Another nun, who was much older than the first, appeared in the hall. Instead of the look of disgust her sister wore when Harmony arrived, her kind eyes had a light of worry to them. And dare she hope, understanding. "Child? What's happened to you?"

"Go back sister. She's upset. She's leaving."

"No!" Harmony turned on the nun. "Do you know my brother? Willie Jones. The father is taking money from mobsters to keep him hidden here." She shot him a hot glare over her shoulder. "Aren't you father? Tell her the deal you made with the devil."

"That's enough!"

"You take me to him now…" The gun dropped from the inside of her dress and between her legs to noisily hit the floor. Both the priest and the nun drew back stunned. Harmony quickly picked up the weapon but aimed it to the floor. "Please. I'm not here to cause trouble, but Romano's men are coming and I will do anything to keep them from taking him."

"Father?" The nun said alarmed.

The young priest's face twisted with conflict. She didn't care if she had to turn the gun on them both. She intended to collect her brother.

"Come with me."

"Thank you."

Quickly he led her down the hall, and it veered toward a narrow stairwell. Harmony braced her hand to the wall unsure of her steps in the darkness. She held tight to the gun. *What if it was an ambush and Vinnie's men were already below? What if she walked into a scene where she'd have to fire the gun at another human being?* Even now her heart was his. She'd never be able to shoot him.

They reached the lower level in darkness. The nervous priest pulled a string to the center of the room and a bulb blinked on, chasing shadows to the corners. "He's in there. I want you both out of here. Do you understand?"

"Yes. Yes."

Harmony hurried to the door. She sucked a deep breath and waited for the priest to unlock it. She entered. Willie sat on a cot pushed to the wall. He had a haggard look on his unshaven face and he wore the same clothes she'd last seen him in. He shot up to his feet startled over her sudden appearance. And she was by his as well. He looked frightened, and thin. His eyes were the only sign of vitality, they burned bright white and stretched with shock. The small room had a cot and a chamber pot. She saw a table with a few books and magazines. There was nothing else. How long had he been in the dungeon? And with the door locked, was he a hostage or there willingly?

"Willie!" she sighed, nearly dropping with fatigue and relief. She forced her body to move and rushed him. Her arms went around his neck and she buried her face there. "You're alive. I thought I wouldn't get here in time. I was so scared."

CHAPTER TEN
The night of reckoning…

St. Nicholas Avenue was unusually quiet, absent of the stream of cars and taxis driving in and out of Manhattan. Word had spread of the trouble brewing between him and Mickey Collins. Romano suspected many had called the night short. He parked in front of St. Mary's and glanced up to see Antonio parked behind him. When he opened the door Antonio was already out of his car walking straight toward him.

"I'll stay out here. Let you talk to the boy alone. Might work better if we don't ambush him."

Romano nodded that he agreed. He turned for the walkway then froze. Parked two blocks down he saw a black and tan Packard. It looked like Mabel's.

"Something wrong?" Antonio asked.

He studied the car for a minute. He would have sworn it was hers if not for the smashed in headlight. He dismissed the nagging feeling of familiarity. There were plenty Packard's like it on the road. Besides what would Mabel be doing there this time of night?

"No. Nothing's wrong. Wait here, shouldn't take me long."

"Mony? They told me Romano had you. Thank God you're safe."

To have him in her arms again made all the anguish of the past weeks intensely real. For a long pause she couldn't speak. She squeezed her eyes shut and held him. "Mony?" he said with a ring of alarm in his voice. Gently he pushed her off him and scanned her face. "Who did this?"

Too many emotions had a hold of her at once. She stepped back trying to calm herself. She wanted to strike him, hug him, and run from the church, wielding the gun toward anyone that threatened to hurt him.

"Answer me! Did Vinnie Romano hurt you? I'll kill the bastard!"

"No!" She shouted back through her tears. "You care now? After scaring the hell out of me for weeks? Now you care? He didn't hurt me."

"I'm sorry…"

"You should be."

"Let me explain."

"Yes. Explain. Explain how could you do this? Do you know what's happened, what we've been through looking for you? Milo is dead."

Willie shook his head in disbelief. "That's not true."

"It is Willie. He's dead."

Willie dropped down on the cot. He wouldn't look her in the eye. He stared straight ahead processing the news. "It's my fault if he's dead. All my fault."

"Why are you here? Locked in the basement of a church? This church? How did you know that Romano had me? Who put you in here? Milo?"

Willie shook his head sadly. "He told me no one would get hurt. He said, we just had to settle the score, set things right for a change, and then it'll be over."

"Who? Who said that?"

Willie dropped his head and refused to answer.

"Okay, forget it. We can talk about it later. We need to go." Harmony glanced back. She heard voices and feet approaching. "Now."

"There's nowhere to go. Antonio will find me."

"Antonio?" Harmony paused. "What does Antonio have to do with this?"

Willie's gaze finally lifted and focused on her. Harmony stared on trying to make sense of the fear and regret reflecting in her brother's eyes. The door behind her opened. She raised the gun and swung it toward the visitor. Vinnie entered. In a trench coat, black gloves and with a fedora low to his head, his presence filled the room and Harmony wavered over pointing the gun in his direction. Their eyes met. Vinnie froze.

"Get up Willie! Now!" She ordered. Her brother stood. Vinnie's gaze switched from her gun to her face, then to her brother.

"You get out of our way. Or I will shoot you," she said in a voice even and exact.

The gun greeted him first. However it was the sight of his woman holding it on him that rendered him speechless. The wild look of determined fire blazing in her heated glare drove the stake deeper in his heart from the words she spoke. Harmony? The side of her face was red and swollen. Her right blood-shot eye had a darkening bruise and was so puffy it had all but shut. The front of her dress had been ripped and he could see stains as if she was dragged through muck. Who the fuck would dare touch her? Hurt her? How was that even possible when he just saw her hours ago soaking in a tub and glowing with happiness? Car accident? Had to be. None of his men would dare lay a finger on her.

Panic, worry, and confusion slammed his heart repeatedly. He would have gone to her if she weren't leveling the fucking gun on him. "What are you doing here?" he said, swinging his gaze left to her brother and clenching his hand in a fist to keep from acting. He didn't need to scare her.

"Don't!" she shouted releasing the safety on the gun. "Come any closer and I'll shoot."

The priest vanished. It was just him and her in that moment of threatening silence. He had forgotten all about her brother. His focus had become singular. "You're hurt Doll. Talk to me."

"Hurt?" she laughed with tears glistening in her eyes. "You have no idea how much this hurts Vinnie!" Her voice was shaky but strong. She kept the gun between them. "I trusted you. I gave you my heart, and all along you and your brother were abusing mine!"

"Who hit you?" he demanded, unable to get past her state. She sounded crazy, speaking of a conspiracy that didn't exist. He'd address it later. First he wanted to know what happened to her. "Who dammit?"

The gun dropped a fraction and she shook all over as if unsure how to respond. Maybe she wavered over trusting him. Whatever it was it had proved to be fleeting. The gun rose again and a firm determined line thinned her lips. Her eyes narrowed on him when she spoke. "Your man Leftie decided to beat on me before he tried to rape me. But I fixed him good. Now let us out!"

"I'll kill him. I swear it." He walked toward her as if the gun meant nothing. He saw panic rise in her eyes. "Give me the gun. I'm not here to hurt your brother. You know me, Songbird. You know my heart. I'll kill them all but I'll never hurt you."

Harmony fired the gun over his shoulder as a warning and he stopped, shocked at the angry defiance blazing in her eyes. No sweet words would grant him access to her. In that moment he knew how deeply her distrust of him was. She fired the gun again at the wall and blew off chunks of brick and mortar. "It's over. Do you hear me? I know you and Antonio had Willie all the time. I know you killed Milo, and if you don't move away from the door I swear..."

"You'll what?" he asked. "You'll put a bullet in me? You'll have to if you think I'll let you go out there believing I could be responsible for this! Any of it!" he shouted.

"Shoot him Mony, he's lying. He'll kill us both."

"Shut up!" Harmony's voice rose higher than theirs. She gripped the gun with both hands to keep her aim steady. "Move Vinnie. It's done. Don't make me do this. Please don't make me. Move dammit!"

"I can't do that, Songbird. There's something wrong here and I need to know what it is." He put his hands up in surrender. "C'mon Doll what's it going to be? Either you trust me or you don't, but you draw a gun you have to use it. A man like me isn't going to back away from it."

"Maybe I can be of help."

Harmony blinked away her tears and Romano's head turned. They both froze when Antonio entered. He walked in with his gun trained on his brother. Now Romano stood with two guns drawn on him and his mind reeled as he tried to unlock the key to how it all unfolded.

"The day of reckoning can be postponed no longer, can it Vinnie?" Antonio chuckled.

It was Antonio all along? The sight of Antonio pointing his gun at Vinnie snapped clarity into Harmony's panicked mind. She lowered the gun, not sure where to aim it. Her gaze switched from brother to brother. He sneered at his brother and extended his arm to point the gun dead center between Vinnie's eyes.

"What the fuck is going on Antonio?" Vinnie asked through clenched teeth.

"Tsk, tsk, tsk. What the fuck indeed. Watch your language Vinnie. Did you check the sign out front? Naughty, naughty," Antonio laughed. No one in the room dared breathe. The wild glint of madness in Antonio's eyes and echoing in his laughter held them all still. He touched his chest. "Oh don't worry about me cursing big brother. My soul was damned long ago. Ain't that right Lil Willie." Antonio winked at her brother.

Harmony's gaze swung to her brother who surprised her by snatching the gun from her hand. She stumbled back, shocked that he would. Willie raised the gun and pointed it at Vinnie too.

"Good boy," Antonio nodded.

She stared into her brother's eyes and it dawned on her. Something she'd never admitted to herself before. Right in her face was a truth she should have seen.

"Where's Willie?" Harmony rubbed the sleep out of her eyes. "Did you forget your key again?"

Lewis stalked through the tiny front room. She closed the door, awake and a bit concerned by his frosty mood. The pounding on the door had woken her with a start. She closed her robe to ward off the chill Lewis tracked in behind him. Frost and ice covered all the windows, in this type of weather, neither of them should be out. But out he went, and Willie was in tow. Now he's back and as usual she'd spend the night worrying because her brother wasn't home. Willie had been in the streets all day. It felt like the hour was closer to midnight. She didn't understand why her brother often disappeared and why he and Lewis fought so much lately.

"Where is he?"

"Leave it alone Mony, damn." Lewis grumbled. He shed his coat and tossed it to the sofa. It would take an act of Christ around here to get him or Willie to hang up their things, instead of having her picking up after them. She swallowed her objection to his sloppy behavior, though her arms c folded tightly to the front of her chest and she frowned deeply at the clumps of dirt he tracked all over her freshly swept floor.

"Did you leave him out there? Alone? It's the third night this week he hasn't come home and I know you two were together. I'm not stupid."

"Trust me Mony, he can handle himself. You keep wanting to baby him. He ain't no fucking baby." Lewis slurred a bit. He was either drunk on hooch or smoking those funny cigarettes that smelled bad and made her eyes burn when ever she caught him trying to smoke them in their home.

"I'm not babying him, he is a baby, he barely sixteen."

"To hell with that! He's no baby! Wait." Lewis gave a cruel snort. "He ain't a man, either. To be honest Mony I don't know what the fuck he is.... but trust me he can take care of himself."

"You been drinking? Have you lost your senses? He sixteen years old. I want him home, go out there and find him and bring him back."

Lewis shot her a glare that stopped her cold. He leveled a finger at her when he spoke. "I'll spare you the nasty details baby because I know you love the boy. But he's not worth your prayers, or tears. Turn him loose before he breaks your fucking heart." Lewis marched off to the bathroom and slammed the door. Harmony stood there stunned, unsure of the meaning of his unsolicited advice. How dare he tell her to cut ties with her blood? The man wouldn't even put a ring on her finger. She was sick of it. She walked to the bathroom and threw the door open. Lewis blinked at her surprised, holding his penis aiming it toward the toilet in the middle of a piss.

"That's enough Lewis Jamal! I don't care how juiced you are, you go out there and find him. Bring him home!"

Lewis shook his penis and tucked it back into his pants. He went to the sink and ran water over it. "Give it a rest, will you? I'm tired baby. Sorry for earlier, but I'm in no mood to fight with you."

"No!"

"You gonna have to, or better yet, stop getting in my face over it. Talk to him your damn self. See if he will tell you his secret."

"Secret? What secret?"

"Nothing, forget it. Can a man take a shit in peace?"

"You're queer," Harmony said. "That's the secret. That's what you've been keeping from me. What you and Lewis kept from me?"

Willie averted his gaze. He stole a quick glance at Antonio, Vinnie, and then lowered his gaze to the floor. He looked everywhere but at her. Antonio kept his gun trained on his brother. She remembered Leftie's nasty accusation. Said he often had to clean up the messes of the younger Romano. Paulette told her she often saw Antonio and Willie meeting together behind The Cotton. Milo warned her to let Willie go, that she couldn't help him. How many people knew of this sickness her brother had? Why didn't Lewis tell her the truth if Willie wouldn't? Her heart felt as if it stopped beating and the tightness in her chest made it hard to concentrate on fact versus fiction. How low did the depths of her brother's betrayal go? She glanced over to Vinnie who continued to stare at his brother and the gun in his face. He looked so coiled tight with tension she feared he'd strike despite the danger he faced.

Had he heard her? The nasty grin Antonio wore when their eyes met said no. Oh how she wanted to lunge for his throat. Her brother was young, impressionable, and confused and she knew Antonio Romano had exploited all three. "You both are queer," she spat toward Antonio as if the truth tasted bad on her tongue.

Antonio laughed. The scar on his face stretched grotesquely under his wicked smile. He returned his attention to his brother. "Do you know what *queer* means Vinnie?"

Vinnie blinked out of whatever state he had slipped into. He frowned at Antonio then glanced over at Willie. She knew he didn't get the meaning.

"Look at him Lil Will. He doesn't know what it means. I told you he'd have to catch me with my dick in your ass before he got a clue. Ain't that right brother? See his face. He gets it now. Oh yes he's got it now." Antonio pushed the gun into his brother's face with a cold murderous look hardening his features. "I've been waiting for a long time for this. I'm sick of being invisible next to the great Vincenzio Romano! It was like this in Sicily and nothing changed in America. You were the same as Papa! The same! I wanted to get out of here, Teek and I would leave and try Chicago, or Detroit. Do you remember when I asked you for the money? Remember what you said Vinnie? Told me to stay in my lane, that you had big plans for me and you. Fucking hypocrite. The only plans you ever made were for your own selfish purposes. You said you loved Annie, but you didn't give a shit about any of us. Just wanted us all to stay in our lane. Not anymore!"

Vinnie's eyes narrowed into slits of rage. Harmony held her breath and watched as his gloved hands clenched into tight balls of fury.

"It's your fault he's dead. The only person I loved. You and your fucking war for power and respect. The Five Points Gang would have never started that race riot if they hadn't wanted to go after you. They knew about Annie. Everyone did. They knew if they killed that kid and dropped his body off in Harlem the blacks would be blamed for the kids murder and the race riots would begin. You'd have to choose sides Vinnie and you did. You left Teek out there to fend for himself."

"I couldn't have stopped it," Vinnie said.

"Bullshit! Your thirst for power divided us all. It's time you pay for your sins. I've been a bad boy big brother. I wish you would live to see your kingdom burn to the ground. I've given the keys to Mickey Collins. Right now he's wiping you clean. And you didn't even know it."

Vinnie's gaze slipped to Willie, but he didn't move. "What are you saying to me Antonio?" he asked calmly. "That I divided you and Teek from being what? Lovers?"

"You're a hypocrite! You can fuck Annie, playhouse with her, but you would never accept me and Teek. They started that race war because they knew it would separate you from your girl. Instead it destroyed the only person who ever loved me unconditionally." Antonio shouted so loud spittle coated his lips. "Teek and I didn't split up because of the gangs, we split up because Leftie found out about us. He threatened to tell you what he walked in on, and ran Teek off. We were going to run away together after we got the money but you wouldn't fucking give it to me. I ran all the fucking errands you gave me and didn't get shit! Nothing! That's why he joined his gang and I joined mine. We had it all worked out. We loved each other. You hear that Vinnie! Your brother's a queer. What you think of that?"

"Antonio, it's done. He gets it. Let's go," Willie said.

Antonio laughed. He glared at Willie. "Go where? I only put up with you to draw her in." He tossed his chin toward Harmony. "The moment I saw her I knew Vinnie would want a piece. She's his type all right. All I had to do was make her desperate enough to go for him." Antonio returned his attention to his brother. "That's your weakness. We all got one. The dame in distress, needing a hero, is what my brother likes. How many times did Teek and I have to hear Annie talk about how you saved her life? And it worked like a charm. You got weak enough to be sloppy. Easy as pie Vinnie."

Harmony cringed when he addressed her directly. "I had another reason too toots. I couldn't have you running around Harlem telling everyone that Romano was responsible for Willie's sister's boyfriend's murder. It would have ruined my plans."

"You killed Lewis?" Harmony asked in disbelief.

"I didn't know his name," Antonio said, his face red and flushed. He held tight to the gun but spoke to Harmony. "Lil Will told me he was your man. He got between me and Teek the night of the riots. Willie saw it all. I was trying to save Teek but he thought I was attacking him. I shot him."

"Is that true Willie?" Harmony asked.

"Yes."

"And you never said anything to me?"

"I tried to get Lewis help but I couldn't. I brought him home."

"Tell her the rest." Antonio interjected. "Tell her how you came to me and struck a deal. Told me that you and Teek were friends, and you knew all about us. How you helped me plan this. Tell her that part. Tell her how you were glad Lewis was dead, and you were free."

The gun lowered down to her brother's side. Harmony put her hand to her mouth. The pain and disillusionment was too much. "You did all of this, why?"

"Teek was a good guy." Willie explained. "He told me nothing was wrong with me Mony. But Lewis said differently. Lewis thought I was some kind of freak. All those nights you thought I stayed out late wasn't because I was in the streets. It was to avoid Lewis. He'd hit me, curse me, threaten to tell you my secret. He worked me hard for Grease then took my money night after night. When I saw Teek die, and how Antonio tried to save him I knew Teek hadn't lied about them. I thought Antonio understood me."

"You could have told me!"

"No! I couldn't. Lewis took you from me Mony! He moved in on us and set up house and you were too blind or too in love to see it. What could I say to make things different? How could I do anything when my secret is the biggest sin of my life? I'm not going to lie to you, I was glad Antonio shot him. I never meant for you to get hurt but you didn't need to be with Lewis. Look at you now. You sing at The Cotton, people come from everywhere to hear you sing. You a star, and Lewis would have never let that happen. So don't ask me to care that he dead. I don't care."

Harmony felt Vinnie's hand ease to her backside. Gentle but firm he pushed her away from him. He winked and she made no move to return to his side.

"Bravo!" Antonio said. "You got a smart brother here Jazz Singer. We planned it all out. Taking my brother out, destroying him." He grinned at Vinnie, shaking the gun in his face. "You'll love this part Vinnie. I was gonna shoot you first. But then I found her here and decided on a better plan. Shoot you both. Leave the guns, and say she came in here with it and fired on you. Perfect set-up huh?"

"No!" Willie said. "That wasn't the plan. You were going to kill him and make it look like one of Mickey's men did it. Then you'd get the money from Queenie on the booze and we'd leave. That was the plan."

Antonio chuckled. "Shit I forgot. Yeah, that plan. Not quite Lil Will. See I already moved the booze and sold it to Queenie. Got the money."

"Fine, then let's go."

Antonio didn't move.

Harmony noticed her brother stood there perplexed for a moment.

Antonio smiled. "Where? You and me? You aren't Teek, and I got no plans to drag some colored boy across the country with me."

"I don't understand?" Willie said.

Vinnie cleared his throat. "What he's telling you kid is you were on the menu first. He lured me down here to make it look like you shot me. Then he planned to kill you. Right little brother?" Vinnie asked.

"Right." Antonio raised the gun and fired. Willie was thrown off his feet and fired his weapon out of reflex, blowing a hole in the floor. Harmony screamed and ran over to her brother as more gunfire rang out behind her.

As soon as the gun swung toward the kid Romano lunged for his brother. He heard Harmony scream and prayed the rapid fire of Antonio's gun sent bullets into the floor and ceiling and not his lover. Disarming Antonio had to be his top priority. He gripped Antonio's throat and struggled to wrench the gun free from his hand. They turned into the wall and Antonio fought back. The rage on his brother's face broke his heart. He didn't know his madness, but he swore to end it then and there. The gun fired again. Antonio's eyes stretched. He spat blood and let go of the gun.

"Meet you in hell Vinnie," Antonio coughed out and slouched against him. Romano closed his eyes and lowered to the floor with his brother in his arms. He clutched him to his chest and cried out in agony.

Harmony lifted her brother's head and placed it gingerly in her lap. Vinnie held his brother in a similar way. To hear him struggling through his grief made her ache to comfort him.

"Mony?" Willie grabbed her by the front sleeve of her dress, and spit up more blood. "I don't want to die," he stammered.

She gazed down at her foolish brother with love and wept. "You won't die. I promise. Just hang on. Please." Try as she may she could not stop the bleeding. A crimson stream pooled along his left side and soaked her hands. There was too much blood. "Oh God, help me. Please help me!" she shouted through her tears.

"Harmony! Move!" Vinnie said. A pair of strong hands pulled her away and she realized Vinnie had come over to help. She relinquished her hold on him struggling to catch her breath, never in her life had she known such pure, undiluted fear.

"He's dying Vinnie. We got to get him some help."

"Go get the priest. Now. I'll need help to carry him out to my car."

Harmony stared down at her bloody hands, shocked to her core. Blood, so much blood on her, there was blood everywhere.

"Now! Go!" His strong voice blasted away her paralysis. She leapt to her feet and ran for the door. One glance back, she saw Vinnie stripping his shirt off and using it to add pressure to Willie's side to stop the bleeding. In her haste she nearly tripped and fell over a dead Antonio. She ran for the rectory in the church hard and fast.

The next three hours were the worst in his life. Romano would always remember it as such. Harmony's weeping would echo in his head for many years to come. The confession of his brother's dark secrets would haunt him for the remainder of his days. Nothing would be the same. His mind kept turning over memory after memory. The days of Teek and Antonio's special bond and how he encouraged them. Still he had no warning or inclination about the depths of their feelings, and the madness that consumed them both to become lovers. Romano pushed all of it to the back of his mind and buried his regret and grief deep in his heart. He had to focus, and stay the course. The desperation he felt made his foot ride the gas pedal as if it were made of lead, and he sped away from St. Nicholas.

Harmony and her dying brother were his new priority. He'd driven them out of Harlem to the Bronx. It was a wonder the kid didn't bleed to death in the back of his car. He kept glancing up in the rearview mirror at her. His Songbird sang softly and hummed to him as he lay on her lap, and she stroked his head. She did her best to soothe him.

The most discreet and highly paid doctor on his payroll was surprised to find him carrying a bloody Negro man into his door. Together Romano and Harmony waited in blood stained clothes for news. When the doctor announced that Willie needed blood he volunteered to save Harmony the ordeal. But the doctor promptly declined stating the boy needed Negro blood and his sister would be the match. He tried to object. She looked so fragile and distraught, but his efforts were in vain.

Romano paced the floor for over forty minutes, his chest tight with worry. When she returned she sat away from him while the doctor's wife served them tea with a shaky hand and her husband patched up Willie on his kitchen table. No words passed between them. The sordid mess would have to be sorted out later. He wanted to comfort her, but the gulf between them seemed impossible to cross. Her suffering was great. She wept so hard and strong he thought it would drive him to madness.

"Mr. Romano?" The doctor said. He walked out wiping his hands on a clean white towel. "Stitched him up best I could. The boy'll live. We need to make sure he doesn't gain an infection, the next few hours are important. If he survives the night he'll make it."

"Can I see him?" Harmony said rising to her feet. Romano stood as well. The doctor glanced over to him for approval. He nodded it was okay. Before she could pass him he held his arm out and stopped her. She refused to look him in the eye. "I have to go. I need to deal with the fallout of what Antonio done. I'll… return for you. We'll talk."

She didn't respond.

"Songbird… I love you."

She stepped around him and walked away. Defeated, he didn't bother to stop her. Instead he got in his car and drove back to the church. Father Michaels had cleared St. Mary's after the first gunshot fired. The priest helped him carry a wounded Willie out of the basement to his car and promised to send word to his men to come and collect Antonio. Romano arrived after Antonio's body was taken away and the massacre in the church's cellar was wiped clean. Gio waited for him.

"Mickey Collins?" he asked.

"The shipyard is on fire. It's a bloodbath boss. And it gets worse. He had help. That bitch Queenie and her band of Forty Thieves. They hit us all boss. Cleaned you out. I just can't get my head around how they got the jump on us. It makes no sense. So many of our boys are down."

Romano knew exactly how. Mickey had the jump on them from day one. Antonio had been true to his word; he sold him out and gave his fucking enemy the keys to his kingdom. He had no idea his little brother hated him so. Even now when he thought of the tough love he gave, and the iron rules Antonio was forced to heed to when he came from Sicily, a pang of guilt ripped his gut. He had become the terror that his father was. It was no wonder Antonio hated him as much as he himself hated their Papa.

"Mickey's not dead. He's put a price on you. That's why I came. The boys are heading to the cabin to hold up. We need you to go there. To be sure we can keep you safe. Keep a low profile and let us sort through the mess."

"How many men dead?" Romano asked, his voice hollow and void of the stormy emotion raging inside of him.

"Not sure, like I said there was an ambush waiting for us. Worst than the first. We were surrounded. They knew our strategy, everything. Got to be an inside job. When I found out who the fucking snake is I'll cut his balls off."

Romano wiped his hand down his face. "Where's my brother's body?"

"They're taking him out to Woodbury. Who killed Antonio, in a church? Was it the kid you were going to see? One of Mickey's men?"

Romano rubbed his brow. Suddenly he felt bone-tired. "Head to Woodbury after you confirm that Mickey's dead."

"The booze? Did the kid tell you where it was? Maybe we still got a chance to strike back."

Actually it was his brother who delivered the news. His booze was sold to Queenie and the money stashed God knows where. "The booze is gone, all of it is gone just like you said," he mumbled. "I'll follow you out. I need to take care of something at home."

Gio stepped aside and Romano returned to his car. He drove to Woodbury with the moon illuminating the way. The night and darkness covered him, making the hollow emptiness he carried complete.

Again the events of the night plagued him with questions until his mind connected all the pieces and the story fit. Antonio had worked against him from the day Teek died. And none of it was for territory or infamy. All of it was for revenge, and in his warped way to excuse his own insecurities over the man he'd become. He wasn't sure how he felt about his brother being queer. For that reason and others he'd never speak it aloud, he'd not mourn him a day after he shoveled dirt over his grave.

When he arrived at the cabin several cars were parked out front. Antonio's wrapped body was probably taken to the barn. Romano reached over to the seat next to him and palmed his gun. He threw open his door and eased it into the back of his pants. One of his boys approached.

"Boss, I think…"

"Where's Leftie?"

"He was inside earlier. Mabel had to fix him up. Tony says your lady friend did a number on him. The side of his face took a banging."

So his Songbird had fought back? Well Leftie would wish she'd offed him before he was done. "Does Mabel know that Antonio's dead?"

"Yes boss. She's at the barn with his body. We haven't been able to get her out of there. She's given to hysterics, and she's started to clean his wounds."

A flash of wild grief rippled through him and he recalled the same tortured tears Mabel shed when her youngest child was beaten to death. He suppressed the memory of Teek and now Antonio. He exhaled deeply. He wouldn't share the details of Antonio's demise or what was said regarding her son. He'd let her grieve. "Give her another hour then bring her out of there. If not she'll stay with him all night." He headed up the stairs. "When you see Leftie you make sure he comes to see me."

***

"Hi there, how you feeling honey?" Harmony asked. She stroked the side of her brother's face. He looked at her briefly before averting his gaze. It didn't matter. The fact he was awake, breathing, alive, filled her with such joy. Harmony had to keep blinking away her tears as she smiled down at him.

"You stayed?" Willie said in a dry tone.

"Of course I stayed. I had to make sure you were okay. Doctor says if you don't get a fever then you'll heal. I'll be able to take you home."

"Even after... now that you know, what I am? What I've done?"

"We'll talk about that later. Right now I just want you alive. And God heard my prayer. You need to rest, get your strength back."

"Doctor?" Willie scanned the modest furnished room he'd been taken to. "Where am I?"

"Nevermind that..." she shushed him.

He turned his gaze to her, unable to move his head. "This doctor have a look at you Harmony, your face?"

"I'm fine." she leaned over and pressed a kiss to his brow and masked the discomfort she felt.

"Mony, I'm sorry," he said. "Forgive me. I wasn't going to hurt you, never you. Maybe I was trying to hurt myself. I should have never trusted Antonio. Can you really forgive me? "

She closed her eyes and nodded. "I will, give me time and I will."

***

After the third shot of whiskey Romano heard the door behind him open. He poured another glass and swallowed down the contents before the door closed again. "Where have you been?" he asked.

"I was with the men near the barn. We got some major problems. Those coming in say Pier 7, 6 and 4 are cleaned out. While we mobilized and moved in on Collins he had us wiped out. He turned the tables. The men aren't sure you can bring them out of it. And what happened to Antonio? Mickey Collins do that too?"

He rolled the tension from his neck and cut his gaze over to the man he once called friend. Leftie stood before him with the side of his face bandaged from brow to cheek. Though Mabel had tried to patch him up he saw the evidence of his fight with Harmony reaching grotesquely to his lower jaw. "I want to know what happened to your face. What happened here with Harmony?"

Leftie shoved his hands down in his pockets and stepped forward. "Sorry to tell you she flew the coop. I caught her down at the barn trying to steal Mabel's car. When I tried to stop her she went fucking nuts. Tried to attack me."

"Attacked you did she?"

"Look at my face. She stole my gun and Mabel's car. I couldn't..."

Romano drew on Leftie, dropped the pen on the revolver and fired. The first bullet hit his friend in the chest and the second nearly took off his arm. Leftie crashed backward to the floor kicking his feet from under him and spitting up his own blood. Romano walked over and aimed the gun directly at him. He pressed his foot down on Leftie's throat and the man's eyes stretched to the point of bulging, but gurgling choking noises were cut off. Leftie's nostrils flared to the size of quarters as he struggled hard to breathe." I told you not to touch her. No one is to ever fucking touch her. You should have listened to me."

Leftie kicked his feet and clawed at his throat with his good hand.

"I'll make it quick. Tell Antonio I'll see you both in hell, soon." Romano fired the kill shot and Leftie went still. He turned easing the gun into the back of his pants and walked away as men that worked for him rushed in. "Bury him, and clean up the blood. I don't want Mabel to see him like this. I'm going to clean up. Can't move Harmony's brother this far. Will have him taken to my place in the Bronx."

"Not wise, Mickey's men might try to get to you."

"Let them try," he said bitterly. "Tell Gio to see me in the morning."

With that said he stepped over the man he'd trusted as a brother and walked up the stairs.

***

The night's events had drained the fight out of her. Harmony didn't object when Vinnie arrived to collect them. The men removed her brother gingerly from the doctor's house, and they drove only ten minutes to Vinnie's place. Harmony stood outside of it watching them carry Willie in. She glanced up to the brownstone and remembered the first time he had brought her there. In less than a week the woman who thought she could control it all had vanished. Nothing would be the same for them.

"It's cold out." Vinnie said. He stepped behind her and draped her shoulders with his trench coat. She dropped her lashes quickly to hide her deep hurt. Earlier she had tried to take his life. Before that she had gone after him with a knife. How could she explain her lack of faith in him when deep down she needed him still?

"Are you okay?" he asked. She managed to nod, though a heaviness centered in her chest. "Let's get you inside." He held her close, his arm locked around her waist as he walked her up the steps. Her trembling limbs welcomed the warmth and strength his embrace always provided.

Vinnie had Willie placed in his spare room. She wanted to thank him but she turned to find he had gone. She didn't know what to do or say. She joined her brother and stayed at his bedside.

An hour passed and he didn't return. Harmony began to believe he'd left when the door opened and he stood there staring at her. His face was cast in shadows. The light spilled in from behind him and his profile spoke of inner control and self-restraint. After all he'd killed his own brother and hadn't said a word against hers since the ordeal began. Harmony slowly rose from her chair. It was time they said the things they needed to. Her life had become one bitter battle after another. However, with Vinnie it was different, from the first day to this moment, it had always been different.

Vinnie walked over and took her hand in his. She allowed him to lead her out of the room and up the stairs toward what she thought would be his bedroom. At some point during the silent climb she found her voice but when she opened her mouth to speak she decided against it. There were no words to express all the pain and raw hurt that weighed heavy on her heart.

"Does it hurt?" he drew her closer and inspected her face, particularly her swollen eye. Shame curled in her breast and she recalled the nasty things Leftie said to her when he attacked her. Should she tell Vinnie the gory details? They were in the bathroom outside of his bedroom. He flicked on the light and stiffened visibly when the glare revealed the horror of her ordeal. He cursed under his breath, then softened his gaze and brushed his lips over her left swollen eyelid. Vinnie rolled up his sleeve. He went to the cabinet and removed a small tin box. He dug out a tube of some kind of ointment and she leaned back against the sink, bracing her hands there for support. She knew it would sting. His touch, however, was gentle. Yet everywhere his finger grazed burned. She tried not to cry, or show weakness. The loss of trust between them was beyond tears.

"I want your forgiveness," he began.

She blinked up at him surprised. "You do?"

He continued to clean away dried blood and add a cooling ointment to her bruise that made the tightness on the side of her face lessen.

"I do."

"Okay," she said.

"I'll have to earn it. My brother acted alone Harmony. I had no idea he was… what he'd done. I don't blame your brother for going along with him. Antonio can be quite convincing when he wants to be. He certainly had me fooled."

"I'm sorry your brother is dead."

Vinnie stopped tending to her face. His gaze lowered to hers. "Don't be. I know he wanted me to kill him, just as I know most of what he said about me tonight was true."

"No, Vinnie."

"It was. But not anymore Songbird, I'm not that man anymore. How can I be? Too much blood has been spilled in my name. I'm not my father."

"You're better than him, all of them."

"Shhh. Tonight… neither of us could have known how far things would go. It happened. I accept it, I can't change it."

She nodded that she understood. Who they were, what their brothers' had become wouldn't change.

"Can I bathe? I… I have Willie's blood on me." She said.

His hand fell away. He stepped back at her request and she turned over her hands. Blood ringed her fingernails and was caked beneath. Her hands were stained pink with it.

"I'll get you some towels."

Harmony breathed easier when he left. She shed her dress and underwear, then ran water in the tub. When he returned she stood nude. He glanced at her body and the frozen look of concern made her gaze lower as well. Leftie had hit her with his belt and though she ached all over the red scarring of welts across her breasts, abdomen, and thighs shocked her.

"The fucking bastard!" Vinnie said through clenched teeth. She was so embarrassed, so stricken with shame and disbelief she broke down. Her hands went up to her face and she sobbed hard. Before she knew what was happening his arms were around her and she was pressed against his chest. She clung to him so tight she thought they were joined as one. She wailed against the injustice of it all until the fear and frustration eased her into small whimpers of acceptance. Vinnie never let her go. He kissed her brow and stroked her tenderly.

"Stay, Vinnie. Don't leave me, I don't want to be alone," Harmony pleaded.

Compassion softened his granite like composure and she knew he understood what she needed. His fingers clamped her trembling chin. "I had no intention of leaving you, Songbird. I love you."

"You do?"

"I do. And I'm going to take care of you, for as long as I can," he said.

Her heart fluttered at the ominous note in his voice. What did he mean? Was he leaving? She couldn't stand a night alone with all the memories of the day. She wouldn't let him go. "Can we get in the bath together? You and me."

"Yes." He reluctantly let her go to stop the running water. When he turned toward her she reached for his shirt and began to unbutton it. He pulled it off when it fell open and she undid the belt to his pants. He shed his clothes and she stepped into the tub making room for him. When they were seated with her back resting against his chest she felt safe. Harmony closed her eyes and let his arms fold around her. It hurt less when she was in his arms. After awhile he began to bathe her. He scrubbed her hands then lowered them under the water to rub the bar of soap over her wounds and scars gently. She cupped water in her curled palms and poured it back over her face, over her hair letting the rinse take away every reminder of the night.

"You said you love me." Harmony spoke. She could feel his erection grow stronger against her spine. Vinnie didn't answer. She didn't expect him to. She closed her eyes to the circular massage of the soap over her tender abdomen. "I love you too Vinnie."

He inhaled sharply and released a deep sigh behind her and she managed a smile. Vinnie let go of the soap and once again folded his arms around her. She sank against his broad chest and sucked down deep calming breaths of her own. Together they floated on a soothing silence and his closeness felt so male and protective. Harmony wanted to stay this way forever.

"Tonight was my fault. All of it. I should have known not to trust Leftie with you. I should have worked harder to protect you. And Antonio." His voice broke. Harmony waited and listened. "He had problems, and I never cared. I was too focused on training him, grooming him, just like my father did me."

"Antonio's issues were his own. I should have trusted you too Vinnie. I wouldn't have shot you. I'm sorry I pulled a gun on you."

"Do you know how to fire one?"

"A gun? No."

"I'll teach you. Soon."

"Uh, alright."

He turned her face so she could look back at him. "I'm sorry Leftie hurt you. He won't ever again. I swear it."

Harmony turned in the tub and water sloshed over the side to the linoleum floor. She eased on his lap forcing his legs closed and her knees to the outside of his thighs. She gripped the back of the tub over his shoulders, her face close, drawing closer. He kissed her first and it was such a relief. But the action stung through her bottom lip all the way to the left side of her face. She winced.

He wrapped his arms around her and sighed against her lips. "You sure about this, Songbird? Does it hurt?" Vinnie asked, his tone soft with concern.

"Not any more," she said settling on top of him, her arms locked around his neck and her sex grooving in slow sexy swirls over his hard cock. His thickness pressed between her inner folds. The water was cool now but the blood boiling her veins had her warm and tingly all over.

"I don't think we should. You've had a rough night. Let me take care of you." He tried to lift her from his lap. Harmony refused to release him. Instead she reached in the water and grabbed his shaft in her hands. Before he could stop her she guided him to her core and eased down on his length. Vinnie went stiff and she closed her eyes, allowing his girth and length to fill her completely. It was all raw emotion now. Having him inside of her seemed to anchor her to reality. She didn't want to think the dark layers of their love over, she just wanted to feel something more than regret and pain.

Vinnie's head dropped back and his lids lowered then closed. Harmony rose and fell on him using all her strength in the lower half of her body, rewarded with deep shudders under wave after wave of her rolling hips. Pleasure filled her to the root and she kept going, kept moving, and kept driving them both to the edge. Her inner walls felt tight, and his cock unbearably thick, but she kept going. He ran his hands down her sides gingerly. She winced and continued loving him. Soon he forgot the need to go soft and slow and was slamming forged steel up into her. She cried out, dropping her head on his shoulder and shuddered though another release.

She kissed his neck and the side of his face. "I feel better now. Do you?"

The lovemaking wasn't his choice. But he was so weak for her he didn't put a stop to it. He felt ashamed of how he ravished her knowing what she'd been through. Romano dried her, and himself. He only joined her in the tub to keep her close to him. The sight of the bruises on her body had him panicked with worry. Leftie had died too easily. He felt the insane urge to dig the bastard up and carve her name into his chest. He should have done exactly that before he sent him to hell.

Together they returned to his bedroom. She was wrapped up in his oversized robe, and he wore a towel tied around his waist. He tried to lead her to the bed, but she rejected the idea. Instead she wanted to sit on the soft rug near the fireplace he'd lit. He joined her and they lost themselves in the dancing flames.

"I don't understand my brother," Harmony whispered. "He could have come to me."

"Could he?" Vinnie asked. "You love him, yes, but if he came to you and told you about Lewis and the things he'd done to him because of what he is, what would you have said?"

She closed her eyes and dug deep in her heart for the truth. "I love him Vinnie. There has to be something I can do for him now."

"You can do for him what I didn't do for Antonio."

Her eyes opened, she half-turned in his arms, curious. "What's that?"

"Let him go. Let him be his own man, make his own mistakes. It's time to let go Harmony. If I had given Antonio the money he asked and set him free, he and Teek would be alive today."

She sniffed. "I let him go then what will I have? I'm twenty-four and I have no kids, no family, no real friends left but Paulette."

"Yourself for starters. I saw what you did to Leftie, saw how hard you fought to save your brother. You're stronger than most men I know, Doll. Strong and brave."

"Myself? Is that all I'll have?" she pressed.

"Me. You'll have me. For as long as I'm alive. Always."

She settled back against him. He leaned to kiss her cheek.

"I'm thinking we should leave New York. Go West," he said.

"Together?"

"Eventually, yes. I'm thinking you should leave first."

Harmony sat upright. "First? What do you mean first?"

She turned and faced him. She sat facing him, her legs parted, his parted as well so that her bottom rested on the floor. Vinnie leaned back on his hands studying her face. She tried not to be self-conscious but she'd caught a glimpse of her red, swollen eye and it wasn't her best look. "I don't understand. Why do I have to leave first?"

"Antonio made a mess of things. I'm not sure how bad. I need to fix things and I have a responsibility to these men. I can't explain it further than that, and you can't stay here Harmony, I need to know you're safe."

"Where will I go?"

"You decide. It's time for you to be free. It's what you wanted, right? Freedom, a life of your own?" he touched her face. "Pick a place. Any place."

Harmony stared in his eyes for a moment. She managed a smile even though he was sure it pained her. "What places are coloreds and whites free to marry?"

Romano chuckled. He smiled sadly. "If I remember correctly, besides here, blacks and whites can marry in Kansas, Iowa, Washington, Michigan, Ohio, Pennsylvania and New Mexico..."

"Wait. I like the sound of it."

"Of what?"

"New Mexico. A new place, where I can be free to be me, and love who I want."

"I hear it's hot there, with desert like weather. Small towns, no real cities."

"Doesn't matter. It's where I can start over. We can start over."

"You sure you still want me?"

"What do you think?" she took him by the face and drew his mouth closer to hers. He gave her a snort of laughter. Her lovely lids dipped and shut and he lowered her to the rug. He paused to kiss her, whispering his love for each part of her body. Instinctively her body arched toward him and he made sure to caress every bruise with his lips and gentle hands. His body moved to cover hers. Before he could love her properly he had to be inside her. A single thrust had his toes curling. The heat of her skin ignited his lusty, urgent needs. She was so moist, so welcoming, her body beckoned him to go the distance. He stroked forward, not stopping until he was balls deep. Her inner vaginal walls clamped down hard around his shaft, then released, and clasped and released again.

"Yes baby, don't stop." She exhaled.

He thrust harder and she rolled her hips in response. It wasn't enough; he burned for more of her. He widened his legs and eased up with his free hand on her hip to keep himself steady, and then he unleashed. He began to fuck her, go deeply in and out of her tight channel. Her whimpers became full-bodied groans. The moment she crested he knew it. Her back arched up from the rug and then sank back down as she released the loveliest sigh. Vinnie fell on top of her and pumped his ass full throttle until his balls emptied every bit of his seed into her core. He couldn't sing her praises, or catch his breath. The shared orgasm slammed against him making him weaker than a newborn.

Harmony wrapped her sweet arms around him and held him to her chest. "I love you." He panted. "I love you so much, Songbird."

"I love you too."

CHAPTER ELEVEN
Sacrifices…

Three Days Later

Sun burned bright over his face , he squinted, turning away from the heat. After a few minutes he awoke. The room appeared as nothing more than a blur of shadows. He waited and his vision focused. Songbird had left his bed. Waking to her soft warm body pressed against his had become a satisfying consistent in his life. He missed her before his lids parted. He and his men were all keeping a low profile. Every newsman in the city ran a story on what they labeled 'Bloody Sunday'. So many men's lives had been cut short, even the connections he had with the police gave him little cover. All he could do was wait out the heat.

"Morning."

His head dropped over to the left. She sat next to the window with the curtain drawn. She stared out at the street, sipping something from her cup. The home remedies he'd rubbed on her face and body had healed her bruises quickly. There was little evidence of what that bastard had put her through. He was grateful. Each time he saw evidence of her pain, murderous rage churned in his gut.

"Come back to bed," he said, missing her deeply.

"In a minute. I like sitting here," she smiled. "Watching you sleep."

The night had been sweet, and his cock twitched with remembrance. He wanted to roll over to her soft body as he had done the past two days. How the hell would he ever be able to let her go now? "How's your brother. Check on him this morning?"

There was a lovely gleam of happiness bright in her chocolate brown eyes. She turned her sweet smile back to him. "Good. He's in a lot of pain but I think that means he's on the mend. No fever, so I know that's a good sign. This morning he was sitting up. I made him lie back down so he wouldn't overdo it. We are leaving today? Right? Going back to the cabins? I think I want to ride Mary again."

"Yes." Romano placed his arms behind his back.

"Were you serious about joining me, in New Mexico Vinnie? Be honest please," she said rising and walking over to the bed. He shifted his legs so she could sit on the edge of the mattress. He lifted his hand and brushed the side of her face with his knuckles. She caught his palm and kissed it.

"Yes. I never want to break a promise, Songbird. If there's breath in my body I'll always find my way to you."

"Remember when I told you I would dream songs? I dreamt one last night. Want to hear it?"

His eyes stretched in surprise. Her singing was the second favorite thing he loved about her. Morning serenades seemed too good to be true. "Yes. I want to hear it."

True to her word she favored him with her lovely voice and a familiar song was cleverly altered with new lyrics that spoke of their adventurous love. Her breath hitched between verses and she released a soft sultry moan before easing into a sweet melody. She sang of a new start and fresh choices, and he was lost in her voice. He barely heard the words. There was something uniquely serene about how he felt when she sang. She brushed his lips with a very faint kiss. Romano reached for her thigh and waist to bring her to his lap and she straddled him on the bed. He cupped the back of her neck and kissed her, ending the sweet song with her moaning through their kiss. He rolled her and dragged his lips from her mouth to her neck then tore open the front closed collar of her robe so they could travel down to the lovely breasts he'd previously ignored. Harmony yanked the sheets from his waist that had him wrapped tight, and he kicked them free as well. With his mouth he worked his tongue licking and sucking her plump nipple. She responded with mewling whimpers that excited him.

He eased down and tossed the bottom half of her robe open so he could dip his tongue in her navel. She spread her thighs wider and started to sing again. After all the many times he'd made love to her, it was the first time she ever sang to him this way. The temperature of his blood spiked and his heart beat at an uncontrollable rate. Her voice was as smooth as milk and honey. Romano groaned, trailing his tongue through the spry hairs of her thick bush down to her sweetly swollen pussy. His tongue toggled her clit and her voice lifted into soprano.

Vinnie chuckled.

He took her hand encouraging her to assist, and she plied herself open for his exploration. The tip of his tongue did a delicious swirl at her center and her hips undulated upward with quick jerky movements. Her singing stopped but her desperate pleas for more increased. She came hard for him and he buried his nose, lips, and chin in her essence. Harmony rolled away groaning. Her tormented groans were a heady invitation for him to give her more. He turned her to her stomach and flipped the robe over her ass to her back. Romano wiped his face over the plush mounds of her round ass cheeks and smacked the left one hard. She giggled. She lifted her hips, spread her knees, and buried her face into her pillow. He placed the head of his cock at her entrance and slowly pushed inside until he was balls deep. He halted and held her by the hips to prevent her from moving and causing him to break control.

"Vinnie, don't stop," she groaned in disappointment. Her inner walls tightened then loosened, and then tightened again trying to draw him deeper if that were possible. Romano pressed the side of his legs against her outer thighs and urged her to close them. She did as he ordered and her pussy clamped down even tighter on his shaft. He exhaled noisily almost dropping his load.

He closed his eyes and began to move in and out of her slow and easy. He rubbed her ass and down her spine with one hand and held tightly to her hip with the other. She pushed back against him repeatedly forcing him to return to her tightness after every withdrawal. Soon another orgasmic explosion was unleashed and he was pounding his love for her into her backside, spraying her womb with his release.

Harmony dropped first and he fell on top of her. She giggled. "I don't think we can leave this bed."

"Good, I don't plan to let you."

***

"Any news?"

"None of it good," Ignacio said.

Two men sat across from his desk stiff and unrepentant. The only light in his office came from the lamp on his desk. The darkly paneled walls, mahogany furnishings, and closed drapes cast the entire room in bleak shadows. It served well for the mood he'd found himself in. And now he had the best men in his crew acting against his wishes and returning to deliver more news of their failures. Romano couldn't blame them for trying to strike back against Collins. The casualties of this war between Collins and his men had bled the soul of his operation dry. Antonio hadn't only robbed him of their brotherhood; he'd given his enemies an unfair advantage by allowing them to steal from him, but his reckless actions had cost him the respect of the men that had sworn allegiance.

"How many?" Romano asked.

"Twenty, maybe thirty of the men are loyal. Lucky Luciano has stepped in. He's calling a meeting. We hear Sottocapo, Costello, Genovese are said to be furious as well and siding with Collins. You aren't invited to the table." Ignacio slipped Gio a sly glance. "We sent your message to Marrazano. You know he doesn't approve of Luciano, and his dealings with Collins or Costello."

"Marrazano will not work with anyone who is not full blood Sicilian. Yes I know. He's old school Mafioso, believes in honor and respect, which none of those fuckers do." Romano seethed.

"Times are changing," Gio finally spoke up. "The old ways are no longer working. This isn't Sicily. Look at what's happening. Luciano is gaining power and friends by aligning with non-Sicilians. If you were to go to him and tell your story, then maybe a deal can be made."

Romano slammed his fist down hard on the wood surface of the desk. Gio silenced. There would be no way in hell he'd go on his knees to Luciano. He ran the slums on the lower east side with him when they were fifteen. They were from the same village. He owed him shit, and wouldn't grovel now.

"I meant no disrespect, boss," Gio said.

The apology sounded as hollow as the excuses he'd received over their inability to neutralize Mickey Collins. With Luciano and his alliances now in the mix, the situation had become even graver. Romano watched them both silently. The side of his face rested between his thumb and his trigger finger. Ignacio swallowed and continued with the message. "Marrazano follows the old ways and... well..."

"Say it!" Romano seethed.

"He's heard about the colored jazz singer you have with you. He doesn't approve of your lifestyle. He's not willing to step in."

"I see." Romano said. He figured it was a long shot. The rumors were flying with Antonio's death and the cops circling. He even had a detective stop by to ask a few questions regarding his brother's whereabouts. His moving Harmony in with him cost him the respect of some of his men. No one called Antonio queer to his face, but if somehow it was indeed known and shared with Don Salvatore Marrazano, the old man would certainly cast him out of his favor.

"Then it's done."

The men exchanged surprised looks.

"Don't worry boys. I expected as much. We all make our beds, I've made mine."

"We think you should move back to Woodbury," Gio said. "We can't keep this place safe much longer. It's the best option."

He wiped his hand down his face and released a long heavy sigh. He knew the score the night it all went to hell. Mickey Collins wanted him dead, and with Luciano backing him they'd move on him soon. He'd lost over a hundred men to the turf war. Sixty of them had abandoned him. The boys who remained were jumpy and on edge, questioning his authority and defying his orders. Instead of ruling them with an iron fist he'd spent three days held up in his brownstone with his lady in his arms avoiding it all. The truth of the matter was simple. He was tired of the war, the battles, and ready for the end his father always predicted for him.

"We'll leave today while it's daylight." He opened his drawer, and removed two envelopes. Both were tossed on the top of the desk. Ignacio and Gio lowered their eyes to the money and neither man could speak. Many thought him penniless. Rumors had it that Antonio had cleaned him out. Much of it was true. But growing up hard on the streets, hungry and lost he learned to save. For every dollar earned in his hustle he saved three. That was no one's fucking business. "Pay the men, find out who wants to come with me and who wants to stand. Either way it's time."

"What are you doing?" Mabel's sharp voice cracked like an overseers whip behind her. Harmony whirled to find the maid glaring, her face pinched in a deep scowl. To add to her shame she'd been caught with her ear pressed to the door. A clumsy stammer of excuses tumbled from her mouth.

"If he catches you spying he'll be furious."

"I know. Don't tell him. I don't want to upset him."

"Hmpf!"

"Can I talk to you? Please," she lowered her voice. She hurried away from the door before Vinnie appeared hoping Mabel would follow. Reluctantly she did. Harmony had been desperate to find out what had him so silent and despondent before and after he met with his men. Every time she tried to broach the subject he changed it. Mabel could be her only hope to understand what she heard through the door.

Willie opened his eyes. He first thought the visitor to be Harmony. She checked in on him at least once an hour. He faked sleep several times just to avoid her hovering. He loved her, but he needed time. So much guilt and conflict churned within him, he wasn't sure of what life would throw him next.

Clarity of mind returned and he focused. Mr. Romano walked inside and the door fell shut behind him. He looked tough, dangerous and unforgiving. Why did Harmony float around this place and blush every time he asked about her relationship with the man? His sister was a smart woman, and not prone to taking up with a white man on a whim. It didn't add up.

He'd only had one meeting with Romano. The night they brought him in, he woke hours later to a very uncomfortable conversation where he had no choice but to confess the dirty truth of Antonio's plan. He shared everything, including the lies Antonio whispered in his ear regarding his fake feelings for him. Romano asked two questions. None were about Mickey Collins's operation. No. Romano wanted to know about Teek's death and his brother's grief. Willie shared the history he knew and tried to spare him some of the things he had heard about them.

After the inquisition ended, Mr. Romano spoke in a direct unyielding manner. "Harmony tells me you're feeling better?"

"Yessir." Wilie nodded.

Romano leveled his gaze and Willie held his breath for what was to come next. "I'm glad to hear it. In a week I need you on your feet."

"Sir?"

"Harmony's leaving, heading to New Mexico. You will need to be strong enough to make the journey with her. A week is all you'll have."

"I can do it."

"Good. I expect you to be sure she arrives in New Mexico and never returns to Harlem or New York. Do you understand?"

"No? I can't say that I do. Harmony has different plans."

"Is that so?" Romano left brow arched.

"Yessir, she told me she wouldn't be leaving for a month or so. She said that you would be joining her right after?"

The mob boss stepped closer to the bed. He eased his hands in his pockets and a small smile flashed over his face before it faded. "She's a special dame. Always has been. But she's wrong. If I can join her I will. There's a strong probability that I won't be able to. If it comes to that she'll want to return here, look for me. You'll make sure she doesn't do that."

Willie nodded.

"I expect your word on this. I'm going to ignore the debt you owe. The fact you drew a gun on me should have you pushing up daisies. I'll let that go too. Not because I'm soft on you Willie, but because I am on her. That's my final gift to her, your life. *Capice?*"

"Yes."

"Then repay the debt to your sister. You owe her your life. Protect her with yours."

He swallowed and nodded. Romano's gaze swept the room then returned to him. His squared jaw tensed visibly. "We'll be traveling out to my cabins. I plan to teach her how to fire a weapon and a few other things to protect herself. You up for a quick trip?"

"I can manage," Willie blurted.

Romano nodded then turned and left. As soon as the door closed Willie let go a deep breath. Finally he understood his purpose. He will protect Harmony from men like Romano, Lewis, from all of them. He owed her that and more. It would be his sacrifice.

"Sit down child, your pacing is giving me a headache."

"Can't. Something's wrong," Harmony said. After a few minutes she gave up and pulled out the chair to the kitchen table. She sat across from Mabel. "Vinnie's different. He hasn't left the house since we got here. I don't see anybody but Gio and Ignacio visiting him regularly. And not as many men patrolling either. And he has trouble sleeping Mabel. In the middle of the night he leaves our bed to go down to his office and drink, and pace, I know something's wrong. What is it?"

"You the one listening to the door, you tell me." Mabel huffed.

"I ain't heard nothing that makes any sense to me. Would you stop fighting me on this? We both care for him. Don't we? I'm scared for him. It's bad what Antonio done, isn't it?"

"Antonio dead. What can a dead man do from his grave? Don't go talkin' about what you don't know. Antonio was a good boy. Vinnie has it under control. Men respect him, fear him. He can handle whatever it is."

There would be no getting through to Mabel. Her loyalty to Vinnie blinded her to his weaknesses and faults. It was clear to Harmony why Annie ran away from her mother. If she had this attitude even after the death of her son, it would break any daughter's heart. Yesterday, Harmony heard two men talking of the war brewing in the streets while outside cleaning her brother's linen on the washboard. Vinnie didn't seem like the kind of man who would hide or cower from a battle. And now he kept talking about her leaving. She felt it in her gut. He was in trouble. She stood, and pushed the chair back to the table. Mabel would be of no help. She needed to confront him and get the whole story.

"There you are." Vinnie entered from behind her and she went still. Her eyes stretched to warn Mabel not to reveal what they discussed. Mabel rolled her eyes and pursed her lips with stubbornness. "Miss my girl." Vinnie said kissing the back of her head.

She turned and smiled brightly. He glanced between her and Mabel, his eyes narrowing with suspicion. "Something up ladies?"

"Nope." Mabel rose. "Only thing up is the linen. Done finished hanging your clothes out on the line and got ironing to do, gonna start dinner in an hour. What you want tonight, Mr. Romano?"

"Delay it." Vinnie said. "I want to talk to the both of you." He wrapped his strong arms around Harmony's waist and pulled her tight up against his chest. "We're leaving in an hour. Pack what you can and leave everything else. I'll send one of the men to pick it up."

"Where we going?" Harmony asked. He kept his hold firm on her so she had to lean her head back and to the left to look at him. Still she couldn't see beyond his profile.

"To the cabins. We need some fresh air. Nothing to worry about." She released a breath.

"Mabel. In two days you will be going to Chicago. Annie is going to meet you there."

"What?" Mabel gasped.

"I spoke to her."

"You did?" Harmony asked, and felt her heart sink in her chest. She held her breath and tried to wait out his news without interjecting again. But she wanted to turn on him and demand to know why he would call his ex-girlfriend, even if the reason was plain. He must have sensed or felt her tension. He kissed her cheek before he addressed Mabel. "Annie misses you. She wants you to know your grandchild. It's time."

"I'm not leaving. You need someone to take care of you." She shot Harmony a withering look of contempt. "You've been through too much."

"You're going. I'm not selfish about this anymore, like I said your daughter needs you now. I think it's time for us both to move on."

She stood there silent for a moment. A great sense of compassion for Mabel overwhelmed Harmony. However, the emotion didn't overshadow her greater sense of relief. She wanted Mabel gone. She wanted to take care of Vinnie and her brother alone. Start their new life again on their terms. Mabel was an anchor to his past and Vinnie needed to be free.

"But…" Mabel began.

"It's done." Vinnie said firmly.

"Fine. Since I have no say." Mabel sulked, her voice shaky. She rose and Vinnie let Harmony go. He walked over to Mabel bringing her to his arms. Harmony watched them embrace. He kissed Mabel's forehead and spoke softly against her ear. Harmony couldn't hear his words but the last of Mabel's strength and stubbornness drained from her face. The older woman wept against his chest, and Vinnie held her until she got it all out. After a moment he released her and Mabel hurried from the room with her hand to her mouth.

"You okay?" Harmony asked. She walked over and touched his face, then let her hand drift down his neck to rest against his chest. "That had to have been hard."

"As long as I got you Doll, I'm right as rain. Now get busy, we're leaving soon."

Harmony rose on her toes and kissed him. She then turned for the door. Stopping there she cast her gaze back at him. He could no longer disguise the weariness in his eyes. "No worries Vinnie. We'll make it."

He winked, and she left smiling.

Two days later –
"Steady, steady…"

"Would you stop? I can't concentrate."

A large shadowy grove on the summit of a hillock is where he'd chosen her lessons to take place. Harmony rested the butt of the rifle against the front of her shoulder and aimed it at the rusted can he placed on a decayed log. She closed one eye and concentrated on the target. Perspiration beaded across her brow, she felt moisture above her top lip and along her nape as single tears of sweat slowly coursed over her skin. The sun was relentless and so was the pressure to prove herself a good pupil. She wanted to make him proud. Thinking of him and protecting them from whatever was out there in the world that would try to divide them, she concentrated on her target. Vinnie stood silent but watchful. She intended to show him that two days of lessons had made her kills sharp and exact. She pulled the trigger. The can flew off the log and tumbled to the ground. "See that!"

"I sure did."

"I knew I could do it."

"You're a good student."

"Nope, got a good teacher, and he's cute too!" she grinned, ignoring the soreness in her shoulder from the kickback of the rifle. He walked out and picked up the can to replace it on the log. He returned removing a pistol from the back of his pants.

"This one here is called a Johnny Ringo, Doll. It's my first piece, my favorite."

She accepted the revolver handing off the rifle to him. He'd taught her how to load a Colt .45 but the Johnny Ringo was a bit different. It had a wider cylinder and shorter nozzle. "Nice." The gun was shiny with a brown wood grip and weighed heavy in her hand. She dropped the cylinder, spun it, and then clicked it back in place. He nodded his approval at how good and comfortable she was now.

"Should I shoot it?"

"Go ahead, it's yours."

"What?" Harmony gasped. "But you said it was your favorite gun?"

"Still is. Always will be. That's why I gave it to you. Now show me what you can do."

She raised the gun and squinted with one eye closed. She aimed it steady with both hands gripping the gun. The cannon blast was stunning from such a beautiful piece, she fired and blasted the can off the log. He clapped and she nearly cheered herself. Each time she pulled the trigger she felt a rush. "I can't believe I'm out here in the woods playing with pistols."

"No game, Doll." Vinnie came behind her and massaged her shoulders. He paid special attention to the tenderness on her right one from the rifle. How he knew her needs, aches, desires without her explaining them confounded her. But she guessed it was part of their connection. She never felt so loved and in love before. He lowered her raised arms and forced her to point the gun south. "I want you to be able to protect yourself. Always. No man will ever put his hands on you. Next time you draw your weapon, no matter what you're carrying, you use it. Understand?"

"Yessir." She sidled up close to him. He stared down at her and she pursed her lips for a kiss. He swept her weightless into his arms. His demanding kiss caressed her lips but urged her to return the fervor. Her tongue swept through his mouth and clashed with his and her bones melted against him. She groaned deeply when he withdrew, her mouth gaped for another taste of him. "Another one of those kisses and I'm gonna hike up my dress and make you mine." She teased.

"Haven't you guessed it by now, Songbird? I'm already yours."

"Yeah, but I like making you prove it." She grabbed his groin and squeezed.

He threw his head back and laughed. Vinnie knew she went without panties unless it was time for her monthly. Suddenly, Harmony realized it was the first genuine laughter she had heard from him since the death of his brother. She pressed her face to his chest and wrapped her arms around him holding the gun with one hand. "It's good to see you smile again, Vinnie. I hate that you've been so sad."

"I'm not sad."

"Okay, maybe not sad, but you have been tense."

"I'm okay, Songbird. Let's start back. Mabel leaves today."

They began the walk out of the woods. He kept his arm draped around her shoulder and hers fit comfortably around his waist. "Vinnie?"

"Yes?" he said strolling at her side.

"Where did all your men go?"

He looked up, a bit surprised by her question. She glanced at the three lingering to the front of the main house. There had been fifteen camping out the first day they arrived. And that was far less than the thirty she saw roaming the land before the mafia war began. Now there were only six? Three on patrol at the house and three at the front gates a mile up the drive.

"Business, you know."

"Oh," she said, trying not to be alarmed. The men that remained walked with rifles and guns, faces drawn in deep scowls and bodies tense. It was a bit unnerving.

When they arrived to the main house Mabel came out of the door with her hat and gloves on. A white purse was hooked over her arm. She locked eyes with Vinnie, ignoring Harmony altogether. It didn't matter. Harmony had respect for the strange relationship he had with his ex's mother. She could see the gamut of emotions passing between them. Mabel descended the stairs and Vinnie approached to take her by the hand and lead her to the waiting car. "You travel safe."

"I won't see you again, will I?" Mabel said, her voice cracking with emotion.

Vinnie smiled. "No."

"I love you, I loved Antonio. We were a family no matter what any of them said. I just wish you and Annie would have seen it the way I had. Things could have been so different."

He kissed her cheek and helped her in the car. They again spoke in hushed tones. Eventually he withdrew and closed the door. Vinnie hit the roof of the car. The cab that had driven in to collect her rode off.

Harmony walked over and eased her hand into his. "How did you find her daughter? Reach her?"

"Got a telegram from Annie over a year ago asking for me to do what I did today. I was too angry and full of pride to let Mabel go. To let Annie go." He squeezed her hand. "I was a different man."

"So you wired her and said you would send Mabel to her?"

"I did."

"We really are going to leave here. Start over somewhere fresh. Aren't we?"

"Things will be different Harmony. Much different."

***

Harmony knocked on her brother's door. She balanced his dinner on the tray in her hand.

"Come in," he said.

She pushed the door open and found Willie sitting up on the edge of the bed. His chest was wrapped tightly around the ribcage. She kept his bandages clean and replaced them often. He had his color back. His usually vibrant chestnut skin had an ashen look to it over the past few days. Now he seemed stronger.

"What you got there?" he asked.

"Mabel made some stew. I figure we should eat it all up before I get in the kitchen and start whipping up my recipes for you guys."

Careful of her load she lowered it to the dresser next to his bed. She turned to bring in fresh sheets and stopped when Willie grabbed her hand. "What is it?" she asked when he didn't speak.

"You a housewife now? What about The Cotton. You said after Lewis died jazz was all you needed."

Harmony grinned. "Jazz was all I had. Now I have something more. I'm done with The Cotton and smoky speakeasies. I'm ready for something more." She cupped his chin and kissed his nose. "You should be too."

"Mony!" he said firmly. "Get your head out of the clouds. You've been through a lot. The bruises ain't all healed. Besides we still haven't talked."

"No!" She snatched her hand away. She smoothed down her dress. "I don't want to talk about the mistakes we've made. I'm trying to focus on the good now." She turned for the door. He couldn't believe her refusal to see their lives for what they'd become.

"We leave tomorrow," he blurted when she opened the door to leave. She paused and looked back at him. Her eyes narrowed.

"No we don't."

"I just spoke with Mr. Romano. He wanted to be sure I was well. He done made plans Mony, to get rid of us. We leave tomorrow."

Harmony slammed the door shut. Earlier she had delivered Vinnie his dinner to his closed door meeting. She had been intent on proving Mabel wrong. She could indeed take care of the men in her life. The look of surprise and pleasure on his face was her big reward. She envisioned many more nights where she would cook for him, love him, take care of him until they could begin again somewhere away from their shared history of pain and blood. Now her brother sat there saying it was done. No way in hell it would end like this. "Vinnie is mistaken. We ain't leaving for awhile. Definitely not before this silly war going on in the city stops."

"You hear yourself? Silly war? Those men are dangerous, and this place ain't safe."

"I meant to say…"

"No! Mony things are serious. Antonio set his brother up. All his money, warehouses, territories and numbers banks were shut down. That was his brother's plan. To break and humiliate him, and he did it Mony. I don't know what the man whispers to you in bed, but he's in big trouble. That's why we gots to go."

"Vinnie can handle it!"

"He can't. Not anymore. It's too many of them and too few willing to stand with him. That's how it works. I'm not sure why he ain't being plain with you but I ain't got no reason to lie to you sis. He wants us out of here and I agree with him."

"You ain't got no reason to lie?" Harmony gave a bitter snort. "After all the damn lies you done told you sitting here pretending to care about honesty? We ain't going nowhere. You ain't well enough to travel and I… I'm not ready. That's the plain truth, cause I got no reason to lie."

Willie tried to stand but winced and plopped back down on the mattress touching his side. He sucked down several quick gasps of air. "I'm not trying to upset you…"

"Well you are. Eat your damn dinner, and stay out of it with me and Vinnie. I got to go."

"Mony!" he shouted.

She froze at the door but didn't turn around. Her heart hurt. Deep down she knew Vinnie had gone to him and set the wheels in motion for her to leave. She felt him finalizing things everywhere she turned. She thought if she ignored it and changed the subject each time he tried to broach it, she would have more time. But time was up.

"He's doing this for you, Mony. Don't know the man. Antonio hated him, said he was evil and cruel. I haven't seen that since I've been here. I know he loves you sis. But he's one of them, and sooner or later they coming for him. It's best we be gone before they do."

"Eat your food," she said and walked out. In the hall she closed her eyes and touched her heart. The fantasy was far better than the cold reality of her brother's words. Quickly she rushed down the stairs to the bottom level. She went to his door prepared to throw it open. She sucked down several breaths and pressed her ear to it to listen instead.

"It's done boss. Luciano has given the order. Collins wants a meeting, says you can choose the place."

Romano chuckled. He picked up his glass of imported whiskey and downed the contents. The burn of the whiskey soon soothed along his tongue and cleared his head. "Tomorrow Harmony leaves. Do I have until tomorrow?" Romano asked, he closed his eyes and rolled the tension from his neck.

"I believe so. The Irish delivered another shipment today. Word is there's a big deal that Collins will control. The Atlantic City deal."

The contents of Romano's stomach soured. He glanced at the stew and cut of fresh baked bread and wanted to throw the plate into the wall. The bastard now had his deal. He swore under his breath in Italian. On his mother's grave he intended to fire a single bullet into Mickey Collins face, before they sent him to hell. "Tomorrow. We can deal tomorrow. But we know it's not going down the way they expect."

"Meaning?" Ignacio.

"We'll be waiting for them. Here. And we'll remind Luciano of *La Cosa Nostra* by sending him what's left of Mickey Collins. I want the men, those who choose to remain, to arm themselves tight. If Mickey tries to ride in tonight and take us by surprise we'll be ready for them," he said in deadly earnest.

Ignacio cleared his throat. "Maybe you should consider another way. Take your lady and the kid and leave tonight, under the cover of dark. We'll cover your back, out of the state."

Romano let go a deep ball of laughter. There wasn't an ounce of humor in it. He glared at Ignacio with murderous intent. "No. My time is over. I won't fucking run like a coward. They want me they can come for me."

"NO!" Harmony yelled throwing open the door. The men looked back in surprise. No one was more surprised than him from her sudden appearance. Had she been listening at his door? He narrowed his eyes on her. Harmony marched into the room glaring in return. "You lied to me! Didn't you? You had no intention of going to New Mexico with me!"

"Leave us alone boys and do as I said."

"Answer me dammit!"

Romano rose from his chair. Ignacio and Gio both made a quick exit. Not before giving his Songbird curious looks. He figured no one would understand them, how deeply he cared for her, and she the same for him. He didn't give a shit. It had been the wild panic and anger in her eyes that set him on edge. He couldn't deal with her breaking down on him now. It was hard enough to make the choices he had.

"You were going to give up. You coward! Why not tell me the truth, instead of making me think you cared?"

"That's enough Harmony!"

"Go to hell!" she shouted back. "You're a coward!"

"Coward? Coward! You think this is easy for me? Do you?" He leveled a finger at her. "I don't owe you any explanation. You do as you're told!"

Harmony laughed. She crossed her arms. "I'm not those men, or that scared boy in another room hoping you won't take out your vengeance on him. From day one I did as I please. You don't order me around!"

Romano ran his hand back over his head and tried to calm himself. He paced before his desk to keep his anger in check before he spoke again. "There are things you don't know. I won't go into it further…"

"I know enough! I heard enough!"

His gaze whirled to her and he stood still. "You've been spying on me?" he seethed.

"Just like you've been lying to me. Funny thing is Vinnie, I believed in you. Believed you could fix this, truth is you're giving up! That's not the man I love!"

"Let's be clear Songbird, you don't know half of the man I am. If I say you're leaving you're leaving dammit!"

"No! No! NO!"

The woman was making him crazy. He reached for her, only to try and get a hold on her screaming at him, but she reacted swiftly. She swatted her hands at him and went on the attack. The more he tried to contain her the wilder her fury grew. She hit at his face and shoulders all at once. Sharp stinging slaps that knocked him back. He grabbed her by the waist to stop the abuse and she howled with outrage. "You bastard! I won't let you! I won't!"

Romano lifted her bodily from the floor as she clawed, shoved, and kicked to be free. There was nothing he could promise that would undo the reality of the situation. He had screwed this up with Annie. Lost her, with her hating him in the end. Though he was furious that she spied on him and spoke to him the way she did, he couldn't finish things with the men hunting him now if she didn't promise to love him. He brought her down on the sofa and pinned her arms above her head. Harmony screamed to the top of her lungs. She bucked beneath him crying and shaking her head furiously side to side.

"Listen! Listen dammit."

"I hate you! I hate you for making me believe that we... I hate you! Noooo!"

"I hate me too. Don't you understand that?"

She stopped, blinking up at him, her chest rising and falling with her heavy breathing. He nodded. "I hate myself. I always have, Songbird. I tried. I really did. But this is over. And I need you, if I'm going to see it through. My way."

"Please don't," she wept. "Please don't do this." He brushed his lips over her wet cheeks. He tried to kiss her mouth but she turned her face away and refused him, exposing her slender neck. Romano inhaled her skin and pressed a soft kiss over the bulging vein along her neck. He put every ounce of his weight down on her to keep her pinned beneath him. There was an ongoing struggle to catch his own breath.

"You're right," he panted. "If I were stronger Antonio would have never robbed me of everything. But I'm no coward, Songbird. It's taking everything in me to release you. Everything."

She cried harder.

The flaming heat of his humiliation burned in his chest and flushed his face, which he buried against her neck. He hated weakness in any man, least of all him. Antonio knew this. Their father had taught them both how to exploit an enemy's failures. But if his brother hadn't steered him in the path of her, he'd never know the love she'd brought him. So for that, on the eve of his downfall, he found a measure of gratitude in his heart.

"Let me go," she moaned.

Harmony's misery and his was complete. Didn't she know this? Romano squeezed his eyes tightly shut to prevent his own tears from falling. "I'm trying," he wheezed.

The deep sobs escaping her were unrelenting. How could a woman so strong come apart completely over the end of him? He wasn't worthy. She didn't become his willingly. He exploited her desperation to find her brother to lure her into his bed. That was the beginning of their love song. Even he believed that this ending fit his crime.

Romano released his hold on her wrists and let his open palms run gently down her arms. Her sobbing began to ease. It didn't matter. Her tears and the sounds of her pain had broken his fragile hold on control. If he was to see this through now, he'd need her help.

"Don't punish me." He captured her lips and tried to force her to respond. "I love you so much," he said against her tightly pressed lips, then eased his tongue between her teeth. "The last thing... I want... is... to lose you," he breathed between deep throating her. If she stayed he couldn't protect her. And if she left, his death would be the only guarantee she'd be free—he'd seen to it. This sacrifice was the only repentance he had left. He'd done a lot of bad things since he crossed the shores into America. He's murdered, robbed, bootlegged, turn friend against friend, and brought about the death of his own brother.

"I'm sorry." He dragged his mouth from hers and leaned his forehead against hers. "I'm so sorry, Harmony."

She grabbed his face and returned his kiss. Her lovely tongue licked his lips and stroked inside before sweeping deeply and he felt a surge of lightheadedness. Romano closed his eyes and shut out the sight of her pain. Instead he focused on the heat between their bodies and the safety he felt to be himself in her arms.

The hard tightness in his groin made him selfish. He should just hold her and talk out their goodbye. Find the comforting words to give her so she would remember him fondly, and not like this, broken and needy. But he craved the physical more. He grabbed the bottom material of her dress hiking it up her thighs. He'd fuck her now. The urgency twisting his gut into a tight knot told him so. Damn if she didn't kiss him harder, forcing her passion to consume him, making him fumble with clumsiness. But he managed to ease his zipper down and release himself. He had no time to remove her undies, pushing the seat of her panty aside Romano flexed his hips and thrust into her.

To his relief he found her wet and ready for him. Her thighs cradled his hips. Her silken walls squeezed and suctioned him. With another push he braced himself by gripping the arm of the sofa and sank deeper. His strokes were slow, measured for pleasure, hers and his. When she tried to wrap her legs higher around his waist, he lifted and pushed her right thigh down and away to open her to his invasion, so he could slam unimpeded into her juicy pussy. Harmony's soft cries were music to his ears, yet tears still trekked down her damp cheeks.

Oh how he loved her body, her spirit, her ability to care for him even when they both knew he was undeserving. Nearly mindless he thrust into her repeatedly edging them both toward a new release. He'd take the sweet feel of her with him to his grave. He lifted his belly to look down to where their bodies joined. A deep shudder of pleasure and lustful need sliced through him. Her hand eased between them to ring his shaft and slow his pumping so he glided easy through her fingers into her tight pussy. And his strokes began to gently tunnel deeper, driving them closer to their breaking point.

Romano tossed his head back and closed his eyes moving in and out of her molten channel, and she let go of his cock, digging her fingernails into his butt cheeks. The love he carried for her made his sacrifice burn his gut. He groaned and felt tears form behind his closed lids as he pumped harder and faster, trying to outrun the doubts and weakness that made him want to grab her now and drive away from it all just to live his days with her. His hips circled, grinding the base of his cock to her clit. He thrust harder, deeper, until the pressure in his balls exploded and he couldn't think of regrets or second chances. The built-up passion between them exploded and he released his seed deep into her womb. A brief flutter of hope passed through his racing heart that tonight a baby would take root and a little person in his image would be his legacy.

When his eyes opened he gazed down at Harmony. She burst into tears once more and he collapsed against her breasts, breathing hard. Her legs eased down and she rubbed his head as she wept.

"I'm sorry, Doll. Forgive me."

Harmony rolled silently to her side. Vinnie slept next to her, his arms and legs thrown across her. Her move forced him to shift and drop to his back. He'd been half-drunk when she barged in on his meeting. The emotional attack they waged on each other had wiped him out. Before his head hit the pillow he was asleep.

Careful not to disturb him she eased out from under the covers. The room was so frosty her skin prickled with tiny goose bumps covering her. Vinnie rolled and she thought he'd wake. He didn't. But she stood perfectly still to be sure he remained sleep. When a soft snore escaped him she bolted for the chair and grabbed her robe, throwing it over her naked body. She hurried out of the room to the stairs. It was Saturday morning, near dawn. The Cotton Club would be nearing its final act and the girls would be changing and dressing to leave. If she was lucky she'd reach Paulette.

Harmony crept into his office. Careful, she closed the door softly behind her and locked it. Then she went for the phone. She rang the club and prayed Charlie answered. He did. She begged and pleaded with him to get Paulette. She wasn't sure why Charlie granted her wish but after a ten-minute debate on the subject her friend was given the phone.

"Mony? That you?"

"Yes. I need your help."

"Mony… listen to me girl. Don't come back here. It's crazy now and the mess with Willie has dragged your name into it. There is so much crazy talk. People say you living with him. Out in Woodbury?"

"I don't have much time. I know how bad things are. I need your help Paulette, I'm in trouble."

"What can I do?"

"Ever been out of New York?"

The bed squeaked and the mattress dipped. Romano blinked awake. Harmony's warm body eased up against him and he relaxed. He shouldn't have fallen asleep. He needed to be outside with his men waiting on the sun. But if this was to be his last night, he'd want to spend it in heaven.

"Where you been?" he yawned.

"Bathroom," she lied.

He rolled on top of her and rested the side of his face in his hand propped up by his elbow. "Want to talk about it?"

"About what? You planning your death? Sending me away like some great sacrifice? Talk about that?"

"You still pissed with me?"

"What you think?" she cut her gaze away and closed her eyes, shutting him out again.

He chuckled at her stubbornness. "I think you're extremely sexy when you're angry. And you're the most beautiful woman I've ever known. I think these past few weeks with you have been the best in my life. I think you will have my son, and raise him to never forget me."

She returned her gaze to his.

"We made a baby tonight."

"Who said?"

"I say." He kissed her lips. "I feel it. A little Songbird, or mobster, who knows?"

"So now I'm to be alone with a child and this is funny to you?"

Romano sighed. He wasn't saying the right things.

"Get off me..." she said pushing him off.

"Wait. Okay, I'm sorry. I'm doing this wrong. I love you."

"Then please, stop this," her voice broke. "I can't lose you this way. Think about me. What you leaving behind if you don't fight."

"Who says I won't fight? You think I'm just going to roll over and die? I plan to fight with everything in me. If I survive this I will find you. If I don't I'll go to my grave knowing you're safe."

"I can't! Dammit! I can't do this!"

"Shhh...." He cupped her face in his hands. The swirl of pain in her hazel brown eyes shone back up at him. She gripped his shoulders hard. He could feel her trembling beneath him. "We have tonight, can we spend it not fighting?"

Her head lifted from the pillow and she kissed him. Returning her passion he raised his hips to angle himself at her core and inserted his hands beneath her ass, changing the angle of his penetration. He broke their kiss to focus on her nipples, giving each a quick suckle before giving in to his urgent need to possess her.

A single thrust drove him half way in. Harmony's inner walls had clutched him in creamy heat and he released a cry of relief over their union. Her back arched and she shoved her chest upward, while her legs cinched tighter around him. The tight warmth rippled up and down his shaft and he surged into her groaning as he went. He had to lift his face to study her. She had been so beautiful to him on stage, but now her beauty stole his breath away. Her high exotic cheekbones, dainty nose, full pouty lips and chin of iron determination were God's greatest creation. Loose tendrils of her raven dark hair were spread across the pillow. She wore it wild and curly for him now. She was gentle, serenely wise, and all his.

He loved her, bringing his mouth closer to hers breathless gasps gust against his lips. She pumped up into his downward thrusts. He kissed her shoulder and continued to drive in and out of her clenching channel. The pulsating beat of their union tugged at him, and her slick walls made his glide unbearably decadent. All of it combined pulled him down toward an orgasmic spiral that had him beating out his love into her. Harmony dug her nails into his shoulder and her head thrashed, her eyes remained squeezed shut before she shattered as well. They both collapsed exhausted, believing that this may be the very last time.

CHAPTER TWELVE
Last stand...

Harmony knocked twice before she pushed open the door and
stuck her head inside. Her large satchel hung from her shoulder and
her luggage waited by the front door. She wore a yellow dress with a
baby blue belt tightening it snug to her waist. The shifting hem swayed
at her knees. She'd taken extra care with her hair. He seemed to like it
when she wore it loose and not pinned down flat to her head. So she
washed it and let it air dry in plaits so she could undo them and make
the ringlet curls reach her shoulder. Vinnie sat in his office alone. They
both avoided each other with the rise of the sun. Neither could face the
other without the same argument erupting. She hated and loved him all
at the same time for what he was doing. In his mind the sacrifice was
worth it. To her his abandonment was the greatest betrayal. And those
mixed emotions confused her deeply.

"Paulette's here. We're ready."

He pushed up from behind the desk. She wanted to fight with him
again. Plead her case. Make a reasonable argument against his suicidal
crusade. But she didn't. She waited patiently for him to retrieve
whatever it was he had for her out of the drawer to his desk.

"Come here, Songbird. Have a seat." He nodded toward the sofa.
She did as he asked.

He carried a large envelope stuffed to the point of the seal splitting. He walked over to the sofa and sat next to her. He tossed it to her lap and then another folder. "In the envelope is fifteen thousand cash. The folder has a bond with the certificate. I put it in your name. It's worth fifty-three thousand dollars. You can deposit or cash it."

"Are you seriously sitting here giving me money? Money? I can't believe you!" She tossed the envelopes to the other side of the sofa.

He put a hand to her knee and she resisted the urge to smack him. She had never laid her hand on another human being, but with him she wanted to kick scratch and scream until her voice gave out. She wouldn't suffer through the grief she felt over Lewis again. She couldn't mourn him. *And sweet Jesus if I'm pregnant, what then? A child to remind me of him? A life alone to raise him or her?* No. She was solid in her determination to help him even if he wouldn't help himself.

"Hate me later, just listen to me now. I want you to drive through the day and night. Stop only for gas. If you are followed, and I want you to pay attention to be sure you're aren't, stick to the main roads. I doubt they'll come for you, but I need you to put as much distance between you and the city before you stop." He rose and removed a three times folded map from his back pocket. He flipped it open and spread it across the small coffee table before them. To her surprise he had taken the time to mark the roads he'd drawn with a red line that led to New Mexico. "Promise me Doll, you'll see this through."

Harmony trembled all over. She swore she wouldn't cry. She had planned to be stronger, but everything in her said she needed to stop him and quick. "I…"

"Promise me," he said firmly.

He seemed to relax a bit. He let go a long sigh and slumped back. "Okay. Let's do this."

"No. Wait."

She put her hand to his chest and moved over to straddle his lap. He held to her hips as she stared down into his haggard, yet handsome face. He hadn't shaven in days. She touched his jaw and savored the feel of his prickly stubble brush over her fingers. "I love you Vinnie. I don't want this to be our goodbye, but if it is, then there is something you can give me."

"Name it."

"I don't want money, I only want you."

"Harmony…."

"Wait. If I can't have you then I need a part of you. The painting. Let me take something you made…" she dropped her head to his brow and swallowed hard. He rubbed her back. "Don't send me away."

"I'll have a painting brought to your car. Take as many as you can fit in the trunk. Okay. Shhh, stop, look at me." He lifted her chin and smiled up at her. "C'mon, Doll. This ain't the end of us. I'll always be with you." He touched her belly with his hand. "I made sure of it."

She nearly released a gust of laughter. She shook her head smiling and hugged him. He held her while she remained firmly seated on his lap. It seemed like the embrace went on forever, but when he tried to stand she realized how short their goodbye was.

"Let's go babe," he said assisting her. She wiped the tears from her cheeks and accepted his hand. Vinnie drew her to his chest one final time and kissed her sweetly before releasing her. He collected the things he had for her, including the map, and she accepted the money and bonds shoving all of it down in her satchel. He lifted her chin and kissed her once more.

"Paulette here?" He asked nuzzling her hair.

"Yes. The car is packed. We're all set to go."

"Not quite." He walked her out. One of the few men that remained loyal to them waited in the hall. He told him to go to the cabin and collect the paintings, to put them in the car. Harmony remained silent at his side.

He'd gotten her a new car. Paulette sat in the front seat and Willie was stretched comfortably in the back.

"I love you."

"I love you too. Always, Songbird."

"Always."

She turned and walked down the steps to the car, passing her satchel to her friend. The man hurried back with three paintings. She didn't care which ones he chose. For Harmony this would not be their end. She had another in mind. He stood there smirking and for a minute she thought he knew her plans.

"You look as stubborn as you did the first night I brought you here."

"I am." She winked, then blew him a kiss and forced herself to get in the car. Driving away was the hardest thing she'd ever done. She bit hard on the inside of her jaw to hold back the tears.

"You okay?" Paulette asked.

"I will be." Harmony said, her lips pressed into a thin line.

Romano watched until they disappeared off his land. He returned inside and dropped in his chair. He closed his eyes and tried to relax. Seeing her leave was harder than he imagined. Sitting forward he'd placed his face in his hands. A soft groan escaped him. The tension in his body was so tight.

"Boss?"

"Not now."

"I have to ask."

"Don't. It's done." He lifted his face from his hands. "Antonio cost me too much, he won't cost me Harmony. We see this through and when it's over everyone gets what they deserve. I'll be ready in an hour to see what you brought in. Make sure everyone else is."

Ignacio nodded and turned to walk out. Romano pushed up from the chair. He walked over to his phonograph and picked up his favorite record. Harmony sang the song for him on their first night together. Dropping the needle on the vinyl disc he exhaled. Everyone has to make sacrifices. It was time he made his. "For you, Songbird."

***

"I won't do it!" Willie said stubbornly. He wore a suit she'd taken from Antonio's closet since his clothes had blood on them. He looked older, more like his own man, and it made her proud of him. Paulette stood at his side, the tail of her coat flapped behind her. The wind gusts were stronger on this end of the tracks and they still felt winter's last bite as it washed over them.

"You will do it. In all the time I've sacrificed and loved you unconditionally I've never asked you for a thing. Nothing. This you will do for me."

"Will you talk some sense into her thick skull? She talking crazy. No way this plan of hers will work. She'll get herself killed."

Paulette turned her sympathetic gaze back to Harmony. "He has a point suga. Vinnie Romano's a walking dead man. I doubt they'll help you save him."

The train's whistle blared, drowning out the rest of Paulette's warning. Harmony reached in her satchel and collected the money she'd peeled off for her brother. He stared at her curious, not sure what she was doing. Discreetly she pushed the wad of bills on him. Paulette's eyes stretched seeing the exchange. "It's time for you to be your own man. Here's a thousand dollars. Go to Chicago, hell maybe after you feel better you can head south, or go wherever you want and be who you are. On your terms Willie."

He shoved the money in his pocket glancing around to see if anyone was watching. "Where did you get this kind of money? Romano? It's dangerous for you to walk around with this money sis. Come with me."

"I belong with him. Don't you see that now? You of all people should know we can't help who we love, only the choices we make. I've made mine. Paulette agreed to go with you. It's why we chose Chicago. I'll be in touch in a day or so. Send you a wire of where I am and more money if I can. Just go."

Paulette touched Willie's arm. "She's going to do this suga. I suggest you listen to her."

The whistle blew again.

Harmony pressed two hundred dollars in Paulette's hands. Her friend promised to see her brother settled in and to make sure he recovered well before they parted. Paulette picked up Willie's suitcase and hooked her arm around his good one. The other was in a homemade sling. Harmony leaned forward and kissed him on the cheek. "I love you baby-boy. Always."

Their parting tore at her resolve. She knew he had a point. What she planned could very well get her killed. This could be the last time she saw him. Willie's eyes glistened with closely held tears. He blinked them away and managed a small smile. "I'm sorry sis, for everything."

"Let's go suga, we'll miss the train." Paulette said.

Harmony nodded for them to do so. He reluctantly let Paulette help him. He boarded the steps, paused and looked back at her. Then they disappeared in the train car. Harmony wiped her tears away and turned. She headed for her car. The Johnny Ringo remained tucked deep in her satchel, but she needed to get somewhere to count the money and stash the bond before she saw part two of her plan through.

***

Red Hots was located off 125th and 7th Avenue. The place looked no different than the market to its left and the Chinese laundry to the right. But at night Seventh Avenue was bumper-to-bumper with Negroes dressed in their finest and trying to get through its doors. Harmony closed the door to her car and stared up at the sign. She'd never been inside. Lewis would come home drunk many nights from this place. When Paulette told her Madame St. Clair and Grease Man would only meet at this place she knew the gamble would be great.

"Hmm, something smells sweet this morning." Came a long drawl from behind her. Her gaze shifted from the sign to the man now standing to her left on the sidewalk. Flat unsmiling eyes pinned her. "Waiting for someone, sweet thang?"

The stranger was taller than most men, but very thin. He wore a deep purple suit with a bright red tie. His wide brim hat was purple with red trim. He shifted the toothpick in his mouth and she caught the gleam of a shiny tooth that looked to be golden. Living in Harlem and working the jazz scene she'd run into this kind of man before, a street pimp that hustled girls into selling their bodies for him. His gaze was sharp and assessing like that of a cobra. She eased her hand inside her satchel and held to the Johnny Ringo. "I have a meeting with Madame St. Clair."

"Harmony right?"

"Yes."

"I knew your old man. Lewis." His sly grin spread across his face. His skin was so dark the whites of his eyes were quite startling when they stretched in recognition. "Queenie waiting to see you. Come with me."

She sucked in a brave breath and followed him to the door. He pounded on it and after a pause it opened. The darkness beyond made her stomach quiver with nerves. Paulette left The Cotton after her call and raced down to Red Hot's to make the request for this meeting for her. According to her friend, Madame St. Clair was pretty pissed at Willie for selling her stolen booze. Paulette warned Harmony that the meeting would be on the mob boss's terms, so if she entered to an ambush no one but her brother and friend knew she was here. She just had to keep her wits about her and stay on guard.

"So? You going in or what?" The pimp asked her.

"Yes." She walked inside the musty, narrow corridor and descended a flight of stairs. The burn of oils, cigarettes, and spicy cooked meet singed her nose and burned her eyes. The club was pretty small with a low hanging ceiling. Lighting was either focused on the stage or relegated to the bar and the candles on the table, which made it harder to see. She scanned the bar to the left and saw several men seated, both black and white. She had heard of Madame St. Clair's band of Forty Thieves, and didn't believe a black woman could run a gang of white men. But there was no black woman wielding as much power and control in Harlem, New York as the revered Madame St. Clair.

"Keep moving." She received a gentle pat to her backside, and cringed at the unwanted touch. There was a stage to the back and a few tables and seats around a hardwood dance floor. It was only a third of the size of The Cotton. Still she knew for a fact some of Harlem's elite dined and performed there.

"Bring her here *cherie*!" A sweet Caribbean voice called over to them. Harmony's gaze swung to the right. The woman those on the streets referred to as Queenie sat waiting. Seated inside the circular booth with her were two men. The man to her left had a deep tan, and dark black hair oiled back from his face. He looked like the Sicilians that frequented The Cotton. He leaned forward with his elbows resting on the table, hands clasped. He had severe dark brows over clear blue eyes that made his stare cold and unreadable. On the other side of Madame St. Clair was a black man. He wore a dark suit and his skin was a deep chestnut. He sort of leaned back into the booth seat with his arm thrown over the back, slouching. A cigarette was pressed to his lips and he drew hard making the end burn bright orange. He exhaled a cloud of smoke removing the cigarette and his features were shielded in the milky wave. Still, Harmony knew it had to be the infamous Grease Man she had heard Lewis and Milo often speak of. She'd never seen him in person but his presence was felt as was Madame St. Clair's.

Harmony swallowed hard and walked toward them. Her legs were stiff but her back was straight. "Madame St. Clair, thank you for seeing me."

The woman snorted, in disgust. Now before her, she could see her clearly. She had beautiful skin, like warmed honey and a colorful head wrap that contained a wealth of dark curls. Harmony guessed her age to be mid-thirties, but she could easily pass for ten years younger. Lewis said she was French, and from the part of the Caribbean where blacks were quite wealthy. Madame St. Clair carried an air of superiority. "You got a lot guts coming to see me *cherie*. Don't you know what your brother has done?"

"I do."

"Still you stand here, unrepentant?"

"No ma'am. That's not it at all. I am repentant, and I intend to make up for what he's done."

The white man chuckled. "Give her to me Queenie, I have some ideas how she can work it off. I hear she's fond of Sicilians."

Harmony held her tongue but she cut the bastard a warning glare. The idea formed after the fight with Vinnie and their subsequent lovemaking in his office. He had confessed it all. What Antonio had done, how the old Dons had turned their backs on him because of the messy turf war and his taking up with a black woman. All of it. He even told her a few things she didn't know about Madame St. Clair and her thirst for power and control over Harlem. So she directed her answer to the woman who controlled the snakes slithering around her. "I'm not a whore, or a thief."

"That's not what I hear *cherie*. I hear you done took to sleeping with a dead man. As his jezebel."

The men at the bar snickered, so did the Sicilian sitting next to Madame. Grease however didn't. He continued to watch her with a steady gaze. Harmony felt her courage soften and the sharp edge of fear pierce her gut. She felt her knees go weak but she tried to keep her focus. "Whatever I am or ain't, shouldn't be of your concern. I'm here to make amends. That's the purpose of this visit between me and you."

"And what you giving up to Vinnie Romano." The Sicilian spat.

"Something you'll never get." She shot back.

Queenie let go a rambunctious peal of laughter. Harmony waited until the humor faded from her eyes. She reached in her satchel to bring her deal to the table but froze. Immediately she felt the business end of a revolver press into the back of her head. "I'm not going for my weapon."

"Put it on the table all the same." The man said to her. Harmony reached inside and removed the Johnny Ringo. It hurt to even reveal the gun to them. It was Vinnie's gift to her, and the only thing that she carried that gave her faith that she could help him. The hoodlum behind her snatched it from her hand. "Holy shit. Man, you see this. Bitch has a Ringo? Fuck. Wanted one of these."

"I want it back when I leave."

"Who says you leaving?" The Sicilian snickered.

Harmony ignored him. She addressed Queenie. "My brother owes you a debt, and I mean no disrespect in thinking I can set a price for it. But it is indeed what I intend to do."

"How much?" Queenie asked.

"Three thousand dollars." Harmony put the money on the table. Grease Man sat upright out of his slouch and a silence fell over the room.

"Where the hell you get that kind of money Jazz Singer?"

All eyes went to her. "Is it enough? To repay my brother's debt?"

Queenie narrowed her eyes on her. She glanced over to Grease who counted out the money. He nodded that it was three thousand dollars. Queenie nodded. "Consider it paid."

Harmony let go a deep sigh. "Thank you. I wanted that business cleared up so I could uh, ask for, uh, request... I came to..."

"Spit it out!" Queenie shouted.

"I want you to save Vincenzio Romano. I'm willing to pay for you to do so."

"You ain't got enough money for that." Grease's voice commanded equal authority as Queenie's. The glare he fixed her with would have made her a believer. She refused to give in that easily.

"I have seven thousand dollars." She removed the money and placed it on the table. "And after it's done I have the other three thousand hid. Is that enough money?"

"Everybody be quiet." Queenie leaned forward. "What's to keep me from taking that money from you right now bitch?"

"Honor, respect. I showed you respect by coming here and paying the debt my brother owed first. I'm showing it to you now by offering the money up front to save him. I think you want Harlem, well those Sicilians are trying to take it from you." She cut the man to Queenie's left a nasty glare, making sure her point was plain. "Antonio Romano is dead and the cover of protection he gave you from the cops is over. The war could spill on to the street, your streets. If you were to strike back and send a message to Luciano wouldn't that make you truly the Queen?"

Her words took on a life on their own as they lingered and lengthened the silence between her and these evil people. Harmony seized on the silence. She tried again to get through to the woman who could end her life at any moment.

"Helping me save his life sends the kind of message you need to. Vincenzio never stole from you Queenie. He never moved in on Harlem. His brother is dead for what he dragged you and my brother into. And I'm offering ten thousand dollars to get the Romano's out of Harlem for good."

"Syl, take her to the back while I discuss this with the boys."

"Wait!" Harmony stepped forward. The Sicilian however eased out of the booth ready to seize her. "My time is short. I don't know how long..."

"I've heard enough of your mouth bitch. Get your ass to the back and we'll let you know how this goes down." Queenie sneered at her. The gentle lovely features she possessed when she smiled disappeared into the threatening scowl she leveled at Harmony. The plan wasn't working and she had to think of something to do quick.

Harmony whirled on the hoodlum who took her gun. He had it shoved down to the front of his pants. Before he could react she snatched it from his loop. She heard several men around her draw on her. "I'm not going anywhere without my pistol. Period!"

Queenie chuckled. "Crazy, ain't she? Jazz Singer you'd be dead before you pull the trigger *cherie*."

"Then it won't be a problem if I keep it on me."

"Not at all." Queenie shrugged.

She nodded and let them lead her to the back. She glanced back over her shoulder. Grease Man was watching her closely.

***

Romano rolled up his sleeves. He walked the line of the dining room table and scanned the arsenal spread over the surface. Weapons of his choosing were brought in. He had enough ammo to get him through the battle, however, not enough men to win the war.

Ignacio entered and the four men gathered turned their gazes toward him. Gio had a family and had left hours ago. Those still gathered were like him, drifters, lost without a purpose. None of the men among them feared death. Each lived as if this day would be their last. Maybe in Sicily they'd have been gladiators in a different time. He reflected on a lot of nonsense lately. Many of his desires were lost on the future he'd forged for himself through fist and blood.

"News?" he asked, snapping his mind clear of wistful wants and focusing again.

"None." Ignacio said, his voice grim. "Streets are quiet. They could ride on us at anytime. My guess is we'll get a visit tonight."

Romano chuckled. Mickey Collins was as predictable as he was a coward. The advantage would be to settle things in the light of day. The cabins were exclusive enough for it. But of course his nemesis had no tactical plan, and that was to his advantage.

Another truth burned his gut, one his pride and reputation withered under. He simply wasn't enough of a priority for the men he used to command respect from. He drew out a chair and dropped in it. "Let them come."

***

Four hours had passed. She sat behind a locked door for four long hours. Harmony kept the gun in her lap and her eyes trained on the only entrance in the room that felt more like a prison with each passing minute. Vinnie could be dead by now. They had the seven thousand dollars already. She'd been dumb enough to leave the money with them. The longer she waited the more she saw the flaws in her plan. She gave up her only leverage and showed her hand too soon. The situation was grave.

The door opened.

Harmony picked up the Johnny Ringo with a loaded chamber. She'd put a bullet in herself before she let any man rape her or worse. But first she planned to take out whoever came for her. The hold on the pistol tightened and her hand shook with nervous tension.

Grease Man walked in. When standing he was much taller and imposing. Lewis said they called him Grease because he was one of those black men who straightened his hair with axle grease. It was true, slicked back over his head it shined like hot tar. Grease was tall, like Vinnie, but a bit leaner. He dressed nicer than the Negroes in Henderson's orchestra, with a fancy tailored grey suit and newly polished shoes. He wasn't a man to be teased or tested. Grease had a serious reputation for having a short fuse.

He didn't bother to close the door behind him and she felt a bit at ease for it. He had no weapon on him either. Harmony lowered the pistol. She still couldn't calm her racing heart to breathe normally.

"You got a lot of courage coming down here the way you did Jazz Singer. Queenie respects that. Lewis said you were tough." Grease Man wagged a finger at her. "But he never said you were stupid."

"I'm not."

Grease laughed. "We shall see."

"So Lewis talked to you about me?"

Grease pulled a chair over, and turned it around so he could straddle the seat. He studied her for a moment before he spoke. "He did. Talked about you quite a bit. Mostly about your singing. I heard a few others drop your name when you started down at The Cotton."

She nodded, unsure if he waited on a response.

"Like I said you got balls."

"Has Queenie… uh Madame St. Clair decided?"

He nodded.

She waited for her answer.

He stared.

"And?" she pressed.

"Here's how it is. We don't give a fuck about Vincenzio Romano. In fact if I had a say I'd tell Queenie to take the money you gave and the money you got stashed probably in that car you drove up in, and be done with it. Thing is Queenie's smarter than that. And you knew that didn't you?"

"I only took a chance and guessed she could help."

"Right." He paused a breath, licked his lips and lifted his gaze from her breasts. "Your deal couldn't have come at a better time. Planning to open our own numbers bank, and ten thousand would make it happen. Queenie is pissed at the Sicilians, how they keep moving in and pushing us out. She wants in on this fight. She likes the idea of sending Luciano a message."

"So she *will* help me?"

"We sent Syl to get more info. They'll be riding on your man in an hour. Mickey Collins wants to put the bullet in him, himself."

"No!" she stood. "We have to leave now."

Grease sneered.

"I said we have to leave now!" she lifted the gun and leveled it at him. Grease Man's sneer faded. He narrowed his gaze on her. Vinnie told her if she pulled a gun she'd have to use it. If Grease Man didn't give her a reason soon not to, she intended to do just that.

"When this is done Jazz Singer, where you planning to land?"

"On my feet and out of Harlem. That's where." She held the gun on him with both hands. "I want to see Madame. Now."

"It's not about what you want, haven't you got that by now?" He stood, and she did too. The chair between them and the gun in her hands made her braver. He glanced down at the pistol then back up into her eyes. "Ever fire it?"

"Wanna find out?" she asked.

He snickered. "Hot damn! Fine and feisty, just how God intended to make women. Until they get so bogged down with being a lady. That's not you, is it Jazz Singer? I've heard what the girls at The Cotton do. After this is done you and I need to finish this conversation."

"It was over when you told me that Queenie would help him. Nothing else to discuss."

"Oh I don't know Jazz Singer. Things are going to change in Harlem with Queenie and the boys in charge." He reached and touched a lose lock on her shoulder and she remained very still, but she lowered the gun an inch. "Eventually you'll need another favor, and I can't wait to set the terms."

He turned and walked out. "Leaving soon. We'll come for you when it's done."

"I'm going!"

Grease stopped. "Come again?"

"I'm going. I can take care of myself."

His brows arched in surprise. Then he smiled again shaking his head. "Of course you can."

Sundown –

As soon as darkness spread through the hills and the forest surrounding his land he heard the roar of the first engine. Vinnie glanced up to the other men. Quick and silent each grabbed their weapons and dispersed.

He grabbed his Thompson with a loaded 20 shot magazine and headed for the front of the house. The only choice left to him would be to hold them off from the front and waste as many as they could before breaking out of the back and luring the rest of Mickey's gang into the woods. It was a solid plan. Anywhere else on his property left them too vulnerable. He was grateful for the dark, his eyes adjusted to it well. They kept the lights off. When he approached the window he immediately realized things for him would never go as planned.

Not only had Mickey himself come along for the showdown, he brought a total of ten cars loaded with men. To make matters worse they circled the cabin, men posting up on the sides and to the back. Romano and his men would be boxed in.

"Out here now Romano!" Mickey Collins yelled. "Maybe I'll put a bullet in ya and send you to your queer brother early!"

Romano froze. He thought his favor had fallen because of his affair with Harmony. He was almost sure that Antonio's sins weren't known. But of course his brother's revenge would reach from the grave, and now he understood the reason so many of his men walked away. He had to wonder about the four that remained. The death sentence they would be sentenced to tonight didn't seem worth the sacrifice.

Pushing all thoughts of doubt from his mind he squinted and tried to focus on the scene unfolding outside of the window. Large orbs of lights from the cars glared back. He could see shadows exit the vehicles but couldn't gain a good viewpoint. And it dawned on him, he had chosen his position wrong. He should have gone upstairs and picked the motherfuckers off one by one.

Before he could turn and break for the stairs. One of his boys
inside the house got trigger-happy. He fired off a shot that set off a
firestorm of gun blasts. Romano dropped to the floor. At first he
thought he was hit. His left arm burned so badly he believed it had
been blown off from his shoulder. But he soon realized that wasn't the
case. Every window around him imploded and a shard of glass had
impaled itself in his back left bicep. He lifted and turned his arm to
yank it out and winced in pain. Blood ran down his arm into his hand.
More blood than he expected. But he gripped the Thompson and
raised it, a bit feeble in his aim, and shot off his first rounds. He
intended to drive the fuckers back the best way he could.

Harmony had been forced to travel behind the men assigned to
help her. It gave her less of a sense of control tailing them and not
leading the way. She wanted them to drive faster, needed them to
hurry, but they travelled at a pace far too slow. She chewed on her
bottom lip and thought the rest of her plan through. If they arrived too
late, things would turn nasty quick. If they arrived too early then Vinnie
would be furious with her for interfering. And these men had no
intention of leaving without the additional three thousand she
promised as payment. She lied and told them the money was at the
cabin. If they believed otherwise they probably would have taken the
bounty and done away with her.

However, her biggest problem remained. She'd fired the rifle and
her new pistol until she became fairly handy with a weapon under
Vinnie's instruction, but now she'd have to actually consider firing at
something other than a rusted can. She'd have to kill a man or two,
even three. Harmony gripped the steering wheel tighter. She'd never
hurt another soul in her life. Other than her striking Vinnie and
drawing a knife on him she'd never had violence near her. Lewis was
always gentle and caring. His fits of anger would send him out the door
before he lost control. Now she'd grown harder, colder, and she wasn't
sure of who she'd become.

All because of love?

Harmony shook her head sadly. Destiny and the winding path she
travelled toward it was set. She could no more turn back the last several
weeks of her downslide if she wanted to. And the truth was she didn't
want to.

Vinnie coughed up the stench of sulfur clogging his throat and tossed his useless machine gun. He grabbed two Colts and ran for the back of the cabin. The gunfight had gone on far longer than he anticipated. He heard the howls of at least two of his men somewhere in the house. He knew he'd taken out six of Mickey Collins's men, but had no idea how many more circled. If he didn't make a move they'd be on him soon, and he'd probably be out of ammo. Either way he refused to go down on his knees. So he kicked out the back door and started firing.

The first bullet caught a gun-wielding man by surprise and blew off the side of his face. Vinnie seized the window of opportunity and spread his arms firing from every side, dropping men trying to fire back. Damn it all to hell but there were too many of them. He kept firing. He charged down the steps of the back porch too fast. If he had taken the time to assess the numbers he'd have seen the one behind him. The gunshot whizzed past the right side of his face and clipped his ear. The pain exploded through his skull and he was temporarily thrown deaf. He collapsed.

The man stomping down the steps of the porch behind him aimed for the kill shot. Vinnie braced for death, welcoming the event.

"Don't!" he heard another yell. "It's Romano. Jacob go get the boss. Tell him we got him."

He wasn't sure if the men thought he was dead. He lay face down. Twice in the night he'd escaped serious injury. Would this be a third?

"Get his weapon!"

"Boss the others are dead!" A man confirmed. Vinnie winced, the pain to the side of his face and arm so intense he felt as if his skin was melting from the bone. He inhaled dirt and nearly choked on the damp soil.

"Yeah, but we caught the big fish, and I want to have some fun boys."

The guns were torn from his hands and he was kicked in the side. Vinnie rolled and tried to rise but another swift kick to the head knocked him out cold.

The cars stopped. They were only a mile away from the cabins. *Why stop now?* Panic rioted in her chest. She struggled to calm her nerves. *It could be anything Harmony, don't lose it. Wait and see.* Grease Man got out of one of the cars and strolled toward hers with his gun in his hand. She rolled the pane down and he leaned in a bit to peer in at her. "Last chance, Doll. Hang back here and we'll bring your boy out."

"No. I'm going too."

"You sure about that sweets? No one here is going to take a bullet for you."

"I'm going." Harmony said. "Now let's do it."

Grease studied her for a moment. She knew he questioned her reasons for such loyalty to a mobster like Vinnie but she didn't care. She'd rather die saving him than sit here waiting. She was going to see it through. Grease straightened and stepped back. He tipped his hat and strolled away toward his car at the front of the caravan.

They were on the move again.

Moonlight changed the landscape. Darkness from the surrounding forest trees closed in on them as they travelled down the one lane road. She leaned forward on the steering wheel to peer out of the windshield, prepared for anything. The cars sped up. From nowhere the men drove faster than the wind. Harmony slammed her foot on the gas and did her best to keep up. She heard the gunfire immediately and grabbed the Ringo from the seat next to her, bringing it to her lap. Should she duck, pull over, or drive straight into the mayhem?

Her car cleared the forested path and she slammed on the brakes to keep from slamming into the Ford in front of her. Grease and at least twenty men from the Forty Thieves were out of their cars and firing. Harmony froze in horror. The main cabin was ablaze. The fire and smoke was so intense it curled up into large black clouds filling the sky.

"No. No. No. No," she shook her head and refused to believe her eyes. She could hear the bullets whizzing past her. The car in front of her took a few shots. The men inside were using their open car doors for cover and firing back.

"No, God, please. No! Vinnie!!" she cried out. She grabbed the gun and turned to open the door when she spotted something else. Men ran out of the open door of the barn where the horses were kept. One in particular caught her eye. It had to be Mickey Collins. Harmony saw the doors to the barn were open. There was light inside.

"Vinnie. Please let it be him. Please."

If Mickey Collins was in the barn she knew damn well what was left of her man was there too.

Grease must have seen them too. His car and three others sped toward the barn with men hanging out of both windows firing wildly into the night. Harmony gripped the gearshift, threw the Packard into reverse, and then shifted into drive and sped after them. There was no time for thought or second guesses. She kept going. She drove right into the middle of the fight. The left passenger window shattered spraying glass into the backseat. The men were intent on killing each other and that was a perfect plan. She remembered on a visit to the stables that there was a back entrance. When she veered in that direction a man jumped out in front of the car firing. The windshield cracked and Harmony hit the guy so hard he was thrown to the roof of the car and then rolled off the back. She spun the wheel left and the car did a half-circle before coming to a complete stop.

There was no air in her lungs. Harmony struggled for several moments to remember how to breathe. She shook all over. Did she kill the man? God she prayed she hadn't. Whatever the case she had to get out of the car and get moving. She reached down at her feet and grabbed the Ringo then exited the vehicle.

Moving quietly on a battlefield of blood and bullets she hurried to the barn door. It was unlocked. She had to hold the gun in her left hand and pull hard with her right to slide the door open. It all happened in a matter of seconds. Vinnie was there. His arms were raised above his head shackled to chains that were thrown over a beam and tied to another post. He wore no shirt. His trousers were darkly slick with his blood. The beating and scarring along his back ran red with blood from open cuts. Her heart stopped. She couldn't move or speak. The gunfight outside of the barn indicated that Mickey Collins's men were holding off Grease. There were only two men inside of the barn with Vinnie.

Both men were so focused on the fight to the front of the barn they hadn't heard her enter from the rear. One of the men turned and saw her. Without thought Harmony raised her gun and fired. She hit him in the chest. The other turned spraying bullets her way. She fired twice before dropping to her knees. She had hit her target. Harmony caught her breath thinking she'd been shot. She hadn't. She sucked down another deep breath and struggled to rise. "Vin-Vinnie…." she panted. "Oh God please be alive. Please God!"

She hurried around him though her feet felt as if they were weighted to the ground. He hung with his head bowed and blood dripping from his mouth. Both of his eyes were swollen shut. "Vinnie!" she wept.

The door of the barn opened and Grease walked in. Harmony whirled and fired at them in an extreme state of panic. Both men ducked in time. Grease yelled at her to stop shooting. She was crazed with grief. The other man drew on her but she didn't care. She kept the gun switching from one to the other, covering them both.

"Get him down!! Get him down now or I will shoot!" she yelled at them.

More men entered. All of them stared up at Vinnie Romano, transfixed. No one seemed shocked at her wielding a gun, or the fact that she aimed it in their direction.

"I mean it! NOW!!"

Grease snapped his fingers. Two men hurried over to bring Vinnie down from the chains. Vinnie was lowered to the ground and Harmony was there at his side. She brought him into her arms, trying to see if the blood to the side of his face was because of a bullet wound. She didn't see one. His chest heaved and he staggered a breath but his eyes were swollen shut.

"He's a dead man Jazz Singer."

"No! No baby, you are fine. He's fine. He's just fine."

Grease approached and stood over her. "Mickey and some of his boys got away. We have to go after them. Our work is done here. Where's the money?"

Harmony kept stroking the side of Vinnie's face, weeping.

Grease raised his gun and pressed the barrel to the top of her skull. "Where's the money? I won't ask again."

She looked up through her tears. "Help me get him in the car. I'll give you the money then."

For a brief pause he hesitated. She feared he'd refuse her request. Her unwavering stance may have convinced him. He nodded for his boys to help. They lifted Vinnie and carried him out the back of the barn. Harmony got to her feet swaying a bit. She didn't look at the two men she killed. She walked stiffly to the back of the barn, then went to the trunk and opened it. She gave Grease Man the last of the money. She'd only kept eight hundred for her and Vinnie to escape with, and it was tucked safely in her bra. When Grease snatched her satchel to see if she had more money he could steal from her he found nothing. The bond was under the floor mat in the car.

"That's it. That's all I have." Harmony said, her chin high and face void of her inner turmoil.

Grease Man chuckled. "You do realize he's dead. You can't take him into the city, no one will help him, or you. He'll die on you and if you're caught with a dead white man it's game over toots."

Harmony shrugged. "He my problem. Not yours."

Grease man licked his lips. "Queenie told me to let you go. I got a good mind to teach you a bit of humility. Not sure if I like that mouth of yours, and you took a shot at me. No one takes a shot at me."

"Are we done?" she asked, and tightened her grip on the gun. He continued to glare at her as if he were trying to decide. "You asked me if I ever used this gun. Tonight you know I have. I suggest you and your men leave us be."

He wiped his jaw. "Where will you go?"

She didn't bother to answer.

"Leave Woodbury. Mickey's out there and he's coming for him."

She shrugged.

Grease Man tipped his hat and whistled, counting the money as he turned and walked away. Harmony gripped the gun with both hands. She stood perfectly still watching the cars drive out across the field. Her gaze swept the carnage. The main house continued to burn. Vehicles were abandoned everywhere with shot out windows and dead men strewn about. She and Vinnie were alone.

The tension drained from her body, and she turned to check for him in the car. He was stiff, not moving. She could see his scarred chest rise and fall with shallow breaths. She had to get them out of New York and fast.

Harmony jumped behind the wheel and drove to the small servant cabin that he had initially brought her to. She hurried inside and grabbed a fresh shirt for him, slacks and blankets.

When she returned the night was eerily quiet. She glanced around expecting some survivor to appear, or worse Mickey Collins. It was her nerves. She dismissed the feeling of being watched and returned to the car. She covered Vinnie the best she could and then high tailed it out of Woodbury.

She drove nonstop until dawn bled across the sky. She stopped for gas once they cleared New York. The attendant, a tall thin boy with dirty blond hair and dingy overalls spotted Vinnie in the back seat and glared at her. She thought to explain but instead she gave him a hundred dollars. His eyes nearly bulged out of his skull. He filled her tank and didn't say a word.

Harmony continued to drive. But Vinnie didn't wake and after a few hours the events of the night and her fear for him got the best of her. They were in Pennsylvania when she veered off the road and stopped the car near an open pasture. Harmony wept. She cried so hard she feared she'd lose her mind. She hadn't thought the plan through. All she had on her was just a little over six hundred dollars. He needed a doctor. And she was too scared that it was too late. She couldn't bring herself to pull back the blanket and check his chest for signs of him breathing again. The wounds and the blood covering him had her petrified.

"Sunnng…berrrd?"

Harmony's head turned and her eyes searched his face. He lay perfectly still. "Vinnie? You awake?" She feared she didn't hear him speak. That it was her desperate exhaustion that played on her mind, but he licked his lips and filled her with hope.

"Oh sweetie, you're okay. I'm going to get you help. Hold on."

Harmony heard a horse and carriage. She opened her door and stepped out of the car. A man dressed in a plain blue shirt and an old-fashioned wide brim hat with a long grey beard sat to its center. She ran out into the road waving her hands. She had blood all over her and she knew she looked a state. She had read as a young girl about the people called Amish who lived outside of society. She had no idea what he would think of a bloody colored woman trying to stop him.

He stopped. Harmony, exhausted and desperate half staggered to him. "Please sir. My… I have a friend who's hurt. Really bad." She looked back and pointed to the car. "He needs help. Please!"

The man followed her point with his steely clear grey eyes. He didn't speak. In fact he scowled, then returned his gaze to her.

"Please!"

She feared he'd force the carriage to go on, but kindness flashed in his cold stare and he gave her a nod. It was a welcome relief. The man came off the carriage and Harmony gave him space. They returned to the car and he peered in. He glanced her way once more, then reached in to touch Vinnie. He then spoke in a different language. It sounded like German. Harmony pressed her hands together and nodded the universal sign of thanks. He pointed toward the road that veered right with several homes in the distance. She nodded that she understood.

The kind man got back in his carriage and Harmony in her car. She followed him from behind as he steered the horse drawn buggy toward a large bell tower. She stopped and watched as he got out and rung a large bell. She didn't know what he was doing but she prayed he wasn't getting a lawman after them. If she didn't find Vinnie some medical attention he'd die. She knew that for sure.

When Harmony glanced out to the fields she was taken aback by the others emerging from homes. Women, in plain blue dresses, white aprons and matching white bonnets on their heads. Men, all wearing the same kind of wide brim hats, had trousers with overalls that were a bit short on the leg. They walked or climbed in their buggies and rode toward the stranger house. Harmony held her breath praying again silently that the strange people would help her.

The buggy continued along the dirt road and she followed. As soon as she parked the others arrived and circled the car. When she opened the door several of the women gasped, covering their children's eyes from looking upon her. The stranger spoke to the alarmed people and whatever he said seemed to calm the crowd. Three men hurried to the car and they worked together to bring Vinnie out. Harmony stood there remembering her gun. She hoped on one saw it. It could turn the situation bad. The men carried Vinnie up the stairs of the house and inside.

"Does anyone speak English?" she asked the crowd.

A girl in the group raised her hand. She was small in stature with clear blue eyes and hair so blonde it looked white. She glanced over to the older man, as if she sought his approval for her to approach.

"Tell him I'm grateful. I only wanted help, I don't want any trouble. We just need help."

She looked to the older man who stared at her with hard eyes. It was clear he helped Vinnie because of his being with her. They all looked at her skin as if she had arrived from another world.

"He's my, my friend."

The girl stepped out of the crowd. She walked over to the older man and bowed her head when she spoke. She said something to him in a hushed tone. His gaze went from her to Harmony. He nodded. He spoke and Harmony knew his words were addressed to her.

"His name is Ishmael. I'm Mary. He says I'm to clean you up. They will look after your friend."

"Thank you! Tell him thank you!"

The girl did as she was asked but the older man had already started to walk away. Harmony swung her gaze back through the cloud of staring faces. Many refused to make eye contact with her. Only the children stared at her with open awe.

"Come with me."

"I can get my things."

"No. I will give you something to wear. It's expected. Leave your car and things. No one will touch it."

The request was odd, but she was in no position to argue. The others gave her wide space, making sure she didn't pass close enough to touch them. She didn't care what any of them thought, she just wanted to get to Vinnie. Instead she followed the girl to her home. When she entered the tiny house made of wood and logs she was asked to stand near the door. The girl reappeared with a large washtub and headed out past Harmony. She followed her to the well and under her instruction pumped water. Harmony hadn't eaten or slept and had no idea what time it was, or how far in Pennsylvania they had driven. But she waited for the girl and tried not to seem like a nuisance. She was then led the short distance to a barn carrying one end of the tub while the young woman carried the other. Harmony realized they wanted her to clean up in the same place relegated for the livestock. She swallowed her pride and did so quickly. The girl gave her a calf length plain-cut dress with a white apron.

"Are you hungry? It's time for Jacob to return from the fields and I've already prepared dinner."

"Yes. I would like to know about my friend, if he is okay?"

"They will tell us when there is news."

Harmony followed her out of the barn. They headed back to her tiny home with Harmony in bare feet. "How did you learn to speak English?"

"My father, he felt strongly that we should know. Ishmael granted it for me but not the others. I translate mostly. We do get strangers at times. So it's useful."

"Oh. Okay."

That was the last of their conversation. She was brought into their home and even welcomed at the table. She sat with them and ate in silence. Jacob looked to be as old as her. Mary however couldn't have been any older than fifteen. When dinner was done a knock came. A young man spoke briefly to Jacob and he then addressed Mary. Her eyes turned to Harmony with sympathy.

"Your friend has a fever. He also has severe injuries. They are not sure if he will live, but they will continue to try to help him."

"Can I see him?"

"No. I'm sorry you cannot. Ishmael forbids it. He says we are to give you an area to sleep. In the morning we will know more."

Harmony swallowed her objections. They stared at her waiting. When she nodded her acceptance she could see them visibly relax. It was strange, their community. Though they regarded her as the foreigner, the simple lifestyle and singular thinking made her a bit nervous. How long could she sit with these people and just wait?

After the visitor left Harmony was led to a room and given a blanket and pillow to sleep on the floor. Exhaustion got the best of her and she slept for the rest of the night. And so it went for two days. She worked in the yard with Mary and tended to the animals. They were very kind to her, but denied her even the simplest of conversation. Mary would only speak to her when spoken to, and offered shy smiles when Harmony tried to press for more details about her life.

The solitude gave her time to come to peace with her conflict over the things she'd done. She regretted nothing. Still she refused to justify any of her actions. Vinnie rested behind doors, locked away from her. At night she'd leave her room and sit on the porch, staring out at the stars. He'd wake soon, and he'd demand answers. She prayed he would set aside his pride to see the blessing they had with this second chance she bought them. However, she was prepared if he didn't. Life held much more promise than ever before and she wouldn't give up on her dreams for anyone.

On the third day, while carrying a bucket of water to fill the troth she thought she heard her name. Harmony glanced to the left and squinted at the sun blaring in her face. A man walked stiffly toward her. He balanced his steps with a cane. It was Vinnie. The bruising around his eyes had healed enough for him to open them, but his face was covered in ghastly bruises, the left side of his jaw was a bit swollen and protruded. Harmony dropped her water bucket.

"Vinnie? Vinnie!" She ran through the tall grass for him. Mary glanced up from where she led a horse into the stable and others within distance stopped to observe. She stopped herself from throwing her arms around his neck. But he surprised her by bringing her to him. He held her as others that were around stopped to watch.

"They wouldn't let me see you. I knew they were helping you so I didn't push. But I was so scared."

"Don't be. I'm fine." He let go of his cane to hold her to the best of his abilities. "I'm fine." She lifted her face and the soft press of their lips made the past two days of torture worth it.

"We're leaving. Today." He lifted her chin. "Can you be ready?"

"Are you sure? You aren't a hundred percent."

He glanced up and she looked behind her to see Jacob had joined Mary and was staring at her. He then lowered his gaze to her matronly dress and white head bonnet. "We aren't really wanted here. Besides, I need to talk to you. To understand... how this all came to be."

Harmony bit down on her bottom lip and her stomach fluttered with nervous energy. "I guess I owe you an explanation. I just don't want you on the road if you aren't ready for the drive. It can be tiring... we have such a distance left. We're in Pennsylvania somewhere."

"I made sure I was able to sit upright without much pain before I left the bed. What I want to know, Songbird is how you managed it?"

Tears slipped down her cheeks. "You won't be happy about what I did."

"I'm happy to have you again." he kissed her forehead. "Get our car, and change out of these clothes. We need to go."

They said their goodbyes with Mary's help. Ishmael seem relieved to have them leaving. He did come out and wish them well. They drove off the land and headed back to the main road before she got the nerve to speak. She told him everything, starting with the plan she concocted with Paulette. She confessed what she did with the fifteen thousand he gave her. He cut her a few looks but didn't interrupt. She explained how she found him. How she got him out and why they ended up with those people.

"Stop the car," he said.

"Why?"

"Stop the damn car!" he yelled.

Harmony veered over and off the road. Vinnie threw the door open. He got out of the car and limped away. She turned in her seat to see him behind the vehicle pacing on his bad leg. Releasing a deep sigh she opened her car door and got out.

"Don't!" he warned, turning from her in anger.

"Sorry Vinnie. I know you're angry. Guess you think there's some honor in dying. Well I say it's bullshit. I love you dammit. I wasn't about to let them have you, and I'm not sorry for it! I had to kill someone! Do you hear me? And all you can do is blame me? After everything I've done for you!"

He turned on her and the glare he fixed her with shook her confidence. He stepped to her and the rage on his face had her paralyzed. "You think this is about my ego?"

"Isn't it?"

"NO! For fuck's sake! You could have been killed. Dammit Harmony, I did all of this to protect you and you go to them and into a gun fight, for what?"

"For you! You asshole! I did it for you."

He heaved a deep sigh. "If you had died."

"I didn't. I'm here, and so are you. Frankly I don't give a shit anymore about the reasons we are. We're here, and I'm not sorry for anything I've done to save your life."

With his strong arm he reached for her and drew her to him. She went into his arms careful of the one in the sling. "I'm sorry, Songbird. Of course I'm grateful, relieved to have you again. I'm sorry. It's the thought of you being hurt, it makes me bullheaded."

"You're angry. You wanted me to leave you there to die? Just walk away? How could I do that?"

"I'm angry because I was too stubborn to leave with you. I won't make that mistake anymore." He walked her back to the car and held the door for her. He returned to the passenger side and they drove off together. Her heart lifted when he reached over and ran his hand over her thigh and relaxed back in the seat. From that day forward they never discussed the events of that night.

"To the very end?" Harmony asked.

He cut her a sly smile. "Who says it has to end?"

EPILOGUE
Heart Song

9 Months Later

Romano paced. John Red Horse smoked his pipe and tracked him with his large brown eyes. "You are sure to wear a hole in those shoes from the back and forth," he warned.

"How long does this take? They've been in there for six hours."

Harmony cried out in agony again and his stomach dropped. He felt physically ill.

"Suggest you take a seat. It may be awhile. Maria is with her. Women have babies every day."

"Not my woman! Do you hear how she screams in there? I'm going in." Romano marched toward the hall.

"I wouldn't advise that!" Red Horse yelled to his back while rocking in his chair. Romano reached the door just as a small Native woman named Etoya stepped out of it. Harmony took to Etoya the day they arrived. It was the old woman that told her that she was with child. Her name meant The Greatest. She was from the Comanche tribe. Red Horse and her had been together since they were in their early teens and runaways from the camps in 1865, towards the end of the Civil War. Etoya had more wisdom than any man or woman he'd ever met. She pointed to the front of their house and he had no choice but to turn around.

When he walked back out Red Horse chuckled and blew out a stream of tobacco. "Told you. White man never have patience. Think it's in your blood."

Romano waved him off. He tried to calm himself. He had to stop believing their happiness was on borrowed time.

"Baby wake up." Harmony eased her warm thigh over his leg and the velvety feel of her curves pressed into his body and stirred his arousal. He turned his head on his pillow and squinted against the soft light cast over their bed from under a glass lampshade. Her brown eyes were moist enough to reflect his image within their depths. There were times when she looked at him with such love he couldn't speak. No woman had ever captured his feelings as completely as she had. Harmony's lips connected with his and his lids fell shut once more. "You awake?" she asked running the tip of her tongue over the seam of his pressed together lips and slipping him a deep kiss.

It came to a natural end. He took down a deep breath to resist the hardening of his groin. "I am now."

"Good."

Romano tried to move on her and she gently pushed back on his chest. She kept handling him like some delicate flower. He missed her. They'd stopped and rested in four different cities. And the ones that wouldn't let him rent her a room meant they slept in the car together under the stars. He'd settled for holding her most nights and that was fine. However, his body was on the mend. He could use his arm without the aid of the sling. Now he needed to feel her lush curves underneath him again. "Something wrong?" he asked.

"I'm so happy," she said.

Romano cupped her cheek and thumbed away a tear clinging to her dark lash. "I plan to make sure you stay that way, Songbird."

"Vinnie, what do you think of this place?" she whispered.

The question went right past him. He was now looking down the line of her body with her black nipples against her smooth brown skin. He eased down a bit to capture a nipple with his mouth and tease it with his tongue. Her hand immediately flew up to stroke the back of his head.

"Answer me please."

He lifted his head and glanced up into her dreamy eyes. "What's the question?"

"Do you like it here?"

He let his gaze sweep around the room. It was one of the better haunts they'd stayed in. "It's okay I guess."

"I know we talked about Santa Fe, but… I was out today and I got a good look at the town. It's really lovely."

"Can we talk about this later, been missing you, Songbird." He cupped her between her thighs and he saw a small shiver go through her. "We'll see many lovely towns."

"Yes, but this one, well it's different."

Romano stroked her below, a little curious. "Different how?"

Harmony chuckled. "Haven't you noticed? The town has a Negro sheriff; there are many Negroes, and Natives here. Some whites. It's like home but everyone lives together."

"We're in New Mexico, Doll. It's probably like this everywhere."

Up and down his middle finger went across her slit slow and easy. Her breath hitched, but the soft grunting moan she gave was a sound laced with pleasure. His finger dipped into her tight hole and her lids fluttered shut. They'd driven for two weeks. She took to a few places but something was different about Mandero for her. Santa Fe would be another six hours. Harmony went out to do some shopping while he caught up on his sleep, and she had returned as excited as he'd seen her in days. Even told him about a speakeasy that had closed, now he knew there was more to it. "Talk to me."

"Huh?"

He withdrew his finger and she shut her thighs immediately. He traced his damp finger over her tummy. "You were saying?"

"Ah, yes, I uh, I met a woman today. Her name is Etoya. Older lady, reminds me of my Grams."

"Okay?" He lowered his face to lick her earlobe while he eased his hand up to her breast. He squeezed it and pinched her nipple. Oh how he loved her boobs.

"She said this town is different Vinnie because they made sure it was that way."

"They?"

"The Negroes, Mexicans, and Natives made it that way. Santa Fe is run by whites Vinnie, but Mandero isn't, and hasn't been since the Civil War. She doesn't think we should go to Santa Fe, because it's overrun with wranglers and outlaws since the Mexican Revolution."

The seduction stopped. He frowned. "What does this have to do with us?"

"You're right Vinnie, Etoya said I'm pregnant. I want our child to grow up accepted. I want our life to be on our terms. And I think… I think this is the place. Maybe we can buy the speakeasy and I can sing again. The town needs a teacher and I can do that too. Just a lot of possibilities." She peeked at him wondering about his reaction. Now he understood. She worried that he wouldn't want to live in a town with people that weren't like him. That he couldn't adapt under this town's rules. He surprised himself by smiling. Here she lay thinking she'd have to convince him of her dream, when all he wanted to do was give her everything her heart wanted. He had his dream and it was her. He could give a shit where they landed, as long as they landed together.

"Say something Vinnie."

"I say if we're going to stay then before we buy a place or anything it's time."

"Time?"

"To get married."

She grinned. "I love you so much!"

"Prove it. The old woman said you carry my baby, so stop treating me like one."

She grabbed his face and kissed him deeply. She pushed him off and turned over to her hands and knees. Romano rose behind her and she pushed her ass backwards while widening her stance. She glanced over her shoulder and dared him to go the distance.

Romano smirked. He cupped his hand and swatted her bottom. She giggled shaking her toosh at him. He fisted himself and watched as he placed the head of his dick at her entrance then slowly pushed his way inside. The heat of her, so moist and welcoming, beckoned him. He pumped his hips and stroked forward, not stopping until he was balls deep. Moist heat clamped down on his shaft and he began to fuck her harder and stronger forgetting his limitations as well. He refused to relent. Harmony's arms gave out and her chest dropped to the bed but her ass lifted higher and it made him wild with excitement. He grabbed her hips to hold her still and thrust repeatedly until they both were shattered with happiness.

Two days later —

Harmony held his hand. She wore a white dress with a long hem and a ring of flowers around her head. He was dressed much more dapper. His dark suit and sly smile melted her heart. They stood on the land he bought for them. Etoya had her husband Red Horse perform the ceremony. He was the town spiritualist. They didn't have a church, but maybe they could build one some day. He chanted and spoke in his limited English, blessing them and their union. She promised her heart to him and their child. She couldn't believe the way Vinnie grinned and nodded. He was like a changed man. When it was done he pulled her to him and grabbed her face kissing her deeply.

"I love you, Songbird. Always."

"I love you too, Vinnie. I'm the happiest I could be."

"Not yet, but you will be I promise."

He lifted her in his arms and the six people gathered clapped for them. He had no clue how much happiness she had found with him.

"Oh God! I can't! I can't!" she yelled through her tears, holding her knees.

"Push down. Hold your knees!" Maria said. Harmony threw her head back and cried out as pressure below ripped her in, and then release came. Exhausted she dropped on the pillow. As much as she loved their baby she couldn't go another inch. They'd have to cut the kid out of her.

"He's here!" Maria cried out in Spanish. Harmony had picked up more and more of the language and the native tongue of the Comanche.

She blinked through her tears of sweat and frustration. "He?"

A pink wrinkled little piece of joy was placed on her tummy. The baby squirmed and let go a soft cry. He had a head full of dark black hair and an apple shaped head. Harmony burst into tears. "Get Vinnie! Get him quick!"

"Let us clean you and his boy up first." Etoya said.

She released tears of happiness. "Okay."

"Still holding on to the poison."

He glanced over at Red Horse and closed the door behind him. "What are you talking about old man?" he said taking a seat.

"Thinking that wife and son of yours shouldn't be yours. Thinking the way of the man you were." Red Horse set aside his pipe. He leaned forward. His skin dried and wrinkled from the sun was the color of copper. He smirked, revealing his missing teeth. "In a minute you are going to be introduced to your boy…"

"Don't know if it's a boy." Romano mumbled.

"Your son is destined, I know it's a boy. In a minute they will bring you to meet him. The man he sees is the man you are now, not the man you were before you began again."

"I'm done with that."

"Are you?"

He opened his mouth to speak then gave up. He shook his head and accepted the truth. Etoya walked out looking exhausted. "The baby is here." She said. "A fighter, and stubborn, definitely a Romano." She walked over and patted his cheek. He stood. "What is it?" he asked.

"Go see for yourself."

He hurried into the hall and passed Maria as he entered inside the room. Harmony lay in the middle of the bed. She held their baby in her arms. Her hair was wild and her eyes were red and swollen from tears of happiness. She looked up and nodded. "Meet your son."

He couldn't move. Nothing on him moved. He stood there transfixed. "Vinnie. Come here."

He approached the bed and stared down at the little angel. His pursed lips and fat jaws reminded him of his baby cousin when she was born. "Can I hold him?"

Harmony lifted his son to him and he accepted him gingerly. Once he held him he understood what Red Horse had advised. This boy and his wife were his past, present and future. He could believe.

"I love you." He smiled at Harmony.

"I love you too, Vinnie, always."

Coming Soon!
From Sienna Mynx

38392464R00134

Made in the USA
Lexington, KY
07 January 2015